D1491352

Marble Mountain

a novel

WAYNE KARLIN

Curbstone Press

Cover design: Stone Graphics
Top photo: Nguyen Qui Duc; bottom photo: Wayne Karlin

This book was published with the support of the
Connecticut Commission on Culture and Tourism and
donations from many individuals. We are very
grateful for this support.

Connecticut Commission
on Culture & Tourism

Library of Congress Cataloging-in-Publication Data

Karlin, Wayne.
  Marble mountain : a novel / by Wayne Karlin. -- 1st ed.
    p. cm.
  ISBN 978-1-931896-43-6 (pbk. : alk. paper)
  1. Adopted children--Fiction. 2. Racially mixed children--Fiction.
3. Identity (Psychology)--Fiction. 4. Family secrets--Fiction. 5.
Children of military personnel--Fiction. 6. Vietnam War, 1961-
1975--Veterans--Fiction. 7. Psychological fiction. I. Title.

PS3561.A625M37 2008
813'.54--dc22

                                  2008012856

CURBSTONE PRESS   321 Jackson Street   Willimantic, CT 06226
        phone: 860-423-5110   e-mail: info@curbstone.org
                      www.curbstone.org

In loving memory of
Sandy Taylor

The Vietnamese are very religious but not fanatical. Compared to other categories, cult music was not widely developed. The most significant cult song type is *Hát Chau Van*. This is a kind of incantation music (although it was classified as ritual music), but its purpose was to hypnotize the person who was estranged from the spirits through musical airs, rhythms and lyrics.

It is in essence a cantillation where the tunes and rhythm depend on the contents of the sung text and may be linked together into a suite, used in relation to a mythical happening, with hints at some features of modern life.

Pham Thuy Hoan

http://www.tienghatquehuong.com/FolkSongs/ChauVan.htm

For Ohnmar and Adam

With special thanks to Judd Ne'eman, Le Thi Minh Ngoc, and Phan Thanh Hao

PROLOGUE:

MARBLE MOUNTAIN

Marble Mountain

Alex remembers how it all blended together, a black jagged rim on his horizon, humped back of a dragon, standing between himself and the country. It leapt closer when he was on perimeter duty, and he would squint along the barrel of his machine gun, getting the inverted V of the highest peak balanced on the tip of the inverted V sight at the end of the barrel. The sand flat that stretched in front of him would be distorted by thermal waves, and he would play with the idea that the country was an illusion that would dissolve if he squinted at it hard enough along the barrel. It didn't work. He would find he was still there, lying on his belly in a hole rimmed with sandbags, tented by a piece of ragged canvas that was supposed to provide shade and cover but that served only to trap more of the heat, or as a sighting point for VC mortars. The heat would thicken, thick as rubber under the encasement of his helmet; it made him sleepy and he would shake his head against it so hard he would imagine he could feel the lag and bump of his brain inside his skull.

From the air, when he flew gunner, he could see how the mountain was really a cluster of hills, five irregular eruptions of foliage-splotched stone, little pagodas on the flanks; when the helicopter came in low enough he could see the statuary here and there, the black mouths of caves, glimpsed just for a moment. A hop and skip and you were over all of it and into the war.

He had thought of it as a line between himself and some concept of himself he was trying to hang onto in the heat baking his brain. He wanted to go to it, cross it into some heart of the country that remained as elusive as that

3

shimmering line on the horizon. He knew there was infantry on it, and the occasional medical civil action patrol went out from the base, winning hearts and minds. But otherwise it was forbidden territory. A Marine messenger from Da Nang had been snatched from his jeep on the road that ran through the hills, killed or pulled into the oblivion of captivity, never seen again. At times the helicopter base was mortared from the summit of one peak or another; the formations were honeycombed with hidden and ancient shrines, sacred to the inhabitants. They were, he had heard, stone-carvers, living on and from the heap of marble they carved. The idea excited him, drew him. A village of stone-carvers. It sounded vaguely medieval, or something out of the Tolkien he loved to read, a guild of dwarf craftsmen in their warrens. He wanted to go to them. He was a carver himself, a whittler; in the barn behind his house a circle of figures he sculpted stood and waited, gathering dust, padlocked by his own father, who had vowed to destroy them like unworthy gods if Alex didn't make it home. He was afraid of losing the cunning of his hands, felt the vibration of the gun under them when he fired into the country transforming his flesh into the very echo of chaos, felt his finger's curve on the trigger hardening into a permanent claw; he needed to go to the carvers, shape stone instead of being shaped by metal.

He had broached the idea of a little field trip, some unauthorized sight-seeing, to his cousin Baxter, a few of the other men in his tent, a few days after he got off sentry duty. It was a lull in the war; the end of one operation, the dead counted; the wounded packed into the field hospital or sent to the Philippines or Japan or home, dispersed out of the sight of the unhurt. He and Baxter and Hector Rodriguez and Donnie Dalton. Two other names he will remember.

They hitched a ride with a six-by going to the dump, four helicopter Marines needing some earth, but helmeted, flak-jacketed, their rifles on full automatic against what might be on this ground. They threaded cautiously near the looming, nearly vertical flank of the largest peak, a dark expanse of stepped and colonnaded and ramparted stone, the men maintaining a good interval, moving through a cluster of thatch-roofed hootches and kiosks with sides made from pressed beer cans.

A steady clanging rang out from a hootch near them; it sounded almost like a drum, though the beat was too metallic. Alex stopped, raised his hand, and the others froze behind him. He walked around to the other side of the hootch. Through the narrowly spaced bamboo stalks that made up the wall, he glimpsed a row of statues, stripped with shadow. In front, the thatched roof extended out like an awning, shading a workshop area. An old man squatted there, working a lump of white stone with a hammer and chisel—putting the finishing touches on a Buddha's head. Alex watched him, his eyes fastened on the carver's hands. There were a number of Buddha statues scattered in front of the work area, as well as a Goddess of Luck, a Ganeesh elephant head, and a life-sized dancer, beautifully carved from a rose-colored stone, her face tilted, her eyes somehow wise and teasing at the same time. Her smile, Alex thought, resembled the smile of the Buddha, enigmatic, blissful. She seemed nude, her breasts swelling under three rows of beads, but when he looked closer, the carving that fine, he could see the edge of a diaphanous garment at the neck, a pleated flap of it emerging between the figure's legs. The exquisiteness of the work woke an ache in his chest and stomach and fingers that was not erotic, or perhaps was in the way the dancer was, the yearn of desire she embodied inchoate, what he missed and mourned in himself. He slung his rifle, squatted, and touched the face of the dancer, ran his hands over the cool stone. The fine dust sifting into his pores. The old man stopped, looked at him.

Hallam, what the fuck you up to—copping a feel? Rodriguez asked. He was nervous, having second, third thoughts about the whole venture.

You all shut up now, Baxter said to him, looking at Alex.

Alex ignored both of them. He continued to stare. The old man rose from his squat. He plucked at Alex's sleeve and pointed to the mountain, as if in explanation.

Ngu Hanh Son, he said. Mar-ble. Moun-tain.

No hang shit, Dalton said.

Thuy Son, the old man said, pointing at the formation above them.

Dubious motherfucker can't make up his mind, Rodriguez said.

Alex was aware of the old man looking into his eyes. But he looked into the Buddha's eyes and then again at the dancing girl. He caressed the hair, traced the enigmatic smile with his finger.

The old man went back into the hootch. Rodriguez kept his rifle trained on his back. He came out again, extended a hand to Alex. All the other Marines quickly raised their rifles, pointed them at him.

Relax, Alex said. In the old man's callus-ridged palm was a statuette; a miniature of the dancing girl, carved from the same rose-colored stone. Alex stared at it. It struck him as Indian, Hindu, rather than Vietnamese. The dancer was an apsaras, a stone dancer in the tra kieu style, itself a replica of a famous Cham statue, though Alex did not yet know these names, any more than he knew the name of the girl who many years from this day would become his daughter and would see herself somehow embodied in this same carving. The old man pushed the statuette forward. Alex's hand closed around it.

The four Marines continued up the mountain, Alex on point. On edge. He felt the statuette, a weight in the baggy pocket on his right leg. He should go back; the others wanted to. But it was not enough. Not yet. They rounded a bend. They were walking beneath a series of overlapping slabs, lush foliage thick in the crevices and overlaps. A thick clump of bamboo was gathered in a fissure ahead and to their right. The breeze stirred the stalks, and they moaned and creaked and banged together as bamboo does and suddenly they parted slightly and revealed a face. As Alex's shots echoed against the sides of the mountain, the other men dove for the ground, panting with fear and shaking with adrenaline.

The echoes died. A charged silence. The creak of the bamboo. The men slowly got to their feet, their rifles still trained on the shredded bamboo. Alex moved forward, in a crouch. He cautiously parted the bamboo. It revealed another man-sized marble statue of the Buddha, this one ancient, the marble aged and worn. The head had been shattered.

Rodriguez whistled.

Man, you done killed the Buddha.

Dalton spat. Fuck, man. Let's get outta here.

Alex stared at the Buddha. His fingers were trembling; he felt the claw-curve setting into them. Out of an impulse he didn't understand, a need to hold captive this moment, he took his camera out of one of his ammunition pouches and photographed the ruined statue. He had the vague feeling he was photographing his own corpse.

Fuck you, man, Dalton said. It was your idea to come up here. Let's get a hat.

You the one said you were bored, Dalton, Baxter said.

That was then. This is fucked.

There's some inscription here, Alex said.

Rodriguez looked around nervously. Sarge, we ain't suppose to be here.

Something caught Alex's eye. He squatted and felt around the base of the statue. Then he pushed it cautiously. The statue moved. Behind it, still half hidden by vines and undergrowth, was a small vertical slot in the concave wall of the fissure, Chinese letters carved around it.

Alex, booby-traps, man, Baxter warned.

Check it out, B—it's an opening, probably a shrine or something.

7

Sarge, c'mon, Dalton said. We tell the grunts. Let's go.

I don't think this is VC. This mountain is honeycombed with shrines. Some of this shit's thousands of years old.

So was that mama-san I balled at the dump. Who gives a shit?

Alex didn't say anything. He unclipped his flashlight and, ducking, slid sideways into the narrow entrance. The others hesitated. Then they went in after him.

They must have. Baxter, and then Dalton and then Rodriguez, cursing, but not wanting to be outside, alone. Not willing to let him be alone. They were all gone. They are all gone. Slipped into the rock and out of his memory. When he does remember, he sees only the Buddha outside the entrance, its face pocked and broken, but its posture, as always, serene. Even though the smile is shattered, looking at it in his mind, trying to recreate it under his hands, Alex can still imagine what he can not see, the slight curve of the smile, the calm. The smile remains unchanged, detached. It is as if he, Alex, is frozen behind that shattered face, even as he hears screams, a fusillade of shots, an explosion rumbling inside the mountain. Even as he sees himself emerging from the opening, covered with dust and blood, dragging Baxter, who clutches his face, both hands cupped over his eyes, blood streaming down from under his palms. The rest is gone, chiseled clean from his mind.

PART ONE

HOA SON

FIRE

Apsaras

The statuette of the apsaras dancer stands center stage on a raised podium, a single red spotlight on it. Another light clicks on, finds Kiet. She stands in an identical trihhanga posture. Legs spread wide, but bent outwards at the knees, so that the lower legs touch at the feet and form the base of a triangle, head tilted to the left, right arm held out and then bent back, right hand, thumb straight, fingers down, resting against cheek, and forming another triangle, or an angle corresponding to the angle of the left leg; together the leg and arm are half the twisted cross, the holy swastika. Her left arm is crossed over her body, elbow inwards, left hand resting on her thigh. She wears the garments and jewels suggested by the statuette, rows of beads around her neck, waist and hips, navel exposed between the pleated, diaphanous cloth wrapped around her body, the pleated central flap hanging between her legs, down to her ankles. The spotlight bathes her in rose light, as close to the color of the stone as she can get it. She stands absolutely still, her posture the frozen instant of a dance, the eyes of her audience fastened on her, demanding motion. Restive rustles pass through the people sitting in the rows of seats, as if they feel compelled to move for her, as if the dance compressed into her posture demands release in whatever flesh it can find. But she does not move. Only her lips, which part as she sings:

I am a dancer in stone,
frozen in a spell that can only be unlocked
by words in a language I do not know.

Near her is an old-fashioned record player with a 33-speed vinyl record on its turntable. Beside it, a single potted palm, a movie screen, and an upside-down boat. The spotlight falls on the record player. She dances to it, looks at it, puzzled, pantomimes turning a crank on the side of the record, her movements are exaggerated now, and as she sings, she begins to dance, slowly, sinuously, the music mixing rock— Springsteen's *New Jersey Turnpike* sung by Deanna Carter, backed by the eerie twang of a Vietnamese monochord *dan bau* zither, the twang of an Indian sitar.

I am the apsaras who guides heroes to paradise
I am the apsaras, who lures heroes to their deaths
You pays your money
You takes your chance
It's my show, my dance

Slowly she disappears behind the boat, the spotlight dies and she works quick-change magic and rises again dressed in Viet Cong black, a green checkered scarf around her neck. When the light goes on again, she is in a fetal position on the floor. She rises, grabs the statuette.

I crawl out of my secret mother.
I crawl out of a movie.
I crawl out of murder.

She stares at the audience, pointing the statuette at it. She's the point, the nexus of something now; it is these moments, she tells herself, that she dances to and dances for, the giddiness of connection, the dissolution of the ties between dream and vocation, the lost girl she was wounding the watchers and listeners around her until they are as exiled as she is, until they become home.

And then, as if it were spotlighted itself (it isn't), a face floats out of the small crowd in the college theater, a Vietnamese woman of about Kiet's age. She is staring at Kiet, a look of utter horror on her face.

Kiet shakes her out of her head.

Images begin to flow onto the movie screen: a collage of scenes from American war movies. She stands motionless, assuming again the posture of the apsaras, in front of the screen, letting the images play on her face and body. She collapses into a fetal position. Haberle's photo of a group of villagers at Son My, about to be mowed down, appears on the screen, and then the ditch.

A baby crawled out of a ditch of the dead.
I crawl out of a ditch of the dead.
I crawl out of my secret mother
My mother the ditch
My mother the bitch.

She slowly rises again. The images on the screen shift. *Platoon.* Sergeant Barnes shoots a Vietnamese woman, her daughter watching in horror. Kiet imitates the girl's moves, the mother's moves, exactly, as if she were the shadow or soul of each. Behind her, a helicopter is pushed into the sea, off the deck of an aircraft carrier. She crawls.

I crawl out of a movie.
I crawl out of murder.
I thread into your dreams.
I am a red mist threading like a dream
through brown muddy water
Spreading like time through muddy water
I curse the water
that separates the two banks.

She dances.

Applause, like a fusillade of bullets.

She sat in her dressing room and wiped away her make-up, drained and exhausted, as she always was after a performance. Feeling the same fleeting fear of disappearing she always had afterwards as well. Vanishing cream.

A common fear, she supposed.

There was a knock on the door.

Kiet remembered a science fiction story she'd once read—or rather heard; it was supposed to be the shortest story in the world. *The last man on earth sat alone in a room. There was a knock at the door.*

The "alone" was redundant, she thought. And the story a

relic, un-p.c.: the continuation would or could simply be, *the last woman on earth waited to enter.*

The knock repeated.

"Come in; it's open."

The woman's face in the mirror behind her own reflection; the same black hair hanging below their shoulders, only her, Kiet's, skin, emerging from the make-up, several shades darker.

"You're the one who called," Kiet said. A statement, not a question.

"Mai. Mai Becker." The woman looked down, nervously, at her feet, and then up at Kiet. "I found your performance very compelling."

"Yes, you would."

"Could you explain…"

"Isadora Duncan once said, 'if I wanted to explain it, why would I go through the very great trouble of dancing it.'"

Mai smiled wanly. "How very clever you are."

Kiet flushed. She deserved the sarcasm. The depth of her anger surprised her. She had been determined not to be rude. But she didn't know how to react to this woman, to whom she was, what she was. The last woman on earth.

"I'm sorry."

Mai Becker hung her head again.

"I…this is quite difficult."

" Please, sit." Kiet rubbed at her face.

Mai sat next to her. They both looked into the mirror, spoke into the mirror.

"The first costume—it looked Indian, Hindu." Mai touched the mukuta, the pointed headdress, on the counter. "It's Cham, right?"

"When did your parents die?"

"My mom in 1991; my dad about a year later. I'm sorry you never got to meet them."

She reached out and touched Kiet's face with the tips of her fingers. But it was the image in the mirror she touched.

"You were their shadow daughter. My shadow sister."

"Yes, well, I suppose it's easier to forget a shadow."

Kiet picked up the statuette of the dancing girl. "You're right—it's Cham. But you find it all over South Asia. This type of dancer is called apsaras. A nymph. A dryad. I'll tell you something about apsarases. One of their jobs was to try to distract sages by seducing them. If they succeeded, they would invariably have girl children. But they would never keep them. They would always abandon them to be raised by foster parents."

"Look," Mai said. "I didn't have to try to find you."

Kiet picked up a tissue and rubbed off more of her makeup.

"Sometimes when the sages saw an apsaras, they were so aroused they'd ejaculate immediately. It's said that the only male children the apsaras would have would come from that. Nice huh? What do you think—should I get that into the act?"

"I don't excuse what my parents did," Mai said. "But they were very poor when we came. Poor and desperate. And I think you reminded them of things they would rather forget."

They both reached, gripped the edge of the dressing counter, as if they really were hard-wired as sisters. Or as if Kiet really was a shadow. Someone looking at them might take them for sisters, she supposed, and in a sense they were; they'd shared, like a womb, the boat that had deposited them into their present lives. But their lives had vectored in very different directions since that landfall. Her anger at this woman's parents for abandoning her was long dead, or at least abstract. She had been their passport, basically. It was a shitty thing to do to a kid, but she had to be grateful to them also— the person she was and the people she loved were the unplanned result of that act of selfishness or survival, and to wish they had acted differently would be to wish for a kind of suicide.

After Mai Becker had called and told Kiet who she was, after the shock, it had been relatively easy to get information about her family: Kiet's mother had worked in state social services; her dad, until this year, was a county sheriff. Both had contacts and ways of unsealing supposedly unobtainable records. But Louise had been uneasy at Kiet's interest, seeing it, correctly, as a desire to find out more about her biological family. Given the nature of her daughter's one-woman performance piece, understanding that need in her was not a great leap. But Louise had never liked her act. She never articulated Kiet's own occasional, uneasy fears that she was exploiting the trendiness of her background, her mixed ethnicity, but that was a reproach Kiet saw in the slight rise of her mother's eyebrows, her fleeting frowns. You just feel threatened, Kiet said, and Louise had smiled grimly. "This kind of retrospective scratching at scabs is what you're supposed to do," she'd said. "But, honey, believe me, it's better just to have the mythology. It's the gift of the country. What you want to do is very nice; it will give you a clear purpose for a time, but in the end it's a distraction from your life at best, a *narrowing* at worst. You have too much talent for that."

She stared at Mai in the mirror. For an instant, as if Louise's words had called it, she felt the room closing in on her. She wanted to just get up, without a word. Leave. But she didn't move.

"I don't know what you want, what I can do," Mai said. "I'm afraid I find this very awkward." She touched the table top as if clutching at an invisible cup of tea. Her fingers were trembling.

"What do you want me to say?"

Mai looked angry. "This…this whole show, performance, you do…the way it revolves around lost identity. But when I contact you, when you have a chance to find out something, you…"

Kiet said nothing.

Mai studied her reflection in the mirror.

"I have something for you."

She fumbled in her purse, drew out a folded envelope. She handed it to Kiet. Kiet unfolded it.

She looked at the envelope, with its Vietnamese stamp: the warrior Trung sisters on their war elephants. It was addressed to *Mr. Trinh Van Hai, 4754 Aspen Lane, Gaithersburg, Maryland.* The return address was *Nguyen Binh Duong, Pho Nguyen Du 12, Ho Chi Minh, Viet Nam.* She pulled out the letter. It was all in Vietnamese, familiar English letters tortured and barbed with diacritical marks, fencing her outside whatever secrets it contained.

Mai suddenly bolted for the door.

A River on the Moon

Nguyen Binh Duong's only direct contact with Americans after the war was through the tourism industry. Before he'd been able to purchase a van and concentrate solely on his own company, he'd led tour groups for a number of other companies, and worked off and on as a guide at the Cu Chi tunnels. The money was not bad, but the work twisted his spirit in strange ways, and he had tried, as he knew foolish men often did—even when aware of their foolishness—to heal himself through an illusion of love. He saw his second marriage, to Ngo Thi Bich Dao, a very traditional village girl from the Mekong, as a sanctuary. Like her village itself, their union would be a safe, hidden place surrounded by gently swaying reeds that broke the sunlight into dazzle, and lotus flowers with their fan-shaped leaves billowing around their brilliant blossoms like the robes of drowning queens. Dao's body, when she finally opened it to him, gave off a lush but delicate fragrance reminiscent of those flowers.

That her native village no longer existed reinforced that wistful ache of nostalgia that he had since come to recognize as the central emotion of his love for Dao. In fact, Dao no longer had family in the Delta. The American war had scattered them and eventually had killed her parents. Her father was famous as a boat builder, her mother for the clever reed fish and crab traps she wove. But the material they had gathered for both crafts grew from earth that had absorbed great quantities of that chemical gift the Americans left behind. The couple died miserably but together, entwined and holding hands, as if conforming their bodies into a monument to a kind of love that no longer exists.

Dao had been five at the time of their death; the neighbors found her trying to snuggle between the cold corpses. Her only other relative was an aunt who was a Buddhist nun. She, and the other sisters, had raised Dao in a Ho Chi Minh City nunnery. Duong knew the kind of place: tiers of rickety balconies lined with wooden doors that all faced a quiet inner courtyard paved with cool slabs of stone, a contemplative statue of the Buddha, his back turned to the noise and tumult of the city. Dao brought the quietude of such places to their marriage: a calm silence—Duong allowed himself to believe—that held in its heart, if one listened to it, the delicate tinkle of temple bells, the murmured chant of prayer. She transformed the inside of their cramped flat in an even more cramped alley into that temple of the sacred past they both longed for, as one longs, even in old age, to lie down and press one's face into the surrounding, comforting flesh of one's parents. And she kept the flat spotless. There was always fresh fruit on the small altar, the smell of incense in the air. Duong would enter, and she would help him peel off his sweaty shirt, as if he were shedding the skin he needed to grow into in order to bear the flaying wounds each day brought. She would silently wash his chest and shoulders from a bowl of water in which peach blossoms floated. Dao was clever, modest, quiet, passionate when it was time to be passionate, gently humorous when laughter was needed to quickly shatter the threat of tears, caring, modest, and she cooked meals that fed Duong's eyes and heart as well as his stomach, dishes which brought back the taste and purity of his youth (or what he wished his youth to be) to his mouth. She was a treasure. Of course he lost her.

The reason for that loss, Mrs. Dottie Simpson, had arrived innocently enough into his life; just one more foreigner; the only American in a group of Germans and Japanese thrown together by fate or accident, into a tour bus that had come out from Sai Gon to see the tunnels. Her smell mingled with, was no different than theirs: the rancid butter odor that foreign sweat seemed to emanate and that mixed with the heavy scent of the perfume or deodorant meant to erase it. It contended in Duong's memory with the sharp stench of the dead who had been blown to pieces or buried alive in those hundreds of miles of tunnels under his feet. But can one truly remember a smell? The Cu Chi area today gave off only the wet, fecund scent of the scraggly new jungle that covered the "historical area," transplanted skin clumsily appliquéd to a scar.

As the new group of tourists descended from the bus, he stood next to Minh, the two of them smiling in greeting, assessing the visitors. He was dressed—his own idea—in the same clothing the manikins placed in front of the bunker and tunnel exhibits wore: black cotton clothing, a checkered scarf around his throat, a cartridge belt around his waist, rubber-tire Ho Chi Minh sandals on his feet. The complete Viet Cong guerilla, though of course in the war, when he'd scurried through these—and other—tunnels, he never had on clothing this clean, and often, during the bombing raids, he would lose whatever clothing he had altogether, blown off as if huge, rude hands had ripped it from his body. Minh was dressed in an identical fashion. He treated Duong to a sardonic grin, gesturing down at the clothing. Duong smiled back, sympathetically. Minh was a veteran too, but from the other side, a Sai Gon-regime soldier who'd worked with an American unit. He'd spent several years in a re-education camp after the war, but had not been purged of the English he'd learned and that enabled him to be hired here, reborn into a new life as his own old enemy.

They spoke their own language to each other as well, the coded references married couples or people who have worked together for years use. "Singapore," Minh grunted, as an overweight foreigner stumbled off the bus, evoking an incident when a similarly heavy tourist from that city had suffered a heart attack after he'd become stuck in a tunnel like an undigested piece of meat.

"No problem," Duong whispered. "This one's at least fifteen kilos lighter."

"Any potential Japanese?" Minh giggled.

Referring to an incident the year before when the Japanese actress who played the lead role in the Tokyo show of *Miss Saigon*, removed all her clothing at one of the tunnel entrances, and draped herself in the red and gold flag of the nation, for publicity photos. She'd been quickly arrested and deported, but now the guides tended to eye each new group of Samurai, hopeful for a repeat performance.

But Duong saw no naked, or potentially naked, Japanese among his middle-aged plodders, and when Mrs. Simpson descended the steps, there seemed no reason to view her any differently than the others. Yet there was something about her, the way she wore her clothing, the confidence of her stride, that clearly marked her as American. She was not, he saw, a young chicken—probably his own age, her skin somewhat coarsened, a slight crepe under her chin, faint nests of wrinkles spider-webbed from the corners of her eyes. She was large breasted, rather voluptuous, her hair blond as corn—though neither of those attributes had ever attracted him before. But when he offered her his hand to help her off the bus, he felt an unmistakable little frisson between their entwined fingers. They both looked at each other, her eyes registering surprise.

Their hands lingered together for a few seconds, and when Duong jerked his back, he saw that his tourists had dispersed to the gift shop. He hurried after them, but they were already haggling over NLF flags, Ho Chi Minh t-shirts, and faked G.I. memorabilia: dog-tags mass produced in the same workshops in Sai Gon that made the engraved Zippo cigarette lighters ("Going to heaven/spent my time in hell, Pleiku, 1966-68,"), fake NLF and American medals, and ash trays decorated with real fifty-caliber rounds. He let them buy for a while, not wanting the store manager to be angry with him. Then, just as he started to gather them back together, he heard a ragged volley of shots. He cursed silently. Apparently some of his group had slipped off to the rifle range, where visitors could fire AK-47's or American M-14's at a dollar a shot.

It was an attraction even more profitable than the gift store, and Duong wasn't sure why he hated it so much—by which he meant that he hadn't allowed himself to dwell on the reasons for his discontent, a quality he cultivated. But as he rushed over to retrieve his tourists, he remembered a conversation he'd had with an American veteran a few days before. Duong had noticed him—a black American—standing to the side as the others picked up their weapons and clumsily blasted away, silly grins on their faces. He was staring at them as Duong did, compelled in this place to see everything with two sets of eyes. Then he must have felt Duong's gaze, for he turned and their eyes met and spoke silently and they both knew. He nodded and walked over slowly.

"Hello, bro,'" he'd said

"My name is Duong."

"Bro," he said again, fingering the black tunic, touching the cartridge belt. "Brother. My brother."

Duong had nodded.

"VC or NVA?"

"VC."

"Here?"

"Yes. You?"

"Sure. 25th Infantry." They both winced as another volley went off. The American had nodded at the tourists. "Know what I'd like? Like to take some of those pieces, me and you, go out in the bush, shoot back at them, drop a few. Shred them. Let them know."

Yes, my brother.

***

In the orientation room his tourists shuffled and shifted and sweated on the benches as they viewed the old jumpy black and white film about the tunnels. Afterwards, outside, Duong pointed out the murals that depicted screaming little Americans being blown to pieces by cunningly placed booby traps, falling clumsily into pits to be skewered by stakes, running panicked through the jungle from heroically postured, and proportioned, male and female liberation fighters who would pour from the cleverly hidden tunnel entrances, looks of determination stamped on their sternly beautiful, heroic faces. The looks Duong remembered were quite different; the faces he'd seen around him during the bombings were like his own, stamped with terror or hatred or both, and it always amused him, if that was the right word, that the painters of these murals never realized that the true heroism was that those terrified men and women had simply stayed, their guts turning to water, tears running down their faces, as if they wished they could turn into the safety of liquid.

Cameras clicked, whirred, flashes flashed, voices muttered appreciatively.

A sequence as unvaried as a religious ritual. Duong led the visitors down the soft, leaf-floored trail through the tangled secondary-growth trees and bushes, pointing out the concealed entrances to tunnels, the exits for cooking smoke hidden diverted through small burrows into charcoal fields, the hidden trip wires, punji stake pits, a heavy log bristling with sharp stakes that would whip down into unsuspecting faces. He spoke automatically, his eyes idly following a large green spider that was spinning a web over the path. It had all become ritualistic for him, a chant to which the chorus would respond in the right place with the correct giggles, grunts, or gasps. Before the tunnel crawl, he took the group to a small clearing near some termite mounds, and told them to stare at the ground, see if they could pick out an entrance to a spider hole hidden somewhere in the area. There was a collective intake of breath as he showed them the camouflaged trap door, covered with latex from the rubber trees and crusted with leaves, right under their noses. He demonstrated how one fit into that small funnel in the earth, holding his arms straight above his head. As his feet touched the mud at the bottom, his ankle brushed against a twig or branch, or perhaps a piece of barbed wire: it must have fallen into the hole. Whatever it was dug sharply into his ankle. He shook his foot, but it seemed to wrap more tightly around, bite into him. He looked up at the grinning faces, the unblinking eyes of the cameras, the assault of flashes on his own. The dirt pressed in on him like heated flesh, awakened an echoing awareness in his own marrow of the other bones beneath this earth. He looked desperately up at the faces again. Their mouths jerked and twitched silently. They were giggling. This blind, stupid herd he was leading through the cemetery of his own past. Then two sky-blue eyes stared down at him. With compassion.

"You OK?" the American woman asked.

At her words, Duong gave his ankle a final, vicious shake and was free of whatever had wrapped around him. "Of course."

"This must be hell for you."

He peered at her, at the rest of the tourists, and pushed himself out of the hole. The group began to crowd forward, eager to take their turns in the earth. They lowered themselves into the hole as if they were squeezing into tight trousers. Cameras clicked, whirred, flashes flashed.

"Vos is loss?" A German woman asked a Japanese. "Why is they have these, these holes?"

"Dottie," the tall American said, holding out her hand like a man. "Dottie Simpson." He shook it warily.

"I'm American," Dottie said.

"Yes."

"But I was always against our war here."

They were walking now to one of the tunnel entrances. Crawling through it was, of course, the highlight of the tour.

"Why do you feel compelled to tell me that?" he asked.

She looked surprised. Duong was somewhat shocked at himself. We only held your government responsible, never the American people, was the stock answer he was supposed to give. He'd been in the tourist industry three years; he knew that one only should give the customer what the customer expected to get. But he was tired of wearing the skin other people put on him.

Dottie continued to stare at him, her pink lips slightly parted. They revealed two rows of perfectly even, perfectly white teeth, like the teeth of a doll. He wanted, suddenly, to lick them.

"Because I don't want you to hate me," she said.

The skin other people put on me. It was an odd phrase, like a word someone had whispered into his mind, and for a moment it gnawed at him, and then he remembered where it must have come from. The English passage came into his mind and immediately slipped out of his lips:

"'*He's made someone up, and it's like he put my skin on her. I'm not like that—not like the made-up one.*'"

He gestured at the other tourists, as if to excuse her. She looked at him curiously.

"Is that a quote? It sounds vaguely familiar."

"From an American novel. Steinbeck. A character named Abra…"

"*East of Eden*," she said.

He smiled, impressed that she knew the book at all. In the beginning, whenever he'd met Americans, he'd tried to talk to them about Steinbeck or Whitman or Hemingway, conversations he'd at times been hungry to have during the war. They would look at him blankly, and some would get very angry.

"It was a book I carried with me throughout the war," he

said. "Steinbeck was one of my favorite American writers."

The others were staring at him expectantly. He pointed to the tunnel entrance. This was a special tunnel, widened, as everyone knew, so that the tourists could go through it. So they could get, as Dottie said to him later, the *idea* of it, without undue discomfort. Near it, one of the girl guides, in complete and spotless Viet Cong regalia like Duong's own but with her face carefully powdered and rouged, her mouth covered with red lipstick, pointed her AK 47 at the hole.

"Go down," Duong said to them. "And please keep moving. But if anyone is afraid of being underground, please wait here. We will walk to the exit and meet the rest of you there."

One by one, joking with each other, full of bravado, they disappeared into the black opening. Dottie stayed. Staring at him. The two of them walked, following above ground the route of the tunnel. He pictured the others, under their feet, wiggling like plump worms.

"Steinbeck, you know," she said, "was in favor of the war…"

"Yes. I saw pictures of him, firing a gun from a helicopter, when he came here as a journalist. I sometimes thought of him doing that, as I lay hidden among reeds below, reading his words. It seemed somewhat ironic. But one needs irony, you know, in such situations. It's helpful."

"But how could…?"

"How could I read him?"

"Yes."

"I was a student of literature before the war…"

She put her hand on her heart, as if overwhelmed by the workings of fate.

"So was I. And I used to teach literature, at a university."

"Used to?"

"I'm a buyer now."

"A buyer?"

"I'm here to check out some new clothing and accessory lines we're ordering from Vietnamese factories."

"Ah."

"When I did teach, though, I didn't do Steinbeck. He's considered somewhat passé—his views on women, on the war…"

"I never met an American, but I always felt I knew the souls of your people through your books. In Steinbeck, I saw my own complexities, contradictions, humanity."

"How did it…affect you? I mean, in the war."

"It made me feel like a murderer. It made me hate you that much more."

She stared at him, and then put her hand on his forearm. Touching it, briefly tracing the skin, as if to test his reality. Her eyes were shining.

"Were you here?" she asked. Gesturing around.

The Japanese and Germans began emerging from the other end of the tunnel, their knees and hands mud-stained. Duong led them to the hollowed log, where other "VC" let them eat samples of manioc, the staple food of the guerillas they were told.

"Our staple food," he whispered to Dottie, "was air."

When the tour was over, the tourists said goodbye to him as they filed onto the bus, thanking him, some pressing bills into his palm as they shook hands. Dottie did also, but when he opened his fist what he saw folded there was the name of a hotel and a room number.

***

The Indochine Palace Tower was a 700-room, thirty-story edifice overlooking the river. The front of the building was gracefully colonnaded, and beyond that shaded façade, behind large picture windows whose glass was streaked with condensation from the air-conditioning, Duong could see well-dressed and coiffed diners, their edges somewhat blurry and erased, sitting at tables covered with white linen.

He walked through two large glass doors, embossed with the seal of the hotel. They closed behind him with a pneumatic hiss. The cooled, slightly perfumed air was the atmosphere of another planet. On the walls were large gilt-framed, sepia-tinted photos of the emperor Bao Dai and his wife arriving somewhere by palanquin; Europeans in white linen suits, the women under umbrellas held by coolies, standing in front of a colonnade meant to evoke the one in front of the hotel now, though he knew the building had been constructed in the 1980's. Bellboys dressed in the red and green robes of courtiers or mandarins stared at him suspiciously, but then smiled in welcome, as if suddenly remembering his face. Other staff, the men wearing brown cotton trousers and collarless white shirts, the women in pastel ao dais, scurried here and there, nodding and smiling to Duong and the guests, their grins echoed on their chests: each of the servers had a large yellow button pinned on his or her breast; on it was a smaller circle containing a curved line and two dots—a "Smiley Face" Dottie explained to him later. ☺ On a raised dais, a musician dressed like an emperor's retainer played a dan bau, its resonant monochord vibrating with the notes of an American tune he couldn't identify then, though it was a tune he would come to know well; he seemed to hear it everywhere in the hotel, floating under the huge crystal chandeliers of the lobby, in the roof tea garden, where Dottie and he would sit on cushioned chairs, around tables shaded by umbrellas, and look down at the turquoise water of the swimming pool. Even from the loudspeakers in the narrow French-style lift, paneled with polished wood, that lifted him now to heaven.

The floor of Dottie's room was also made of polished teak, laid out in a parquet pattern. It was cool and smooth under his feet. Paintings of rural scenes—boys on water buffaloes, village girls threshing rice—hung on walls covered with a sateen fleur-de-lis wallpaper. A ceiling fan stirred the already cool air. The bed was covered with a satin comforter and large green cushions. Duong tore his gaze away from it, stared at Dottie. They stood awkwardly, looking at each other, each reluctant to take the step, cross the line they could never cross back over again. Nervously, he hummed some notes from the tune he'd heard in the lobby and elevator.

"What is that song?" he asked.

"'Moon River'." She took a step forward, and he lurched awkwardly to the side and bumped into a mahogany desk, Dottie's laptop on it. His hand wandered down, caressed the keys. Dottie shuddered. Nervously, he opened and closed the cover of an American clothing catalog, lying on a heap of other catalogs, next to the laptop. Dottie walked over. She took the catalog from his fingers, riffled through the pages, and then stopped. She took his hand, pulled his forefinger straight, and laid it on one of the photos. Duong saw, like a sudden visual echo, that it was a picture of the shirt she was wearing, a description and name written under it, followed by the American copyright symbol, a small c in a circle that at first he confused with Mr. Smiley Face.©. He took in all the details, as if they were ropes to which he could cling to keep from falling into a pit. Dottie smiled at him. She read out loud, "'*Ultraline Rib-Knit T-shirt.*'" As if she were reading a fairy tale to a child.

He stared at her. "Say it," she said, laughing. He repeated it.

"Keep reading," she said. "That's one of my jobs—to make up the names."

"'*Comes in Fresh Berry, Light Sand, Gray Heather, or Deep Coral,*'" he recited.

"Bravo," she said, and drew the shirt (*Deep Coral*) over her head, threw it on the bed. "Those are the magic words." Her pendulous breasts, startlingly white and blue-veined with age, fell free. The years of battling gravity contained in their sag moved Duong deeply. He cupped and kissed them. She grinned, flicked through the catalog, used his finger to point again, and he saw her *Teal Mist Freeport pants of cool Stretch-Piqué cotton canvas* displayed in brighter-than-life colors on the page, like the very idea of itself.

After they had made love, she disappeared into the bathroom. She closed the door, and he heard the shower run. He lay for a time, sated, staring at the whirling blades of the ceiling fan. On the night table lay a small laminated notice from the hotel. "Dear Guest. We are proud here at the Indochine Palace Tower Hotel to tell you of our 'Smile Policy.' All of our helpers here at the hotel are trained to deliver their service to you with a sincere smile. Please help us keep the atmosphere here pleasant and welcome for you by letting us know if any of our staff should 'fail to deliver.' As we say, 'A Frown Brings Us Down.' Sincerely yours, the Management."

At the bottom of the note, there was Mr. Smiley Face.

He swung out of bed, and padded across the polished floor, poking here and there. He opened the sliding door of the closet, and a little light went on, revealing a linen bathrobe. A tag dangling from it told him, in English and French, that this was for guests; if he wished he could purchase it. For now, he would just slip a Vietnamese into it.

It hung on him as soft and comforting as a duck's feathers.

He went to the window and stared down at the clogged, odorous streets below, and at the river. A ferry spun in gracefully to the dock and then spewed out hundreds of motor scooters, swarming like starving bees, the black smoke of their exhaust farting into the air, though he could hear nothing through the glass, only the swish of the ceiling fan, and, from the hallway, faint strains of now familiar music spilling from hidden loudspeakers.

How, he wondered, could there be a river on the moon?

He slowly walked home that night. In his alley, the smells of fish sauce and sweat, heat and dust, assailed him, as the neighbors called his name, said hello. Smiles beamed at him from seamed, worn faces, lips back to reveal crooked, discolored teeth. Calloused hands waved at him. Everything closed around him like a prison. When he walked into his own cramped, hot flat, the first thing he noticed was a continent of mildew stain spreading across the ceiling. How had he never seen it before?

Can't you do anything about that, he asked Dao, pointing. She was squatting over the rice pot, her face shining with sweat. She looked at the ceiling, but registered no reaction.

About what?

Are you blind?

She didn't respond, but went quietly back to her cooking. He sat at the table. Dao put the meal in front of him, opened a beer and put that down too. The beer was hot. She was staring at Duong's wrist.

Did elder brother buy himself a new watch?

He looked down at it.

It's a gift. From one of the tourists. It's not a watch.

A *Fitware Pulse Pedometer* © the catalog had explained. Good for a guide like you, Dottie had said.

Oh. Dao looked at it. A dull red light blinked at her.

It tells how far I've walked. Also how fast my heart beats. Can I have another beer?

She served it.

Can't we get some ice for this?

I'll go out and get some.

Never mind. Sit.

Dao stared at the pulsing light.

Ah, she said sadly.

On Duong's third or fourth visit to the hotel, Dottie convinced him to stay the night. Their lovemaking was frantic. As if they tried to use flesh to go beyond flesh.

Afterwards, they lay in bed and smoked, blowing lazy clouds at the ceiling. Dottie leaned over him and switched on the radio built into the bed table. A French song featuring a woman panting like a dog filled the room.

"Duong, darling," she said. "I want to go back out with you."

For a moment he drew a blank. "Where?"

She blew a smoke ring, stuck the pink tip of her tongue through it. "To Cu Chi."

"You've seen it all."

She snubbed out the cigarette. "Have I? I don't think so."

"What do you mean?"

"Duong," she said. "This is hard to explain."

"Is it?"

She began speaking slowly, as to a child. "When I was a college kid, I spent all my time working against the war. It was the passion of my youth—it defined me. Can you understand how much this country means to me?"

"No."

She caressed his chest and stomach, her fingers drawing circles on his body. "I've heard stories," she said. "About the tunnels. That some of the old ones, the real ones, still exist. Not the stuff you guys have made for the tourists. The real ones. I want you to take me in one. One that you don't bring the other foreigners to." Her caress moved lower. "It's true, isn't it?

"Yes," he said hoarsely, as if confessing to an interrogator.

"Great." She rolled over, and kissed his cheek.

"Where are you going?

"Down to the Business Center. I'm expecting a fax."

"From your husband?"

"Shh," she said, and kissed him again.

32

When she was gone, he put on his robe, sat at the small teak desk, looking at himself in the mirror mounted above it. He would not take her; he'd agreed to nothing. In the soft light, his scar was not so much invisible as transformed, representative. His fingers found, spread the short stack of email printouts and business cards she had left on the desk. Her own was on top. He stared at the address under Dottie's name. For a long time he did nothing, only looked at it, the letters swimming in front of his eyes. It was not a portent he could ignore. Some hotel stationery, thick and creamy, also lay on the desk. He opened the drawer, found a pen, envelopes embossed with the hotel's name. He wrote for a few minutes, sealed the letter, addressed it. Someone knocked on the door. He froze. Dottie would never knock, and he was something of an unauthorized guest here, an intruder into this cool sanctuary. He didn't answer. Then he heard the sound of a card sliding into the lock, and the door opened.

One of the hotel staff, a slight effeminate man in a collarless white shirt and brown pants, stood there smiling at him, holding a tray. He bowed his head.

"Oh, I am sorry, sir," he simpered. "This is our nightly gift, sir. For all guests."

He giggled, and took a piece of chocolate, wrapped in shiny green foil, from the tray.

"For your sweet dreams, sir," he lisped. And smiled.

Hundreds of thousands of skulls emerged from the soil of Duong's mind, grinned at him mockingly. Mr. Smiley Faces.

Turn around, he said harshly, in Vietnamese.

He smiled, complied.

Duong kicked him.

"Thank you, sir."

Yes, my brother.

No, of course he didn't. Though his foot itched to feel that boney behind. It was a scene his mind constructed, wishful thinking. Instead he gave the envelope to the man, told him to charge the postage to the room. The man left. Duong went to the window and watched the silent whirl of boats on the river, the silent throngs of people clotting on the hot streets below. He looked north, to the horizon. If he had stood behind this window during the war, he would have been able to see and hear the explosions as the B-52s hit Cu Chi, collapsing those delicate veins through the earth. Can you understand how much this country means to me?

When she came back, he picked up her card from the desk, pretending was seeing it for the first time. "'Gaithersburg, Maryland,'" he read. "Is that where you are from?"

He had tried to speak casually, but she looked at him curiously.

"Yes. What's the matter, Duong?"

"Nothing," he said. "I may know somebody there."

"Well," she said. "I wouldn't be surprised."

"What do you mean?"

"Take it easy, baby. Just that a lot of Vietnamese live there."

"Ah."

"Jeez," she said.

"We can go out," he said. "Tomorrow."

"So there is a tunnel," she said triumphantly.

"Of course."

They drove out on Duong's motor scooter. He parked it in a small bamboo grove behind the main "historical" area. He led the way through some rubber and causarina trees to a small clearing, ringed by thorny underbrush. As he bent down to part the brush, a slim green snake flowed out between them, and Dottie let out a short scream. He watched it silently disappear. Dottie was breathing a little harder, not, he saw, with fear, but with excitement. He held the bushes back as she slipped through. She was sweating heavily and the turned-butter odor he had ceased to smell from her flesh was back now, strong, reeking under her deodorant. He wrinkled his nose. She glanced at him, grinning, her eyes aglow. The crepe of fish-white flesh under her chin dripped with sweat. How had he ever found her physically exciting?

A large areca tree, out of place here, stood in the center of the clearing. A bristle of blackened joss stick stubs stuck out beneath a small shrine one of the other guides had placed in a convolution of the trunk. Near it was a dried creek bed, and the entrance to the old tunnel was hidden in the bank. It was well known to those guides who had been here during the war, but until now they had kept it pure, kept it for themselves. No one who did not know would ever find the door to this world of the past under their feet.

He went to it unerringly and pulled it open. Dottie gasped.

"It's so small!"

"What did you expect," he said harshly. Unlike the tourist tunnels, the tunnel beyond the opening was more or less horizontal, gradually sloping into the earth. "We need to go in headfirst. Do you still want to do it?"

She looked at him and shivered, and then licked her lips.

"It will be tight, and hot." He stripped to his underwear. She hesitated, and then did the same. As her skin was exposed, her smell grew stronger, clogging his nostrils.

She winked at him, and then flicked on her flashlight and crawled into the tunnel.

Duong waited a moment, and then followed her inside.

It was, of course, almost too tight for her, and for that matter, for him also, at this point in his well-fed life. But Dottie wormed her way forward, moaning a little with the effort, the sound rising to a kind of wordless mantra. Dirt spilled down on their heads and backs. The deeper they went into the earth, the hotter it grew. The red light on the pulse odometer winked at him, faster and faster, and its little face tried to tell him how far he'd come. But the lens was obscured by dirt. The tunnel widened a bit, and Dottie rose to her hands and knees. He clicked on his own light. Her full, round behind filled the space in front of him. *Glowing Salmon Pink.* Her scent was mingled now with the strong odor of wet earth, and instead of the revulsion he'd felt before, he was suddenly rigid with lust. He grabbed her ankles. She stopped, docilely, as if expecting his grip. He worked his hand up around her sweat-slick legs, his knuckles and the backs of his hands and his back and neck scraping against the dirt walls of the tunnel. The flashlight went out, and they were in pitch black darkness, broken only by the blink of the red light, pulsing more quickly as his heart beat faster. He got his fingers under the band of her panties, and she crawled forward, whimpering as he slipped them off. In the darkness, he couldn't be sure which tunnel he entered, but he pressed forward anyway, like a good soldier, ignoring her sudden scream. Dirt spilled on their backs. *For your sweet dreams*, he thought. *Do you know what this country means to me?*

He let out a small scream himself then, and he collapsed. The earth quivered around him. In the darkness he could hear her gasping.

Her flashlight clicked on. She was lying full length, face down, the soles of her sneakers near his face, her panties draped around one ankle. She turned to look at him, just able to bring her face around, her chin on her shoulder. The light made her face a ghastly mask. Her lips drew back into a faint smile. It was filled with a triumph that stuck into Duong's throat like a knife.

Panic fluttered in his chest. He began to work his way backwards to the entrance; it was awkward and difficult but he needed to get away, to get out of there. Dottie called his name, softly, querulously. In a while he heard her scuttling softly after him.

He left her clothes piled near the entrance, but he didn't wait for her. It took him fifteen minutes to work his way through the bush to the main entrance. Minh was manning the rifle range. He stared at Duong's mud-covered face and hands, but said not a word when Duong took the AK-47 from the rack, and remained silent as he loaded and fired bullet after bullet, one at a time, as if he were trying to punctuate a sentence that refused to end.

Cul De Sac

On Monday, Kiet drove up to Mai Becker's house in Gaithersburg to see what else she could find out, and to make amends; she had been somewhat stunned, and then hangdog, at the depth of her anger. She supposed some of it had been leftover emotion from her performance. Mai and her husband lived in a brick split-level at the end of an oak-shaded street ablaze with azalea bushes, a house, she had told Kiet, that she had inherited. Apparently her parents hadn't remained poor. Kiet stood outside for a few moments, wondering what it would have been like to have grown up in the little suburban cul-de-sac that held this house cupped in its protective hand, a haven after the heaving seas, the rude displacements.

There were two photographs as well on the altar to the ancestors that Mai kept on a shelf set into an unobtrusive niche in the living room wall. One was a color-tinted print of a man and woman in traditional Vietnamese clothing, he in a blue-silk robe and she in an ao dai, on her head, the pill cap— Kiet forgot the right term for it—that her father said made the women look like Speedy Alka-Seltzer; a figure out of some sixties television commercial he was, as always, surprised she didn't know. The other photo was of a child of, perhaps, two years, dressed in some sort of jumper. A cluster of dusty joss sticks in a small silver bowl. A small teak box. All of it subtle, congruous with the soft gray and mauve of the wall, the pine Ikea tables and shelving, the silver-framed prints on the wall, the white leather sofa and love seat, the blue and tan Isfahan carpet centered on the gray tile floor. A small boy sat in front of the flat screen TV on the other side of the room, his fingers dancing over a control pad, zapping aliens, ignoring her, the alien that had come into his living room. He looked more white than Vietnamese, would never be bui doi, dust, in any life. An uncharitable thought.

Mai came back into the room, bearing a tray with two sweating glasses of ice tea on it. She put the tray down on the coffee table in front of the sofa, and stepped up next to Kiet.

"The other night—I'm sorry for the way…"

"Forget it," Kiet said. "Me too."

They both looked solemnly at the altar. It was a Moment.

"What can you tell me about this man?" Kiet asked.

"Nguyen Binh Duong?" Mai said. "I googled him. Apparently he has some sort of tourist service. In Sai Gon. Ho Chi Minh City. Whatever."

Kiet took out the letter. "Can you translate this?"

Mai looked embarrassed. "I'm afraid not. But we can give it to some friends of mine."

"You said you had another letter," Kiet coaxed. "A more recent one?"

Mai rose and went to the small altar, and then brought the teak box back to the settee. Kiet was moved that she had kept it on the altar. Mai opened the box, handed her the letter. The envelope was different, cream-colored, the paper expensive. She ran her fingers lightly over the raised letters of the return address, the name of a hotel repeated: once in English, once in Vietnamese. The top was slit open. Kiet ran her thumb along the slit, feeling somehow violated. She took out the letter. In this one, Nguyen Binh Duong had written in English. But not very much. *This is to inquire after the fate of the infant girl child…* The words swam before her eyes, spiking and curling as if they were morphing back into Vietnamese.

"And you never replied?"

"I didn't know what to say." Mai sipped her tea. "I don't know what to say."

"Your parents never spoke of him?"

She hesitated. "There was a box of letters. They burned them."

Kiet gasped. Felt her heart turn to ash. Mai's son screamed in triumph at another murder.

"Preston, turn that off and go to your room," she snapped.

"Mom, I'll lose my level…"

"Do what I say!"

It came out in a high-pitched scream, edged near hysteria. Her son stared at her, shocked, his eyes welling. She stared back, but not at him. He turned off the television and left the room.

"I'm sorry."

Kiet said. "I'm not here to complicate your life. Just tell me whatever you know."

"Whatever I know?" Mai laughed, as if the phrase was funny. "I know there was a man who helped my parents, helped us, get out of Viet Nam in '75. I remember *Ma* and *Ba* would pray for him." She looked at Kiet defiantly. "And for you. Believe me or not. From the letter; I suppose it was him, this Duong. You can Google him too."

"I did."

Mai laughed again, a little too loudly. "It's so weird, isn't it? What will you do?"

Kiet shook her head.

"Looking for the missing," Mai said, as if she'd answered. "It's the thing to do, isn't it?" She raised her face and looked into Kiet's eyes for the first time since she'd come into her house. "But you were my missing. And I found you."

"Yes."

She held Kiet's gaze. "My parents weren't bad people…Kiet." A hesitation when she said the name, holding it in her mouth for an instant, as if tasting something tentatively, something that might be bitter. "I'm sure that when they gave you over to social services, they thought it was the best thing. That you would at least have a home."

"So I did. Several of them."

"I can't help what they did." Kiet wondered which *they* she meant. Mai's parents? The series of nightmare foster parents that had culminated with Hiram Johns and his tobacco stained fingers? The way Louise had reconstructed it, the Trinhs had probably taken her because Kiet had been what was called a golden child, with enough of an American—in her case, African-American—look to enable Mai's parents to get American visas for the family, when they'd ended up in a Malaysian refugee camp. But Kiet had no desire to keep fighting this particular war.

She shook her head. "It doesn't matter. And in the end, I, well, ended up OK."

"Your dad...your...what would you call him? Adoptive father?"

"Alexander Hallam. I call him my father."

"Of course. He was in the war?"

"Yes."

"Does he know anything else about your background... your origins?"

"No more than I do. Your parents—did they ever tell you my Vietnamese family name, anything?"

"No."

"When I started doing my act, I discovered that Kiet's usually a boy's name. Did you know that?"

Mai nodded. "It was my brother's. He drowned, off the coast of Malaysia."

Kiet stared at her, her shadow sister, feeling herself sinking, her edges dissolving into water.

Baxter

She turned off the engine. Her father's sculptures guarded the lawn like pickets. The house, her own sanctuary from the heaving, treacherous ocean of her first fifteen years, was an old weathered clapboard Maryland house, surrounded by a screen porch. Behind it, a dock stuck out into the head of a winding estuarine creek, its banks lined with lush green and gold cord and marsh grass, swaying cattails. The patch of yard behind, Kiet knew, would be cluttered haphazardly with piled crab pots, a tangle of nets, wooden boats up on skids, three fiberglass kayaks, stacked pilings, a large wooden crabbing boat. Baxter's trailer, a neat double-wide, was kitty-corner to the house: Alex had it placed there about five years ago. Before that, Baxter had lived in his own cottage, out on Point Lookout. But it was state land, and the state had finally claimed it. Later, she found out—he never said a word about it—that for years, her dad had been paying Baxter's rent on the property, bringing food and supplies out to the house, doing repairs.

She walked over to the trailer. She'd meant to go straight to Alex and Louise, but she realized that she needed to stop here first, talk to Baxter, get what she was doing straight in her mind— something she had done since she was sixteen and had a problem or feeling she needed to articulate before going, as Baxter said, to the Big House for judgment. Before she could knock, she heard Baxter call out her name and ask her to come in. She smiled. It was something he did— identifying people by their footfalls—and something she knew he enjoyed showing off.

He was sitting in a large comfortable chair, upholstered with some kind of bright orange, fuzzy cloth. He wore his sunglasses—Kiet wondered if he had put them on when he heard her at the door, turned his face towards her, tilting it upwards in that quizzical way the sightless have.

"If you ever got your sight back long enough to get a glimpse of that chair," she said, "You might be grateful to be blind."

"There are all kinds of advantages, girl. I often mull them over."

She kissed his stubbly cheek. "Mull?"

He nodded. "Often."

She sat on the couch, kitty-corner to his chair. He reached out and touched her face, his fingers tracing out her features, a traditional greeting between them. She closed her eyes for a moment, trying to listen, feel with her skin the way she imagined he would. Wondering how that sensation could be translated to words, to dance. She opened her eyes. There were no lights on in the trailer, only the daylight coming through the window, and the room was pooled with deep shadows. The spillage of his eyes, she had once thought. She was suddenly conscious of the weight of her bag pulling at her shoulder.

There was a plate with some hardening scraps of egg and a crust of toast, on the low table in front of his chair. She piled the knife and fork next to it onto the plate, picked it up, took it over to the sink. She spoke over her shoulder as she rinsed.

"I'm going to take a trip to Viet Nam. I was given a letter from someone who might know my family there."

"Well, that's exciting."

She dried her hands on a dishtowel and came back over. "I'm a little worried about Alex."

"You didn't tell him yet?"

"Sometimes," she said, "I used to imagine you were my father. My black father."

"I know that, honey. So does Alex."

She put her bag on the table and drew out the stone

dancer. Handed it to him. He touched it, caressed it, as he had her face. Nodded.

"Your dance."

"He gave this to me, when I was sixteen, when the adoption papers came through. As if this was the real sign I was now his daughter."

She felt herself blushing, her own words suddenly sounding melodramatic to her.

"He gave it to me, but he would never talk about it, Uncle Baxter," she said. "In a way that was a blessing—I suppose that's why it's fascinated me, gave me a kind of creative energy." She touched the statuette, closing her eyes, trying to feel it the way Baxter would. "I preferred not knowing. I could make up my own stories."

"And now?"

"It's not enough."

Baxter held up his hand. "Maybe you were right in the first place, honey. There's nothing I can tell you about this—you need to ask your father."

He handed the statuette back to her.

Ice

Le Thi Thanh Thuy woke feeling not empty but emptied. As if what had filled her had spilled out. The feeling was there before the details of the dream came back to her; as they did, slowly, she wanted to sleep again, reclaim it. It was impossible. Impossible also that the tips of her breasts ached for a mouth that had only found them once, only found them dry. Thuy lay next to the empty space where the weight of her husband would have dented their sheets. She opened her eyes, caressed the cool linen, feeling a sense of guilt, as if the dream had been a reproach to him for the child they'd never had. Her hand moving, she realized, the way she would soothe Thinh when she was tired, wanted him to be still, could no longer bear to think of his futile pounding at the door of her womb.

She sat up, switched on the ceiling fan. Lay down again, let the air beat the trapped heat down onto her body. Tried to move off the twisting paths her mind was running along this morning. She became aware that she was singing softly, the words pushing past her lips:

A flag hangs far away in the windless homeland.
I am without enemy and thus have been in pain
ever since the months of anxiety withered my hair.

One of Trinh Cong Son's songs. A few days before she had read about the death of the old folk-singer, rebel; she had known him for years, had last seen him, when? Only two weeks ago, sitting at an outdoor table, a platoon of empty beer and vodka bottles in formation before him. He was poignant as a ruin: beret tilted rakishly on his head, wild strands of brittle silver hair tendrilling around his ears as if in imitation of the soaked strands of tobacco in the cigarette butts disassembling in the puddle of spilled stale beer on the table. A clichéd image of bohemian poet, only he was the original, the thing itself, drinker, smoker, womanizer, mad with words, hated by whatever authority he needed to hate as much as it needed him to persecute, his aging an embodiment of the inevitable withering of some youthful idealism in her own heart and she supposed so many others, the end of a need for peace as if it were an end itself, as if it only meant the laying down of arms.

Paltry sunrays on a distant road,
nights return rhythmically in the heart,
eyes like afternoons underneath innocent foreheads.

That his words were in her mouth now didn't surprise Thuy. Since his death she had been thinking of doing her next cai luong play as a dramatization of Trinh Cong Son's life, put his songs to the warble of cai luong tunes, perhaps even incarnate him as a woman poet, his personality and lyrics recognizable but transformed into a nineteenth-century courtesan, the idea edgy. Or simply do him as himself, dramatic enough. But she was unsure. The last time she had seen Son, he had waved a tobacco-stained finger in her face, admonished her about the futility, the "arrogance" he said, of taking a traditional dramatic form and trying to fit it into modern situations. "You can only reduce it to the political, sweetie," he said, and before she could retort—he should talk!—had launched into a long and completely irrelevant anecdote about a commercial photographer who gave odd instructions to his subjects, when he posed them. Look happily demented. Look demonically ecstatic.

Besides, other playwrights, novelists, artists, the whole flock of vultures were already feeding on the old man's corpse. She didn't want to join them.

But she needed something for the theater. Something original. Her own flock of rare fledglings—the young actors she had lured to live theater from their electric dreams of being on the reality shows, music videos and Korean soap-operas that crowded the television airwaves—waited, stretching their necks out, their beaks parting, desperate for nourishment. Legendary for her vigor, she felt blank these days, stunned with fatigue, filled with reluctance to expend once again the energy a new work would draw from her depleted spirit. That reluctance itself simply a brittle-rough thatch lid pressed over the deep-seated fear that she had nothing left inside herself to draw from.

She tried to comfort herself with the thought that she always felt this dread between plays, worse now perhaps because of Trinh Cong Son's death, the whirlpool of memories his passing left in its wake, a Charybdes that sucked her down into the past, into the dreams she'd had every night.

She needed an image; that was always her starting point. Pearl Emperor, send me an image.

She dressed and went out, had a steaming bowl of noodle soup at the corner, sitting eye level with the traffic, eating soup and fumes. She bought a copy of *Youth* from the old woman squatting near the noodle shop. The literature section had a new story by Phan Trieu Hai, a writer whose work she liked. But as she turned to it, a photo on the opposite page caught her eye. The Chinese had sent an exhibit of ice sculptures; the display would be shown in Dam Sen Park. The article gushed about the technology that enabled the sculptures to remain intact in the heat of Sai Gon, but what had arrested her gaze was a blurry photo of two of the statues, their features vague. She felt a chill, imagined the ice moving through her veins, sharp to her heart.

It wasn't a portent she could ignore. She waved down a motor-scooter taxi, rode to Dam Sen Park. Keeping herself open to the world.

At the entrance, children were whirling around on the octopus arms of a ride, each tentacle holding a tiny airplane, American insignia on its fuselage. She stared at them.

No. Too obvious. Too banal.

Inside the park gate, she strolled along the sidewalks, past ice cream vendors, statues of Roman gods and goddesses, a water puppet performance—could she do a cai luong play as a water puppet show, her actors playing puppets?

Suddenly she was surrounded by brides.

Heavily madeup, full Western gowns, layers of gleaming white satin and lace; they made silky rustling sounds as they walked, the brushing of feathers, a flock descending on her, no fledglings here, but preening swans, squawking ducks, a few waddling geese, bouffant crests piled atop their heads, beaks clicking, eyes heavy with apprehension or dull with resignation or gleaming with triumph, their bridegrooms dark, barely noticeable shadows shifting around them. The brides clustered and queued at "scenic" locations: small arched bridges over lotus ponds, in front of statues and small pagodas. Thuy watched them line up, arms hooked possessively to what seemed to her a single, slight interchangeable groom, as the park photographers clicked away, snipped their single shining moments from the inevitable stream of time. Smile. Look dementedly certain. Look moronically confident in the future.

A couple was standing in front of her, the bride, all lace and white satin, thrusting a camera at Thuy, the new generation demanding what was owed from the old guard. Though apparently, from the quizzical look Thuy noticed now, the young woman had been speaking to her for some seconds, asking, no doubt politely, for Thuy to take their picture.

She tried to capture them in the rectangle of the viewfinder, unused to these digital cameras: the couple floated and bounced here and there, shifting whenever she tried to center them, until finally she gave up, pressed the button, got them on the fly.

She handed the camera back and walked on. A few meters further up the path, an old American helicopter, its interior stripped, its rotors wilted like broken reeds, sat next to the sidewalk. As she looked, another flurry of brides descended upon the machine, giggling, teasing, hanging from the skids, enclosing its faded green with undulating, rustling, fluttering white wings, as if trying to bring it back into the sky, oblivious to its history, its deadly resonance here, as the children at the gate of the park had been, circling in the air and laughing, blessedly blank of the memories those old fuselage insignia on the peeling paint sides of their toy aircraft could awaken.

I had a lover
He died in the A Shau
He died in Pleiku
He died naked under a bridge

The grooms surrounded the grounded aircraft, their cameras clicking and whirring. Smile. Try to look like homicidal spreaders of democracy.

A sign: *To the Chinese Ice Exhibit.*

She followed the arrows, glad to have something that told her what direction to go.

Behind a little copse of trees was a huge humped mollusk, the inflated rubberized shell she had read about in the paper, the generators outside whining frantically in the 40-degree-Celsius temperature of the day. She entered an airlock-like chamber, was given a quilted red coat to wear. Its thickness made her arms stick out from her sides at an angle, another strange bird getting ready to fly. For the first time in her life she saw her crystalized breath pouring from her mouth: one of her seven souls escaping.

Mist swirled around her feet, skittered from her as she walked. The Great Wall, the Eiffel Tower, the Taj Mahal, stood behind a rope barrier, carved from great blocks of ice, white and gleaming, the mist disturbed by her feet keeping them ephemeral and obscuring the dimensions of the enclosed space, so that its walls seemed to keep dispersing, shifting.

The structure was subdivided, hive-like. She walked into the next cell. And stopped. Here were the ice statues, a platoon of them, their bodies and faces prismed and gleaming in the light from the sodium lamps, some life-sized, some larger, a few smaller. Chairman Mao and Uncle Ho held up their guiding hands, their features blunted smooth under the sheen of the ice. Soldiers and workers and peasants, frozen in time, marched heroically, raised fists pumping; near them, Mickey Mouse danced with Daisy Duck. Her father had been a carver and she knew he had led her here, had troubled her sleep, had marked her path past the dead icons of the past. Through the picket of statues, she thought she glimpsed the face of the Buddha. She walked around the roped statues to it. Closer, shuddering, she saw the figure's face was melting slightly, too close to one of the lights. Next to him Quan The Am Bo Tat, the Goddess of Mercy, and next to her a tra kieu dancer, an apsaras. The ice-mist swirled around the white forms like the exhalations of the dead, blurred their features, the Buddha and the Goddess dancing and jerking like the bride and groom in the viewfinder, and the Goddess's face was suddenly her sister's face, the pure white of it a thin shell over a burning yellow inner fire, and the ice hand of the Buddha was the hand of her father, putting a small statue he'd carved into the hand of an American soldier.

I am without enemy and thus have been in pain
ever since the months of anxiety withered my hair.

She turned to run, stopped herself. Her mind retreated, drew back as it had at the soup shop from this inevitable vision, as if it had touched fire instead of ice, and because everything in her wanted to let it melt away through her fingers, her grip, she knew that this was what she had searched for; that this was exactly what she needed to seize.

Someone nearby lit a match. A guard said something angrily, the match was extinguished. But not before it had flared in Thuy's brain. Opened that night, when she had tried to flee with the child. A match had flamed suddenly, its light revealing the tight-lipped faces around her, rendered flat as masks. The match quickly blown out, a man cursing, the upturned faces painted white by the moonlight. As if they were statues of ice. As if they pushed around her now as they did then, their breath visible as they panted in the mist. The ice filigreed, cracked, revealed images frozen in memory slowly warming into flesh and motion. She had stood near the boat, pressed in the middle of the crowd of people, winging her elbows out against them to give the child in her arms space to breathe. The child did not cry. It was if the silent intensity of this desperate group had affected her; they were like a single organism focused completely on what might kill or save them. They stared at the sea, clutching their bags or suitcases or children. Its blackness was scrawled with silver lines of phosphorescence. They stared the way they would stare at the tracks of a train station. They were a silent crowd at a train station. They panted. The heated air felt thick in their throats and lungs. Their tongues hung out. They could imagine in their thirst the larger thirst that awaited them on the sea. They had heard the stories. They were going anyway. They stared at the boat. It was surely too small to hold all of them; the wood in its hull streaked; the boards warped, ill-fitted. A sailor, barechested, wearing a pair of baggy shorts, waved at them, his eyes fierce, whispered, quickly, quickly. A woman near Thuy suddenly, frantically, had kissed the face of the little boy in her arms, and the crowd pressed forward and, as if she were still a small girl with a doll, imitating the behavior of an adult, Thuy kissed the child. As if her action were a signal, suddenly a whistle blew. The blinding glare of a searchlight found them, beams probed, like the accusing fingers of the nation, illuminated individual faces, each twisted in fear or panic or acceptance, as if they were photos in a book, the tattered album her father had kept near the family altar. She saw them like that, suddenly fastened, and it seemed it was only sometime later that she heard the groans. There were no screams. She was sure of that. The soldiers were suddenly around them, their AK 47s raised, and there was the sound of a woman quietly crying. But there were no screams. Only that groan that seemed to burst from all their throats and chests at once; a great and collective moan of pain but also of surrender and resignation, and she had clutched the child hard to her breast, as if she could melt it into herself.

Hands

Kiet stared at her mother's hands, their fingers spread over the computer keyboard. Since Mai Becker's revelations, the loss of her name, she'd had the sense of a basic shift in the world, a kind of lurch that had created the need to inventory what she had and who she loved. Louise's gaze was fixed on the screen; she was unaware of Kiet. She had a soft pouch under her chin now, a minor spread in her hips, her hair only slightly graying—but it was the slight thickening of the knuckles on her mother's fingers, the small constellation of liver spots on the backs of her hands, that caused Kiet to feel a sudden pang, the anticipation of loss.

Once upon a time her mother, as all good mothers should, had helped rescue her from an ogre. It had been at the end of a time marked by hands. Her own hands on a polished black granite wall, trying to carve out with her fingernails the name of a dead and mythological father. The filthy, spatulate, probing fingers of the tobacco farmer who was her last foster father. Her own hands again, the feel of a trigger under her fingers, so that she knows, as the man who became her true father, as Alex does, what it was to squeeze that curve of metal. Louise's hands reaching for her, taking her like a bundle, a gift, from the arms of Alex, as if he, strangely, had birthed her.

She reached down and caressed the skin of her mother's hand.

Louise jerked it away, startled, streaming a uuuuuuuuiiiii across the screen.

"Shit, Kiet!"

"Sorry."

She shook her head, said, "She-it, Kiet," in exaggerated exasperation.

They both grinned. It was a catch-phrase between them, a curse first uttered by one of Kiet's fellow residents at the group home where Louise had been her counselor. She'd been placed there when the state of Maryland found that the man she'd been given over to for foster care was fucking her—the only way she would ever describe it. The Johns, Hiram and Dorothy, had a small farm just down the road from this house. Kiet was fostered to them after the police had picked her up at the Vietnam memorial; she would go there and look at the statue of the African-American soldier, and then at the names on the wall, as if her unknown father's would leap out at her, claim her. The D.C. cops had passed her on to Maryland social services, since her original papers came from that organization, and that office had sent her south, here, to the tip of the state, fostering her to a farm family in a theoretical attempt to shelter her from the temptations of the street, expose her to rural work ethics. But Hiram Johns, twisted by loneliness after his wife died, or perhaps simply liberated into his true form, had taught her other rural values.

She-it, Ki-et. Tonetta—was that the girl's name? It was during a period she had decided to be black, in an attempt to blend in more, or, she supposed, to simply make everything less complicated. Louise had insisted she use her Vietnamese name—what they both had thought until now was her Vietnamese name—but she'd tried to get the other girls to call her Keisha, a campaign that ended one evening when one of the other counselors at the home rented *Platoon*. Watching that movie, she became convinced that the village mother shot dead in front of her daughter was, in fact, her mother, that this was how her biological mother had died.

She thought she had let all that go. Turned it into art, into her performance piece. The apsaras could be, variously, a female spirit of water and clouds, or a muse, or in other manifestations, a dancer before the celestial throne of Indra.

Apsarases were known to help gamblers and heroes; they were also known, as she had said to Mai Becker, to seduce would-be saints, demonstrate to would-be holy men their true natures. They were, in other words, shape-shifters. There was a time when that was an attractive concept to her.

"Dancer in Stone," had started as her senior project at college—she'd double-majored in history and dance. For the first subject she had started, not, as people assumed, in Asian or African-American studies. Instead she had concentrated on seventeenth-century Maryland. It seemed an identity she could tap into—both Louise and Alex were descended from first-settler families, her dad's branch containing both white and black ancestors—and yet far enough away from the war and its country that had shaped her childhood like another, ghostly, hand. But the dancer her father had given her when she was adopted became more and more an object of fascination—its origin and his silence made it so. At sixteen, she stared at it, draped K-Mart beads around her breasts, a towel loincloth swaying between her legs, and imitated its posture, pretended, boobs bouncing, to dance its dance. She found images of it easily enough on line, learned it was a type of figure carved by the Cham people in Central Viet Nam, identical to the apsaras found in friezes at Angkor Wat, Pagan in Burma, and on the temples of India. The Chams had been mostly wiped out by the conquering Vietnamese. She had felt drawn to that history of defeat. It was, her mother claimed, an imagined connection, coaxed out by the exterminated history of her own past. Her mother was probably right. This small statue from her father's time in the war, whatever secrets it, and he, held close to their respective breasts, would have nothing to do with whatever biological family she came from. Alex knew no more of them than she did. Had acquiesced, as she had, in the theft of her name. But the statuette became a way for her to meld the mysteries of her own engendering to the tight-held secret that had been his origin, that froze him in the stone whose hidden shapes his hands tried desperately to chip away, liberate. They were both frozen in stone, they both needed to believe that the recreation of that condition in art, finding its true name, might save them. So she chose to believe, chose a credo. She had attended her first dance class as a way of doing her freshman physical education requirement, and it came to be that only in dance could she liberate and control the strange and conflicting tides of her existence.

She had told Louise about Mai Becker, but not what she'd learned about her name. When Mai had told her, she'd felt as if she had been yanked out of herself, a replicant finding out her past merely a programmed fiction. That night, she felt she was drowning. Her mouth and throat thick with salt water and blood, her chest heaving. It was a feeling akin to what she had felt as a fifteen-year-old as she'd watched the film *Platoon* and became convinced that the village woman Tom Berenger had shot was her actual mother: a sudden, sick-making discovery that she was not who she'd thought she was that had filled her mouth with the coppery taste of blood. In a sense, the name Kiet—even though she knew its origin now—was a name Louise had given her, and in another sense, that was how it should have been, and she was reluctant to take that from her mother, especially now.

Louise turned off the computer. "What's up, honey?"

"I've decided to go."

"Do you know what a quixotic chase it's going to be?"

"You and Dad could both come with me."

Louise smiled wanly.

"You have the time."

"Not really, sweetie. I'm serving on two commissions and the school advisory board. And what about your time? You have a full schedule of performances."

"I wouldn't be there for months. Just in and out."

"Well, we've heard that before, haven't we?"

"It's not the war."

"Yes. 'Viet Nam is not a war.' They keep telling us that now." She reached over and caressed Kiet's face.

"Do you know—when your father wanted to adopt you— I was very much against the idea?"

Kiet drew back from her, somewhat shocked. They had always been frank with each other, but much of what they understood about the cords that had knotted their lives went unarticulated. Kiet knew the truth in what Louise had just said, but not why she had chosen to say it.

"Yes," she said.

"I couldn't accept that you were supposed to be some sort of redemption for him."

Kiet felt her face burn. "I was never only something symbolic for Dad."

"You became more, darling," Louise corrected gently. "For both of us."

"Why are you telling me this now?"

"Oh, honey, I just don't want to lose you. Either of you. That's what I was afraid of then. That's what I'm afraid of now."

The year she had come to Alex and Louise, Kiet had decided to be a Viet Cong. Perhaps it was the beginning of her life as a performance artist. As a shape-shifter. She would dress in black, imagine herself containing the ghost of her Vietnamese mother, imagined seeing the New World through that mother's transported eyes. Haunting Southern Maryland marshes and forests and neighborhoods as well, though few of the people she'd bothered then had any idea who she was supposed to be—with the exception of Alex, who became obsessed with finding her, with rescuing her, as if she were some do-over he could snatch from the world—the fear Louise had articulated. The war had brought her to Alex and Louise, the war could steal her—and Alex—both away. Viet Nam was not a war, her mother had quoted, and Kiet had read the literature too, the sudden outpourings of a generation of Vietnamese-Americans insisting on the complications of the place whose oversimplification into a synonym for pain and loss had littered them across an ocean and across an America that had insisted on seeing Viet Nam in only that way. She understood the concept. But what else could it really ever be, for her, for her father?

Another memory of hands. The night she had finally come to this home, to these good people, she had broken into Alex's studio, torn to pieces a clay statue he had shaped into a Vietnamese woman holding a baby. It was an unfinished piece, its features still largely unformed, blurred, but she had felt he was stealing her soul, her name, would seal it in that form. She wouldn't have said it like that then; she hadn't understood her rage at the time, her need to gouge a vaginal trench between the figure's legs, to tear away its blank face, but Louise, her wise, wise mother, was right. Had named what she had then resented. Had named, perhaps, what she feared now also, the name that could be taken away from both of them in that country which had once taken her father from Louise, held him for so many years.

She kissed her mother and left the house by the back door.

A flock of Canadian geese passed overhead, their necks and beaks strained forward to the direction they were compelled to go, their querulous honking reassuring each other. The line of locust trees behind the house groaned, their dry leaves rustling, whispering, as Kiet stood there, and when she moved closer, a cloud of sparrows exploded from their canopies, rose and switched back and forth like a single organism, as if they were being drilled by the honking of the geese. Those cries had always seemed heart-breakingly lonely to her when she'd first come to this place, echoing in the hollow she had felt thinly shelled around in those days; fifteen years old and so nebulous that her skin felt liquid even then. When Johns had picked her up at Social Services and driven her here, to the south county, she'd gotten out of his pickup truck and stood shivering, the corn stubble and frozen furrows of earth hard and strange under her thin-soled shoes, and she'd heard the geese, saw them flying away, somewhere, and they'd shattered her.

The small barn around the back of the house was a miniature of the larger one that had been on Johns' land: a gray-boarded tobacco barn, its worn boards able to be winged up from the bottom when the plants were being cured. Inside, in that dim striped light, the bristly spears of the tobacco would hang like crowded rows of spectators over their heads, hers and Hiram Johns', and she'd stare at them, fix her eyes to them. But it was gone now, burned down by her father when he was still sheriff and could pretty much do what he wanted in this county. Johns' twenty acres now sprouted ten 6000-plus square foot vinyl-sided wedding cake houses, replete with bay windows and circular windows and arches and fluted pillars, each house fronted with an uneven jumble of faux dormers and gables so that it looked, in her father's words, as if a village had exploded and been haphazardly stuck together into one edifice. He hated the ostentatious, alien squat of them on the landscape of his ancestry; their violation of his need for clean, functional lines and clear spaces. It was a quality Kiet shared with him, but what had fit charmingly into this landscape had been Hiram Johns' farm, and she was fine also with whatever vulgarity could replace it.

She walked to the barn. Alex's studio was around the back. She stood outside it, looking through the storm window set into the back wall. Since his retirement, Alex had been spending most of his workdays here, giving himself a rigid schedule, as if he were still going into the office. The sculptures were draped, ghostly behind the glass, except for the piece he was working on: a replica, perhaps, of a Buddha, sitting in a meditative posture, but its face gone, replaced by a hole that went completely through, an O in the center of the head. The statue's hands were realistically veined, strong, but the fingers bursting, tapering, worms emerging from their exploded tips. Kiet watched his own strong hands, her father's saving hands, moving over the hands he was creating and wondered, as she always did, at his ability to bring out into the world what he otherwise kept so tightly wrapped in silence.

But she didn't enter the studio, not yet. There was only one other undraped piece: the Vietnamese mother and baby she had desecrated when she'd come to this place, when she'd broken in and torn it into whatever shape was wrapped and warped inside herself. Her father had kept that as it was, rutted and gouged, blinded eyes staring. *Because her eyes weren't there*, Kiet had read once, in a poem about a little girl blinded by napalm, *they were there*.

She walked around to the barn door, and came into the studio. Alex looked up and grinned at her, his face dusty.

"Saw you outside. Stalking me."

He came around the bench, clapping his hands against his pants, took her by the shoulders and kissed her forehead. Hey, Daddy, she said. Hey.

He gestured at his workbench. "Cup a coffee?"

She shook her head. He went to the half-refrigerator and took out two bottles of Old Bohemian, twisted off the tops, handed her one. She took a mouthful. It was very cold and bitter and wonderful.

"How's the new performance?"

"Come and see it."

"I will. Sure. But these days, I've been…" He motioned at the sculpture.

Something moved under her heart. *These days*, he'd said, and she knew what he meant as if his two words opened a sentence in her own head, the seep of his nightmares into her own, some of them borrowed from him and some borrowed from movies and now from newscasts of the new war suddenly geysering out halfway around the world, as if it had taken thirty years to work its way underground to a new location, desert instead of jungle, minaret instead of pagoda, brown-side-out camouflage instead of green-side-out, but that was the only difference. As if the past assumed a horizontal and physical direction instead of being a dimension of time. How linked they were by history and wound, this accidental father and herself; how had they found each other? At fifteen, she had hated the morally inferior position of being saved, and she had hated the ones who tried to save her. It took her some time to be finished with all that, but when she was, what was left was a sense of being inextricably wired to Alex that was stronger than blood, melded by that war, the country she wanted now to discover that gave that war its name and had swallowed her own, to this man, to this father.

"Sure," she said.

He brushed at her hair, smiled. On impulse, she seized his hand and brought it, palm first, to her lips, smelling the good dry stone dust.

He turned away, closed his eyes for a moment. The lines on his face had deepened, and his neck had started to wattle a bit, the signs of aging you notice only when you don't see someone every day. She felt the same brief flutter of panic in her chest and throat she'd felt about Louise, a preliminary of grief, that she understood had to do with the leaving she'd do now.

"How's your mother with that? The trip, I mean. You talk to her?"

She shrugged. "She's not happy, Alex. I think partially she's worried that I wouldn't find out anything about my biological parents. And partially she's worried that I will. That's why I want her to come. That's why I want both of you to come."

He just smiled at her.

"I have something for you." She reached into her pocketbook and took out the statuette. She handed it to him.

He held it in the palm she'd kissed, staring. Then he shook his head.

"You should take it now," he said. "Bring it back."

"You never told me how you got it, where it came from."

He said nothing for a long moment. He touched the face, tentatively. But he didn't pick up the statue.

"A place called Marble Mountain," he said.

"Is that where you were in the war?"

"That was the war."

"Dad, come with me now. Please. Even if Mom won't."

"Honey, this is your trip."

"Are you worried about what I may find? Who I may find? Like Mom is?"

He touched her lips, sealing them, his blunt, sculptor's fingers as soft as breath.

"From the first time I saw you, honey," he said, "I knew you were my daughter."

Reenactment

That evening, Friday, Russell Hallam called Alex.

"Been a while, cuz," Russell said. "Enjoying retirement?"

Russell, a former deputy, had been elected sheriff after Alex had stepped down.

"First time in years I can get some work done. Have you protected?"

"I have."

"And have you served?"

"I do."

"Then I'll sleep in peace tonight. What's up, Russ?"

"Listen, Brian Schulman? He wants to know if we can get together, try on the uniforms, rehearse a little."

Alex, Russell, and Brian Schulman were once-a-year Civil War soldiers at the annual reenactment at the Point Lookout state park—a former federal prisoner of war camp: Alex and Russell by virtue of their ancestral ties to the place, Brian an archaeologist digging up the bones of those same ancestors, black and white, guard and prisoner.

"Russ, I don't know. This year…"

"Listen, we get together, we can go out in the boat, kill some crabs. Bring Baxter."

"Sure," Alex said, giving up.

Louise and Kiet sat on the porch chairs, next to a beer cooler, and watched the men emerge from the house. Alex and Brian wore tattered Confederate uniforms; Russell a cleaner Federal uniform; he had a rifle with a bayonet slung over his shoulder and would be a camp guard, the other two his prisoners. Baxter came out of his trailer in a cotton

Washington Redskins sweatshirt and some baggy brown corduroy trousers, all 21st century.

She watched Russell unsling his rifle and pretend to march Alex and Brian, who raised their hands over their heads, in front of him.

"Don't bunch up," Brian said. "One cliché will get us all."

Russell grinned at him. Kiet suddenly sick of the whole secret language thing. The whole camaraderie thing.

The three men formed up in front of Louise and Kiet.

"What about Uncle Baxter?" Kiet asked.

He came and sat next to her, took three beers from the cooler, handed one to Louise, one to Kiet. They popped the tops and drank, Kiet raising her bottle in toast to the men.

"I'm W.I.A." Baxter said.

"Some excuse," Brian said. "You ladies coming this year?"

"You know how I feel about it," Louise said. "This place celebrating its murders.

Kiet said to Alex. "I'll go to your reenactment, if you'll come to mine."

He looked at her, said nothing. Her father.

A series of sensations and images suddenly shivered into a procession in her mind, marched, as it were, out at gunpoint: Johns' boney bare chest pressed cold against her breasts, the cold suddenly vulnerable expanse of his forehead when she jammed the barrel of the gun against it, the sharp whip pain of what she realized later must have been some piece of the man flying into her cheek, the feel of the gun being pulled from her hand, of the blanket Alex had wrapped around her, holding her to him like a baby, of the words, 'my father', coming into her mind for the first time as a blessing instead of a curse, of him laying her down and calling Russell for backup, saying Johns had attacked him, he'd had to shoot, looking into her eyes to seal that story, as he was doing now.

Russell said: "Kiet, how about giving us some tips. As an actress."

She didn't reply.

"Kiet?"

"That's not my name."

"Excuse me?"

"I'm sorry," Kiet said. She forced herself to think about Russell's request. A lifeline she could hang onto. "I don't know, Uncle Russ. If I were doing it, I'd put in something that would shake up people's perceptions a little."

"What do you mean?"

"Blur the lines between drama and reality. That's the only way they'll really see."

"How do you go about that?" Brian asked.

"Well, what I've seen, it's mostly just play-acting. Put on the costumes, play soldier. The photos I've seen of Civil War soldiers; they're skinny, filthy; they have that thousand-yard stare. Young men with old eyes. Most of the reenactors—present company excepted of course…"

"Of course," Brian said..

"…Well, it's a matter of body language. They're middle-aged. They look like middle-aged men in costumes."

She came down from the porch and moved around them, picking up some dirt and smudging it on their faces, strategically ripping their clothing here and there.

"There's guys go all out; only eat beans and hard tack, drink chicory, don't shower, sleep outdoors," Brian said. "They get lean and mean."

"I think the right term is delusional," Louise said.

"Maybe that's what's needed," Kiet said. "Living it. Channeling. Bust the past into the present."

"You all let yourself believe?" Russ said.

"Well, it has to mean something to you. What's it mean to you, Uncle Russ?

"Why do we have the same last name, girl? Black me

and Baxter and your dad there, white as a sow's belly? You know anything about the Hallams?

"Those aren't the ancestors she's concerned with," her father said.

"That's not fair," she said to him, and then turned to Russell. "Sure I know. His side of the family owned your side of the family. One of your ancestors killed one of Dad's, a slave killing his master. Drowned him, I understand."

"Old murders," Brian said.

"Drowned him," she repeated, thinking of the boy whose name she had been given.

"What nonsense," Louise said.

Alex shook his head, said something sharp to Russell—Kiet missed what it was. As he and Russell started to argue, she slipped away, went around to the back of the house. Changed into her own costume, slid silently out of a side door in black cotton trousers and shirt, a conical hat on her head, checkered scarf around her neck, one of the Civil War muskets Brian had brought cradled in her arms. Staying in the shadow of the house, she circled behind the three men. Got down on her belly behind the row of azalea bushes, low crawled, the rifle at an awkward high port, branches scratching her arms. Transported to this earth. Awakened in this alien light, this alien earth and water. Remembering the encasement and violation of flesh. The enemy, silver-haired, skin creased, but still here, waiting across years. She raised the musket, briefly sighted on the back of one head, another, lowered the barrel, saw Louise on the porch, staring at her. Kiet put a finger to her lips. Louise shook her head vigorously. She shook her head back, saw Alex look quizzically at Louise. Kiet sprang up, rushing to the flank of the men, pointing the musket. Ka-pow, Ka-pow. G.I. you die!

Russell spun quickly, pointing his rifle at her, his finger pulling the trigger, the musket's hammer clicking on an empty chamber. The other men crouched, their hands grasping invisible weapons, then closed around her, pressing in, their faces grim—all this in an instant; they looked at each other, stepped back a little, relaxing, grinning sheepishly.

She looked at the faces of these three men, her father and two that she called uncle, not because it was the custom in this Southern place to so name close elders, but because they were her father's truest brothers.

"That's what I mean," she said. Shaken to her heart. "What would you do—how would you treat me?"

"We wouldn't even see you, honey," Baxter called from the porch.

Watermen's Dues

The *Louise* pulled off from the dock at five the next morning, making her way slowly through the water with what Alex liked to think of as ponderous dignity. She was a six-ton wooden work boat, solid built in Crisfield by Evans Boats in the mid-1950's; he kept her expensively in shape, getting her dry-docked, scraped and painted earlier in the year, though he had not crabbed much this summer. That he kept the Louise at all was out of a need, he supposed, to keep some Hallam presence on these sustaining waters.

He baited and dropped off a line of crab pots, each marked by an orange float. The surface of the creek was flat calm, though a breeze crinkled it into a sparkling foil here and there. The men worked easily together, four friends in their late middle age acting out a dream of their youth when coming back to this water had meant still being alive. Brian Schulman's thinning strands of silver hair waving like tentacles in the breeze, Russell, Baxter, and his own close-cropped hair graying, but all of them in shape, moving with quick grace and competence, a rhythm that he had realized recently had passed into Kiet's own dance, as if she had absorbed that from his blood—-did time and love create some estuarine, genetic shift within each other? A portable radio was bungee-tied near the wheel; Alex kept it on the oldies station, Sloopie still hanging on as Alex steered the boat to an orange marker float, Russell hauled up a dripping trap, Brian shook the catch out into the trough in front of Baxter, who—amazingly, for a blind man—culled the crabs, reaching into the basket, quickly pulling out one at a time by their back fins, throwing the smaller ones back into the river, the larger ones into different baskets according to their sizes.

The other three stopped, looked at him, then each other, grinned, and then went back to work. Russell hauled up another trap, dripping with jellyfish. He winced as a stinger got his arm.

"Son of a bitch."

Alex looked at him thoughtfully. "I remember how your dad's eyes would swell up, he'd catch a jellyfish in the face."

"He'd come home, my ma would smear meat tenderizer on him, get the rash on her own self. Waterman's dues, he called the jellyfish. Got to pay back the pain."

"Before the war, I always figured you'd follow him onto the water."

"Thank God for the war."

He gave the trap he was holding a last shake to get the last crab out. It fell on the deck, scurried backwards, its claws raised. A speedboat went by, its wake rocking the *Louise* violently. The three weekend boaters in it hooted raucously at the *Louise* and threw empty beer cans in the workboat's direction.

"Ain't enough they want to stick McMansions and Starbucks every inch a farm land," Russell said.

Put on your red dress, baby, a voice sang from the radio, *'cause we goin' out tonight...*

"We bonding yet, Russ?" Alex asked.

And wear some boxin' gloves, case some fool might want to fight...

"Beg your pardon?"

"Louise call you?"

Russell didn't answer, baited a trap, and then another, threw them into the water.

"That why you're here?"

"Excuse me?"

"You hate fishing."

Russell shrugged. "You got me mistaken with someone who gives a shit about you. Me, I'm just someone worked with you for twenty years." An edge of anger came into his voice. "Who's your blood."

Brian waved around, encompassing the creek, the world. "Hey buddy, we're all in the same boat, right?"

Alex baited another crab pot.

In Fallujah, nine American Marines were killed today in heavy fighting...the radio announced suddenly, as if on cue. The men laughed grimly, at the joke on time each of them had heard buried subliminally in the announcer's words. Alex switched the radio off.

Brian nodded at the set. "Welcome aboard, kids." He started restacking the empty traps, shaking his head. "I can't even watch the TV news these days."

"Me neither," Baxter says.

They laughed. Alex also, though he looked at his friend, wondering at Baxter's need to do the blind man jokes, present the feisty cripple to the world. Wondering at his own feeling of being somehow reproached whenever Baxter did, how long it would go on.

"Well, I don't watch the news either," Russell said. "Know why? Cause all the commercials are for adult diapers, don't-piss prostate medication, Viagra, gas, and heartburn. For all the old farts who are the only ones who watch the news anymore."

"Not this old fart," Alex said.

Russell baited another trap. "Hell, it's not the same war, whatever they say."

"I can't look at those kids' faces," Brian said. "They tear out my heart. They piss me off. I want to kill somebody— and not an Iraqi."

"Hell, we lost more people in a month, they do in a year," Russell said.

Brian held up an alewife, bait fish. "They send you out into Indian country until you get hit. You die, they know where the enemy is. Bait on a fucking hook. Bait in a fucking cage." He put the fish in the crab pot, threw the pot into the water. "Samey-same. For nothing. So some old fart can feel like he has their balls."

Alex said, "Kid's thinking of going over there."

Brian looked shocked. "Iraq? Fuck that."

"Viet Nam. Look for her roots, all that crap. Gets a letter. One name, one address. Do you believe that?"

Russell shrugged. "Why's it bother you?"

"Thing is, I should go with her. She wants me to."

"Then go," Baxter said.

"Thing is, I can't."

"Then don't. Vets going over there," Russell said in disgust. "She's a grown woman. What's eating you?"

"Her path's opened a path in my mind, is all." He touched Baxter's arm. Baxter shook his head, as if responding to a question only he and Alex had heard. He rose, walked away from Alex to the other side of the boat.

"Son of a bitch!" Alex yelled. Russell and Brian gaped at him, but then saw where he was staring. Off the bow, ahead of them, the speedboat had stopped and the weekend boaters had pulled up one of Alex's crab pots and were emptying the contents into a fiberglass cooler. Another empty pot was already on deck. One of them, florid-faced, his toothy smile a white gash in his face, looked up, pointed out the *Louise*. The two men hooted, and the driver put the boat into gear and shot right towards the work boat, swerving at the last minute, the florid-faced man throwing an empty beer can at them. As the wake hit the *Louise,* the boat pitched, and Baxter, standing, trying to figure what was happening, pitched into the water. Russell and Brian shouted at the speedboat. Neither heard the splash, saw Baxter fall. Alex did. He rushed over to the port side, and then stood, rooted, staring at Baxter as the water closed over his face, his blind eyes staring back at Alex. Alex didn't move. Baxter seemed to smile up at him, his lips barely under the sheen of water. Suddenly Brian was there, next to him; he cursed, jumped into the water, got Baxter under his armpits and frog-kicked him back to the boat.

Russell and Alex hauled him aboard, Alex turning away from Brian's stare.

The speedboat was heading back towards them, the two men hurling more beer cans. Russell climbed onto the bow and flashed his badge, pointing at them, motioning at them to stop.

Alex went into the cabin and came out with a .30 caliber rifle. He cocked it.

Russell turned. "What the hell, Alex?"

Alex aimed below the water line. He fired two rounds. Fiberglass splintered. Panicking, the driver spun the wheel, turning the boat. As soon as the stern was towards Alex, he put two more rounds into the motor. They hit with a clanging sound. The motor whined into a high-pitched scream and the speedboat stopped dead, the motor sputtering, dying, smoking. Brian, who had gone to the wheel, took in the sight of the boat and whistled, a broad grin breaking his face.

"Get me alongside," Alex said to him, his voice strained.

"Alex, I'm the sheriff…" Russell said.

"Fuck it," Brian said. "Go with the flow, Russ." He took the wheel, shouted as the boats came parallel. "*Dung lai,* motherfucker! Steal another man's crab pots, will yah?"

"For Christ sake," Russell said disgustedly.

Alex put on his rubber gloves, Brian still looking at him curiously. He roped the two boats together and jumped on board the speedboat, facing the two men. The speedboat was listing, taking water. Russell shrugged and went into the cabin, so as not to see what would happen.

The first boater had a square face with a flap of skin hanging below it like a fringe. His sunburned face looked mottled now, beet-red with anger. "You fucking maniac!"

"Best not let your alligator mouth overload your lizard ass, old hoss," Brian shouted happily. "Know what it means, down here, you mess with another man's crab pots?"

"I'll have your…." the other boater, a pear-shaped man in madras shorts, a lemon-colored shirt and a captain's hat, started to say.

"You missed one," Alex said calmly.

Brian's grin widened. The Alex Hallam legend. He began humming some bars from the *Deliverance* "Dueling Banjos" medley. "Da dah dah dah dah, di da dum dum dum."

"What the hell are you…?" the man in the captain's hat started to stay.

Alex pointed to a float marker. "You missed one of my pots. Pull it up."

"We're sinking, you maniac!"

"Right," Alex said. With one hand, he untied the mooring line, tossed the rope back onto the deck of the *Louise*. "Best hurry then."

The two men looked at Alex. Alex aware of how he would look to them. A sixty year old man with a bull neck and barrel chest and flat belly and roped arms that haven't changed in thirty years, except to somehow take on, not the sag of gravity, but of the gravitas of those years. His blunt stone-carver's hands, his thick forefinger taking up the slack on the trigger. Machine-gunner's eyes. He knew it, used it, had had to use his physical presence during his tenure as sheriff. Used it now.

Cursing, pale, the man grabbed the line and pulled the trap from the water. It was dripping with jellyfish. Alex scooped one up, pushed it into the man's face. The boater clawed at his eyes, screaming. Alex scooped up another handful of jellyfish, turned to the man in the captain's hat. Waterman's dues, he might have said. Something like that.

PART TWO

MOC SON

WOOD

Peace Hotel

Kiet walked out of the terminal. The heat slapped her, the sun blinding her, so that the people milling in front of the exit doors were at first a blurry, shifting mass that slowly distilled into individual faces: cone-hatted, baseball-capped, bareheaded, her own mirrored face breaking into a thousand reflecting shards. A taxi driver reached for her bag, and she showed him the address of the mini-hotel she had booked, the Hoa Binh.

As soon as they pulled out of the airport access, the chaos of the street claimed the car, the way, she thought, a river claims you as soon as you loosen your boat and are in its current, in a different world than the shore. She rolled down the window as they wove through a tangle of cars, carts, motor scooters, cyclos, bicycles, the taxi shooting with sickening, heart-stopping precision through sudden and miniscule openings that presented themselves like the sudden choices of fate, her face buffeted by wafts of hot air and scored by stinging dust, her nostrils assailed by the stink of raw gas fumes. Next to the car, a Honda scooter held an entire family of five; daddy driver, mom behind with two kids pressed between her and her husband's back, one kid on dad's lap, the other squatting, fitted under the windshield. All of them were masked. The traffic surged around Kiet, not a river now but a fantastic dance, the swirl of motor scooters and cars and pedestrians threading confidently and fatalistically through the loops and curves and sharp turns and leans of their own journeys, the machine-gun bursts of unmuffled engines, the blare of horns, the whiff of sweat and fish sauce and frying meat laced faintly under the stink of the gas fumes, and everywhere the press of people, and again the oddity of seeing all of them stamped with her face manifested into all its forms: laughing, screaming, weeping, smiling, greeting, eating—sitting on low plastic stools in front of restaurants, stalls, food carts, fanning chopsticks to their faces, stuffing grilled meat and paté and banana-leaf-wrapped rice and pork balls into their mouths. Roast ducks, their skins crisp and golden, hung from steel hooks in the window of a restaurant. The surprise configured into their duck faces, probably by her own imagination, seemed to again underscore the sudden transformation of idea into sounds, sights, and smells, the heat and dust on her face, the trickle of sweat running down her back.

The traffic knotted into immobility. No, just a traffic light. It looked prosaic, out of place. If she were here long enough, would it become an object of nostalgia, homesick-making? On the sidewalk, an old woman in gray patched pajamas squatted by some bamboo cages stuffed with live ducks. As if she was showing them their karma, hanging in the window. As Kiet watched, one duck wiggled free, stepped out into the road, as if pulled by her thoughts. The traffic heaved suddenly forward and the duck was immediately flattened by a motor scooter. The driver and the girl behind him wore what looked like tennis outfits, their faces impassive behind black Oakleys. They sped off, weaving through the traffic, the old woman cursing after them. One instant the duck was there, squawking, waddling, sure about whatever duck plans it had; the next it was a spilt sack of bleeding meat and a coil of greasy intestines on the road. No one except Kiet looked at it or the old woman. She felt a flash of anger, and then shame. It was ridiculous, racist, of course, to see the casual accident as an exemplar of some Asian indifference to life: She'd grown up in a rural area where she couldn't drive on any road without seeing the burst corpses of opossums, raccoons, and various house pets, some of them run down maliciously.

She had seen something that was in its life in one instant

and a corpse the next, and she'd seen it here. The duck meant nothing. Except what it seemed to call to her, here, in this place. The chanced path of a life.

Kach San Hoa Binh, the Peace Hotel, was in a long narrow building squeezed between a larger building with iron-mesh screens over all its windows, and an alleyway filled with noodle stands. The narrow "lobby"—an extended, high-ceilinged hallway, was lined with parked motor scooters, Jackson Pollock dribbles of oil laced all over the floor. She checked in, walked up to her room on the third floor. A cheap pressed-wood armoire, a narrow bed, a rickety air conditioner above the window, controlled by a boxy remote, its control buttons labeled in Korean; a large thermos and a tray with tiny cups on it on a low carved table. A tiny balcony that hung out over the street. She opened the doors, walked out onto it. The hotel, she'd been told, was near the river, but she couldn't see the water.

She went back into the room, lay on the hard bed. She was in Viet Nam. She said it aloud, like an incantation. As if she feared for its feathering against reality.

The wall across from her was covered, floor to ceiling, with a beige-and-tan photograph of a bamboo forest and, under the sputtering neon light, she could glimpse the vague shapes of animals. Deer or tigers or wolves. She felt floaty and jet-lagged enough that she could squint and let something in herself relax and allow the shapes to flow and shift; she could make them into creatures of menace or promise, guides that would lead her to the secrets of the forest. Lagged. Who she was lagging some distance behind who was lying here in this bed.

She thought to rest before hunting down Mr. Duong. But she couldn't sleep. She got up and went out to the balcony again. It was a rickety affair, just wide enough for her to stand on, her back on the wall. The heat immediately annealed to her skin, like a hand pressed on her face. Inside an apartment across the street, through a barred window, she could see a gold Buddha with an incense jar in front of it, and a bald man in a t-shirt and boxers sitting cross-legged on the floor in an identical posture, eating from a bowl of rice. It was early evening, and the traffic in front of the hotel hadn't diminished and outside the fumes were strong, but laced with the smell of cooking beef and chicken, and the sharper odor of burning charcoal, drifting up from the noodle soup stand in the alley next to the building. A radio was playing the theme from *Titanic,* the lyrics, sung in Vietnamese, somehow more annoyingly cloying than they were in English. Men and women and a few kids were sitting on the tiny blue plastic stools she had seen everywhere, eating, drinking their coffee or tea or beer, eating, smoking cigarettes, laughing, the music of their voices, of the language that teased at the edge of meaning, coming to her ears. She lit a cigarette. The woman behind the huge black pot of cooking noodles looked up at her from the alley and smiled, her existence untroubled by Kiet's doubts, her belly undoubtedly full. Kiet waved at her like an idiot.

Let me stay, she whispered, hearing the voice of a fifteen-year-old homeless runaway suddenly insinuating itself into her mouth.

***

As soon as she stepped out of the hotel door, a motorbike swerved over to the curb, the driver, a skinny young man in baggy shorts, urging her to get on. The model name on the scooter's mudguard was Dream. Kiet showed the driver the address on Duong's letter and he nodded enthusiastically. She climbed on the back, and they began the traffic dance again, her arms around his sweaty waist, the heat of the exhaust pipe threatening to blister her leg.

She felt a sudden stab of doubt. As much as the country

itself, Nguyen Binh Duong had been an abstract concept to her, ghost writing on a letter, and it seemed impossible she would find him, in the midst of this chaos, in a corporeal form, no more than one expected to actually find a legend. She could have—and now thought, should have—tried to get a telephone number or email, contact him from the States. She was afraid, she'd told herself, that he might tell her he knew nothing, or that he might refuse to see her. What she had really been afraid of was it would take away her reason to make this trip—how could one chase a legend already debunked?

They pulled finally into a small alley, the houses old, leaning on each other haphazardly, street vendors squatting before the doorways, near small tables, selling tea, cigarettes, and what Kiet took for lotto tickets. She caught glimpses through window grilles and open doors, into the lives of various families: kids on bare tile floors watching a soccer game on a tiny TV, a grandma who seemed to be little more than a bag of bones lying on a low pallet, her knees, drawn up to her chest, a group of men barechested or in sleeveless undershirts, playing cards and smoking wooden pipes. An old woman, her white hair in a bun, was squatting next to a broken wooden gate, a pot and circle of small tea cups and packs of Vietnamese cigarettes on a tray in front of her; her skinny arms were wrapped around her knees. Kiet looked around nervously. There were no numbers or names. She showed the address to the driver again, and he nodded and grabbed her arm, and then smiled at her reassuringly. She let him lead her over to the old woman, squatted next to her, said chao ba, hoping that was the polite form, and showed her the address. The old woman smiled and nodded, pointed to a blue door across the street. Cam on, ba, Kiet said, and bought a pack of cigarettes. The woman rose, took Kiet's arm from the driver—passing the tourist around—and led her to a door, its paint peeling. She smiled at Kiet, her teeth black, and knocked. There was, indeed, a sign on the door, but the door itself was locked, and no one answered the knock. Another old woman answered, looked at the address, came out and took Kiet's other arm. The two brought her to another door, looked at her expectantly, laughing to themselves. A third old lady squatting nearby, in front of a tray of cigarettes and lighters, called over to her. She handed Kiet a business card:

NGUYEN BINH DUONG, TOUR GUIDE. CU CHI AND BATTLEFIELD TOURS MY SPECIALITY. 283 D. PHAM NGU LAO, HCMC. WELCOME HOME, BROTHERS. TEL: 863 7626

Reenactment Redux

The sound of gunfire still echoed in the air. The man the girl guide had identified to her as Duong was leading a line of tourists, middle-aged Westerners, down a jungle trail, wearing the same kind of VC costume—black pajama outfit, checkered scarf around his neck—Kiet sometimes wore in her act, but more accessorized: ammunition belt, rubber tire sandals, a plastic AK 47 slung over his shoulder—everything too clean, new-looking. Kiet stood perfectly still next to a "VC woman" manikin standing at the entrance to a tunnel, and as the group passed, she fell in with them. At the rifle range, he stood a little to the side, a faint smile on his lips, as members of his group blasted away at the targets. It wasn't, she decided, a smile she liked; it referred one to a well of bitter experience. But it seemed an affectation, part of the act. A middle-aged American woman in shorts and a Montagnard "tribal" shirt sidled up to him. Flirting. He looked at her and sighed with what seemed a sense of resigned inevitability. Her interest made Kiet look at him again: he was a handsome man for someone his age, not tall but well-knit, his movements neat and economical, his slightly scarred face symmetrical and carved-looking, framed by thick, well-combed black hair. Kiet wanted to mess with him.

"I only do my duty," he was saying, pompously. "Then and now."

"I understand," the woman said. "For people of my generation...well, it is as if you and I share the war."

He smiled tightly. "So I've heard. I'm sure it was exactly the same."

"Well, you needn't be sarcastic."

She walked away angrily, as if looking for someone to complain to.

One of the other tourists, an Australian woman jiggling here and there in too-small shorts and a too-tight shirt held up a camera and shook it at Kiet. Another ragged volley of rifle fire cracked through the air.

"Could you snap us, dear," the woman asked.

Kiet took the camera, and the woman waved Duong over, and then "arranged" him against a clump of bamboo, stood next to him, smiling broadly. He unslung his rifle, held it before him at port arms as Kiet snapped the photos.

When the group had finished blasting away their targets, he led them by some thatch-roof structures, models of booby-traps, stacks of rusted shells and bombs, gathered them into a semicircle. A mural behind him depicted crudely painted American G.I.'s, faces stamped with fear or panic, mouths gaped in Münch screams, bodies falling into punji-stake traps, skewered or bisected on stakes, blown to pieces by various explosives.

"The villagers in the Cu Chi area," he said, "dug hundreds of miles of tunnels. Because they were poor, they had to create their own weapons to fight the Americans." He pointed at the mural. "Here you see some of the traps we will look at. Punji stake pits...."

"They look vicious, cruel," Kiet said.

The Australian woman stared at her, shaking her head.

Duong looked surprised at the interruption. "Perhaps. But so are cluster bombs. You see, people needed to defend themselves with whatever weapons they could get...or make.

His tone was mild, condescending.

She went up to the mural. "And these are Americans?"

"Yes, an artist's..."

"Don't you think they look like caricatures?"

"Miss, you must..."

"Like frightened demons? I mean, is it necessary to demonize them? Isn't this art a little silly?"

The people in the tour group muttered, frowned at Kiet.

Duong, for the first time, looked amused. "No, it's all right. I…"

Another volley of gunfire from the range interrupted him..

"Were you in the war?" she asked him. "What do you think of letting tourists pop off AK-47's and M-16's at a dollar a pop? It's kind of Disney, don't you think?"

The other tourists shifted, gave her more dirty looks.

Duong smiled. "Miss, are you Viet Kieu?"

"Bui doi." She turned to the American woman. "That means dust of life. Ask your guide."

"We must move on," Duong said.

He led the group down a path through the jungle. She stayed right behind him. They stopped at a small clearing, the ground covered with brown leaves, which he brushed aside to reveal a hidden tunnel entrance. The group applauded appreciatively. Duong demonstrated how to get into the tiny entrance, feet first, his arms held up above his head. The tourists gasped, took photos. They took turns going into the hole, as others snapped their pictures. There was a great deal of laughter. Kiet slid up next to him.

"Really, don't you find all this offensive? I mean, real people died here."

"It is important to show the world the history of our struggle." He turned away from her, addressed the others. "We will go to the tunnel now."

The tunnel opening was inside a sandbagged bunker structure. She stayed at his heels as they walked over. When they stopped, he glanced at her and then took the scarf from around his neck and wound it around his head, as a sweat band.

"If anybody suffers from claustrophobia…."

"I'm sorry if I was rude—I'm a bit nervous," Kiet said. "May we speak?"

He frowned. "One minute, please."

They watched as the tourists went one by one into the tunnel.

"What can I do for you?" he asked, and smiled. It was what Louise would call a gigolo smile—he thought he had her pegged. Kiet took his business card out of her breast pocket and showed it to him. "Mr. Nguyen Binh Duong?"

He glanced at it. "Yes. So you have my card. What can I do for you?"

She put it back in her pocket, took out another. "My name is Kiet Hallam."

He nodded at the card, annoyed. "Should that mean something to me?"

"No. It's a meaningless name."

"Please, I don't have time...."

She took out his letter, showed it to him.

"It's the dust name of the person you called the girl-child in this letter."

He stared at her. "Please—I can't see you," he said. As if he meant it literally, his eyes flitting away from her face, staring at some point above her head. He held his hands out in front of himself, pushing away at an invisible wall, like a cliché mime. "Go back where you came from," he whispered.

"That's the idea."

He spun around, walked rapidly away from her, and disappeared down into the tunnel.

The Theater of Then and Now

He managed to avoid her the rest of the day, not the first time he'd needed to hide from Americans in that place. As soon as he'd gotten back to the city and deposited his tourists at their various hotels—now that he had the van, his own company, he no longer worked solely at Cu Chi, only included it as part of the tour—he drove to the Theater of Then and Now. The shoddy mud-brown building that held Thuy's company and dreams was indistinguishable from a movie theater, except for the name on the marquee with its explanatory subheading: Traditional and Contemporary Cai Luong Performances in the Style of the South. A ticket booth stood optimistically on the right side of the entrance: it had been Thuy's hope, passion—a futile one, Duong thought—to revive the traditional opera by adapting it to contemporary drama. Sheltered by the overhang, as if from the real world, photos of costumed actors and posters from past perform-ances were imprisoned behind smudged glass like museum exhibits.

Inside, the air conditioning was strong, but the cold air seemed only to increase the smell of mold, itself enhanced by the echoing emptiness of the theater, the rows of seats new and wooden and large by Vietnamese standards; Thuy hoped to fill them with fleshy foreign behinds. At the moment, they were empty, though Thuy, looking out at them from center stage, would feel, as always, the stare of an invisible audience on her skin. A singer was warbling a cai luong song through the PA; he saw Thuy catch the singer's eye, put her hand to her throat in an up-and-down rubbing motion to indicate that the girl needed to get more vibrato into her voice. Her actors in training—Thuy refused the term students—most of them in their late teens and early twenties, were frozen into the positions she had coaxed them into, though Binh, who was on his hands and knees, was staring intently at Tuyet, a stunning eighteen year old Nha Trang girl who, Duong knew, had gone through and left devastated half the males in the troupe and had just added Binh's smashed heart to her pile of trophies. As he watched, Binh slowly lifted one leg into a peeing-dog posture and pantomimed letting his stream loose on Tuyet, who wrinkled her nose in disgust. It was—Duong had to admit—well done, though Thuy called out a warning to Binh.

She looked back offstage. He waved to her, trying to catch her eye. When she saw him, she clapped her hands, as if to repel a demon. He climbed up on the stage. She told the troupe to keep rehearsing, she would be back.

As they went backstage, he saw that Binh, still on his hands and knees, had stuck his right arm down between his thighs and was humping it violently.

Her dressing room was tight and hot and, as she sat at her mirror, she patted at the lines of perspiration making rivulets through the makeup on her cheeks, and then began to strip it off. Duong was the only one she would permit in here. Like a eunuch allowed in the seraglio, he understood. There was an easy intimacy between them now, since the tides of life had washed them both together again, so many decades after the war. It was not sexual—Thuy would never permit that, and his own desire for her had long ago been burnt to ashes on the altar of the history they shared—history, he thought sourly, which had shown its face again today at Cu Chi, drawn by the letters he'd been foolish enough to send. It was rather the closeness of people who had wounded each other so much that nothing was left but a vast weariness, of two people who knew the worst of each other and so could relax with each other, strip off all the masks and makeup that they layered over their true faces.

How can you be sure it's her, Thuy asked.

Look at her face yourself. You wouldn't have any doubts.

He handed her the card. Her fingers trembled as she held it.

What does this mean, 'performance artist'?

It means she is an actress.

What did you tell her? Her voice rose, an edge of hysteria in it.

To go back to America.

And nothing about her past?

I couldn't. I ran from her.

Not for the first time, Thuy said.

The Elements

She lay on her bed, looking at the photograph of the forest, with its elusive animals. She had no idea how to find Duong again. She'd gone to his "office," called the cell phone number on his card. He'd disappeared. The elusive Mr. Duong.

Noises from outside drifted into the room; laughter and shouts, the barking of dogs, a cacophony of horns. At the desk downstairs, the clerk had expressed surprise that Kiet had wanted one of the street-side rooms. Apparently the rooms that didn't face the street were more expensive, more desired by what he called domestic tourists. She understood now why this room would be less in demand, but the noise, the smells, the heat of the city intruding from the streets were what she wanted on her skin.

She dressed and went out, thinking to walk down to the river. The street was lined with high-priced tourist shops—leather goods and designer jewelry and Shesheido perfume outlets. Behind the huge lobby windows of one of the upscale hotels, tourists were eating at linen-covered tables, raising silver forks to their mouths. If they looked out and saw her, would they think she belonged here?

There was an internet café down the block. She hadn't emailed home for a few days. She entered, sat in front of an old Compaq. It took forever to get on line. When she did, she sent an email to Alex, ending it with an unexpected *Dad, it's falling apart*, her fingers tapping out the words as if someone else was operating them. She moved the cursor to "send," hesitated. Her finger twitched, pushed the key as if of its own volition.

She came off line, paid the ridiculously low fee, and went out. The wide boulevard that ran parallel to the river was curb to curb with a parade of cyclos and motor scooters, all honking, all streaming towards a docked ferry, as if the city was suddenly fleeing itself again. "Hey, you come!" a cyclo driver with legs like whipcords yelled at her. A boy with a tray around his neck tugged at her sleeve. "You buy, madam," he said, in English. The tray was filled with cigarettes, lighters, tiger balm, cheap handbags and scarves. "Madam, you buy." She smiled and shook her head. As if it were a signal, more vendors, boys and girls, were suddenly around her, tugging at her. She shook her head more vigorously. "Jus' looking, jus' looking," they chorused, a pre-emptive echo. She plunged into the traffic. The vehicles whipped around her. She froze: the noise, the lights, the horns fixing her in place. Hands tugged on her sleeves again. The first boy and another girl had come up on either side of her, grinning. She let them guide her across. They moved through the traffic without hesitation, the scooters and bikes and occasional cars slowing or swerving slightly around the moving island of their bodies, a dance everyone knew except her. On the other side, she bought a pack of cigarettes from the boy, a lighter and a small Vietnamese phrase book, printed on cheap paper, from the girl.

As she walked beside the river, the two kids stayed with her. Street kids. They were sharp, in all the meanings and connotations of that word: shaped to their purpose, ready to gleam or cut. Once she had been one of them, on streets they probably couldn't imagine, and somewhere inside her she still held their shuck and hustle, could still harden to an edge, could still love anyone with her without borders or hold-backs. Kiet doubted if they, those American streets, were gentler than here, but there had been at least the chance of hope at some of their intersections, there'd been Alex and Louise, and it would have taken only a brief twist and she might have stood on this street, hot and hungry, looking into a hotel window as if at a painting or photograph of an alien world.

The girl suddenly smiled at her. "Relax, baby," she said. "Everything's cool." Her American accent was perfect, and for a moment Kiet felt nauseated, as if she truly were seeing a younger self translated to this place. She took out one of the cigarettes and put it in her mouth, her hand trembling. As she raised the lighter, a small flame blossomed in front of her face. She put the tip of the cigarette into it, inhaled.

"You shouldn't be out by yourself," Duong said. Behind her. Appearing. He said something sharp, in Vietnamese, to the kids. They hurried away. Kiet waved to them, peering after the girl.

"They weren't bothering me."

"Good."

They were standing in front of a row of wooden boats, held up on supports. Eyes were painted on their bows. She reached up and touched one of the hulls, the wood warm under her palm. She looked at the river. Runnels of current veined under an oleaginous sheen.

"I'm sorry if I startled you," he said.

"I'm glad you're here. I've been looking for you."

He reached up also, touched one of the painted eyes.

"Did people leave from here?" she asked.

"What do you mean?"

"Boat people. Refugees. People like the people who took me to America." She threw the sentence out like bait on a line. He didn't bite.

He caressed the eye. "Perhaps."

"Were you here in Sai Gon—Ho Chi Minh City—during the war?"

"Sai Gon was merely a dream of victory for us then."

"Where did you fight?"

"Many places. For many years. It's boring to speak of."

"Yes. Well, grasshopper understands."

"I'm sorry?"

"You're being very enigmatic. Very...oriental. Do your lady tourists enjoy that?"

Duong made a puffing sound, laughed. "Usually."

"Well, Mr. Duong, I don't."

He walked to the other side of the boat. Kiet stayed on the street side, but walked along parallel to him, the boat between them. They met at the stern, face to face, and she was out of patience, tired of being grasshopper. Fuck a whole bunch of enigma, Alex would say.

She slapped the hull, the eye. "What's my name, Duong? Where am I from?"

He reached over and took one of her cigarettes out of the pack, flicked his lighter again and lit it. He let the flame burn, staring at it.

"You are from the five elements. From water, from wood, from metal, from earth, and from fire."

He took his thumb off the lighter and the flame died.

"See," Kiet said. "That's just what I mean."

Hunger

The woman, Kiet—could he think of her by that name?—
stared at him expectantly. He searched for another face in
hers, and when she turned towards him and a slightly ironic
smile flitted on her lips, for an instant he saw what he was
looking for, and other faces as well, and had to turn away—
as if he could turn away—from memory.

"I will help you all that I can. But I think it is good if we
get to know each other a little first."

"Why? To see if I'm worthy?"

"Of course not. But I don't know very much…"

"Yet you wrote letters…"

"I was just a, how do you say? Messenger? But there is
someone I want you to meet."

"Who"

"A friend of mine."

"How will he be able to help me?"

"She. Le Thi Thanh Thuy. She is a theater director."

"Really? What sort of theater."

"Cai luong. It is a…."

She smiled. "I know what it is."

"Please. Let me take you to her."

To his relief, she asked nothing else. Gave up. His van,
Duong's Battlefield Tours stenciled in English and
Vietnamese on the sliding door was parked outside the hotel.
As they walked to it, he watched as the heat hit her, the
sudden line of perspiration on her forehead, springing up in
response to the country's assault on foreign skin. But when
they had entered the van and pulled away from the curb, she
did what no tourist had ever done, pushed the power button
to roll down her window, let the heat intrude, looked around

almost frantically, as if trying to take back at once all that had been taken from her.

And then Duong was surprised at himself, at what he was doing: searching for qualities to like about this American woman. He would think of her that way, he decided. He would think of her that way, or he would have to run as far away as he could from that face.

They passed establishments specializing in Hue food, in Mekong Delta dishes, in Hanoi pho, in his favorite Hanoi food, bun thang, chicken noodle soup, made from just the right kind of castrated rooster, cut exactly and placed precisely on one corner of the noodles, with fried egg and sliced sausage on the other corners, and coriander and dried shrimp, and a black-prawn and beetle-musk paste. It was a dish Dao had learned to make for him, and, suddenly, he missed her sharply. But the sudden aching hollowness he felt probably had nothing to do with Dao. It had edged into him from the presence of this American woman, this impossible reincarnation, sitting impossibly next to him.

He reached over to the door control panel and pushed the button to raise her window. "What do you see," he asked.

She glanced at him sharply. "I'm surprised at some of the new buildings, the amount of business—I spent some time in Thailand and in ways this is like Bangkok."

"In ways?"

"I can't look at it the way I looked at Bangkok. Everything that this city's supposed to mean to me is underneath everything else."

"And what is there—under the surface?"

"The war, I suppose. Don't you still see it that way?"

He smiled at the probe. She was testing his defenses, approaching him from the flank, rather than in a direct attack, being more Vietnamese than American. Or perhaps he merely wanted to see that in her, wanted to see the face that was just under the face of this person, sitting next to him, just as she strained to see the war under the concrete and glass and indifferent hustle of this city.

He waved one hand at the restaurants lining the street. "What I see is hunger."

"It seems quite the opposite. A feast."

"Opposites remind us of…what they oppose. I grew up in Ha Noi," he said. "I left as a child, but came back and lived there after the war, until 1988."

"I don't follow you."

He shook his head, confused at the phrase. Following him was exactly what she did. "I don't understand," he said.

She laughed. "I'm sorry—it just means that I didn't understand."

"When I was a child, millions starved to death. The Japanese made people grow jute for their war, not rice, and the French held food as hostage. But when I came to live in Ha Noi, after the American war—from just after the war until the eighties, we called those times the brick days. When you left your house, you brought a brick with you, to use as a marker if you had to leave a food queue. Any queue. You would get up at five in the morning and join whatever line you saw, wait hours for tiny portions of broken, deformed grains of rice, fouled with rat droppings. That was Ha Noi. But it was no different here, or anywhere in the county, and worse in the countryside."

"Why was that?"

"Oh, because we had won the war."

"Excuse me?"

"We'd defeated the French and we'd defeated the Americans and we thought we could bring down heaven if we wished. But the skills we had to win the war were not what we needed to run the country."

It was an explanation he would offer to those tourists who seemed to desire a daring little jab of political criticism from their commie guide. Usually it was enough—they feltthey had been given more than their money's worth, had the illusion that they'd been privileged to glimpse some flesh of the country's true heart. But she wasn't one of them. He had thought he could keep her in that category, but he understood now how futile that notion was, and when he started to speak to her, he was surprised at the intensity of his own need to explain, as if he could give her through those few words all that had been subtracted from the Vietnamese portion of her life, from the soul that he'd cut from her, that had waited here with him for her return.

The traffic swirled around them, and finally clotted into a honking, frozen mass. They came to a halt. A peasant woman, in from the countryside, squatted next to a basket filled with squawking chickens, a stack of cardboard boxes filled with Hitachi televisions towering precariously above her. His father had told him how, during the great famine of '45, when he'd open his door in the morning, it would bump against the corpses of people who had crawled up to it the night before; Duong born into a city where the walking dead, their breath fouling the air, their bellies pressed against their backbones, stumbled in from the countryside to die by the thousands in the streets, as if Ha Noi was an ancestral tomb to which they felt compelled to drag themselves. It was the obscenity of hunger in a fertile country that had led his father, the poet, to the revolution—in war, Uncle Ho had said, poetry must be a sword—and his stories of that hunger—of trying to fool the hard knots in one's stomach with straw and banana roots, the parents who sold their own children rather than see them turn into skeletons in front of their eyes, the dead piled in the streets—had led Duong to it as well.

He understood that hunger; in the war it was a chewing worm in his intestines, a visceral subtext for slogans of independence and freedom; he'd devoured roots and crumbling, infested rice, honed himself into a knife. His family, Catholics, had gone South in 1954; he'd studied at Hue University, had come to the revolution then, an ideological convert. But it was really the memory of hunger that had brought him to the Party, and hunger took him from it in the eighties, when he knew himself to be a small cog in the apparatus helping to enforce the collectivist stupidities and other Chinese fantasies that brought millions who had suffered through the war to the brink of starvation. As a party member and an officer of state security then, his ration card had entitled him to half a liter of nuoc mam and a hundred grams of meat each month, amounts that, even more than his status as a war hero, attracted his first wife (before Dao) to him. But he'd left state security (and his wife had promptly left him)—he had been tired of arresting the wrong people.

A line of schoolgirls in black dresses, white shirts, and red scarves, books clutched to their breasts, passed the car window, staring at his staring passenger, giggling, ignoring the man in blue shorts and a ragged Tiger Beer t-shirt pissing on a utility pole.

"In those days," he explained to this woman, whose face had reopened a sense of loss in him for which hunger was only an inadequate metaphor, "if you somehow got your hands on a chicken or fish, you cooked and ate it in secrecy, so as not to shame your neighbors."

In those days, a voice whispered in his mind, and he knew the days it meant were not the ones he'd tried to call up; *in those days*, the mocking voice said, *you were shamed.*

The shadowed, cavernous interior of the theater was cool, a stain-map of mildew on one wall. A rehearsal was going on, and so the hall was empty, except for the actors on the stage. The curtain opened as they took seats in the front role. The spotlight fell on Thuy, and Duong felt Kiet stiffen next to him, turned to see her staring intensely. Thuy was heavily madeup and costumed as a peasant woman, an old shawl draped over her shoulders. He had seen her assume characters before—all she needed was one prop: a shawl, a flower, a certain hat—and she became the character, not inhabiting another's form, but molding it out of her own flesh and spirit.

She was standing among some representative boats now, the shoreline indicated by props of palm trees and thatched houses. She held a baby doll tenderly. He caught his breath as he realized what part of her play she was rehearsing. Around her, the young members of her acting troupe were also dressed in ancient peasant costumes. Coils of barbed wire blocked a part of the beach, but they have been cut and parted. The spotlights suddenly flashed on and off, and the music, from Thuy's boom box—a recording of traditional music with dan bau monochord zithers, Dan gao coconut fiddles, and the moon lute, the dan nguyet—became jarring, discordant. Soldiers dressed in crimson-and-black armor ran in, the leather pauldrons of their armor flapping. They surrounded the people menacingly, pointed their swords and spears at the crowd. When the people were cowed, a trumpet sounded and a palanquin, resting on the back of near-naked slaves, entered and came to a halt. A prince, in silken Mandarin robes, descended. He walked over to the baby, snatched it brutally from Thuy's arms. She danced madly, cradling the space where the absent child had been, singing a lament in cai luong style. She grasped an end of the coiled wire and tried to circle it around the prince and the stolen child, dancing, singing:

To you I'll give a coil of wire, barbed wire,
The climbing vine of all this modern age—
It's coiling tight around our souls today.
Take it as my love token—don't ask why

An old Tran Da Tu poem, and once forbidden to their ears and eyes, as Thuy had been to his. He whispered a translation—to Kiet, who was still watching with an intentness that was more than politeness. Thuy danced in front of them, coming almost to the edge of the stage. She looked down and then did something Duong had never seen her do in any of the hundreds of performances he had witnessed—she looked at the audience. At them. At Kiet. She stopped dead, freezing into a stillness that seemed to suck at the edges of the walls and ceilings, as if they were being drawn into a vortex centered on Thuy's slightly open mouth, her widening eyes. He saw her struggle to speak, but whatever words were there crowded in her throat and squeezed out as moan. She ran suddenly from the stage.

Kiet was staring at him, but before she could speak, he motioned to her to remain seated, and then went up the stairs at stage left. The actors were looking at each other, frozen into their positions, starting to mutter.

Why do you stop? he barked at them.

They began going through their motions again, the mandarin warrior twirling, his robes winging out, a girl cooing over the doll. Duong slipped behind the curtain. Thuy had parted it a little further down and was looking out through the slit. He walked up next to her. She was breathing hard, her breasts heaving, looking at Kiet. One of the actors turned up the music. Duong put his hand on her shoulder. Her flesh jumped under his palm, as if electricity were flowing through it.

I couldn't do it, she said, unnecessarily.

He stood next to her, looking at the actors, and what the actors were doing. A chill going through him, thinking how Thuy had created this particular cai luong before she knew the woman would return.

You're already doing it. Just continue. Let her see it through the play. Bring her into it. Bring it into her.

I can't do that.

Then you no longer believe in your own art.

Grammar

Vietnamese pronouns vary depending on age, sex, social position, and level of intimacy, Kiet's little phrase book informed her. *Em: younger sibling, male or female, or a wife or lover.* She closed the book. At the theater, Duong had told her the woman, Thuy, had been called away. He'd insisted on escorting Kiet back to the hotel. But she did not feel like going back to the room, staring at the walls and ceiling. There was a small dining room—a few tables against the corridor wall past the reception desk—and she sat against the wall, her shoulder resting on a mural of a garishly painted leopard stalking through the same bamboo forest on the wall of her room. A small black-and-white television set stood on a round table near the kitchen door. On the screen American soldiers in helmets and flak jackets fired over stone walls, ran down rubble-strewn streets punctuated by the exclamation points of minarets.

When she looked away from it, Thuy was standing in front of her.

"May I sit?" Close to her now, without her makeup, she was a handsome woman, perhaps of Duong's age, her hair done in a tight bun that somehow accentuated a kind of fragility. The faint lines around her mouth, the smile crinkles around her eyes belied that; she had a strong face. The fragility had to do, Kiet sensed, with herself.

"Please." Kiet rose and they shook hands.

"I'm happy to meet you." She glanced at the television. "Do you mind if I close that machine?"

"Of course not."

An American soldier was speaking to the reporter, his voice canceled by the Vietnamese translation. Thuy listened for a moment, shook her head.

"Those children of yours, so eager for their own war."

"I'm not sure how eager that boy is."

Thuy shut off the war. "Yes."

They both stared at the blank screen.

"I'm sorry," Thuy said. "I'm being rude." She laughed ruefully. "I came to apologize for being rude earlier, for not coming over to meet you."

"It's OK." Kiet tried to smile. "You looked at me as if I was a ghost." She reached over and touched her. "There. You see? Flesh."

Thuy clutched Kiet's hand. Hard. The desk clerk came to the table, asked a question.

"What would you like to eat?" Thuy asked.

"Just coffee."

"So what's your relationship to Duong?" Kiet asked, when the clerk left.

"Did he tell you anything?"

"He's being very dark and mysterious."

"Yes. It's tiresome." Thuy smiled, as if they were talking fondly of someone they both knew well. Oh, that Duong. Kiet wanted suddenly to goad her.

"But he does it very well."

She smiled briefly. Or grimaced.

The clerk brought two glasses, strainers, and small metal brewers, strainers sitting like the Tin Man's hat on their tops. The glasses had yellowish condensed milk thick at their bottoms.

"Do you know him well?"

"He's an old family friend."

"Where is your family from?"

"The center of the country."

"I thought Duong was from the North, Ha Noi."

She shook her head, as if amused at the crudeness of Kiet's questioning. "He is."

"And he was a communist, a soldier."

"He was a, how do you say? Liaison to the southern

guerillas. In the war. He was in many famous battlefields in the South. Cu Chi. The Truong Son mountains. Plei-Ku. Quang Tri and Quang Nam. Where I'm from."

Kiet regarded her. Did that make Thuy a southern guerilla also, the VC of her fantasies? "He's an interesting man," she said.

Thuy regarded her sharply. "Yes. Many women find him interesting. He's recently divorced," she added, as if that explained it.

Kiet smiled at her. "Don't worry. He's much too old for me."

"I understand you're a performer," Thuy said. For an instant, Kiet was startled, wondering if Thuy had just made some sly, dirty dig. She grinned. But she was probably misreading the woman. Probably quite a bit. "I want to introduce you to my actors, show you our work," Thuy said. She hesitated, but when Kiet didn't reply, she plunged on quickly, as if afraid Kiet would disappear. "We do traditional cai luong plays—but it's a dying art. We try to liven it up, introduce modern forms and stories."

"You want to blur the lines."

"Exactly—blur the lines. Come to my studio—you'll enjoy it. We'd like you, perhaps, to join us for a performance...."

"Miss Thuy, normally I'd be very interested. I don't want to be rude, but you understand why I'm here."

Kiet put the drip-strainer on top of her glass. Thuy reached over and put it back on top of the little metal pot.

"Be patient, em," she said. "Let it brew."

Dead Ringers

Louise turned on the computer, clicked on her server, waited impatiently to get on line. She had a dial-up, no broadband available in their rural area yet. It was never something she missed, absurd to need to be connected instantly to the flood of real estate and sexual and dietary aid come-ons on line, but now she cursed the clunky slowness of the connection. She needed to be linked. Immediately. Webbed to the world, to her daughter. But when she finally got into her email, there was nothing from Kiet. She could have her breasts enhanced, her penis enlarged, and a nice Nigerian man wanted to place 25 million dollars into her checking account. But not a word from Kiet. Or from Alex, who had gone after her.

She knew, if she wanted to know, that he was still in the air, somewhere probably over the western Pacific by now, winging back to what he had never left. But their daughter's emails had only been an excuse. She knew Alex had decided to go almost immediately after they'd seen Kiet off at Dulles, had seen him staring at the space she'd occupied just before disappearing into the metal detector, until Louise had had to tug his sleeve. That morning, she had woken up at three to find his side of the bed empty. She lay with her eyes closed, knowing that if she listened, she would hear the sound of chisel biting stone from his barn workshop. He came back into the bedroom at dawn, and sat, stone-dusted and fully dressed, on the edge of the bed, looking out of the window, the pink light softening his features, shifting him momentarily into the young man she'd married.

Her last conversation with Alex, in the code-talk of a 40-odd-year marriage:

Everything's copasetic.

Baby, I'm not blind.

No—that's Baxter's job.

You're not funny either.

I told you, it's all good.

Sure. Every bit of it.

OK, but thing is, I never bought any of that stuff. It all seemed Hollywood, vets acting the way Hollywood taught them to act.

You were too much of a man?

None of it had ever happened to me.

And if not you, then nobody.

Something like that.

But we both know it's not true.

But since Kiet…

You being retired now...

I have the time to go nuts?

The time to remember. To redefine yourself. To think. The time when all those things you held away though other problems come rushing back in. And things are happening in the world too.

Déjà vu all over again. But maybe that's just the excuse.

Even the excuses are true, me love.

She clicked off the email. On her server screen a news item popped up: a young American face under one of those Nazi space-alien helmets soldiers wore these days. The boy was one of five who had died in Anbar Province when their Bradley had hit a mine. She stared at the face, touched the screen. The boy morphed into Paris Hilton. She had never thought she would know the words Anbar Province; her vocabulary had expanded exponentially over the last few years. Better to have a daughter in Viet Nam than in Ramadi or Fallujah. A resonant statement only to someone of her generation, she supposed, that word, that *country*, no matter what the culturally correct thing to do, would always be the key to open a box of shit and pain, a stack of photos of young dead faces that would pop up, pop out of the ground. In nineteenth-century England, Brian Schulman had told her, they would bury the dead with strings around their fingers, attached to bells on the surface. If someone were accidentally buried alive, he could wiggle his finger, ring his bell—it was where the term dead-ringer came from. There seemed to be bells ringing all over now, bodies thought to be long dead frantically wiggling their fingers. Since Kiet had left, she had become obsessed with the war news, as if her daughter in going back to the ground of one war had pushed her into another. She refused not to see the dead. She would open the *Post* every morning to see the daily casualty list: names, ages, units. The above, unless otherwise indicated, were all killed in action. As opposed to what? Killed passively? She didn't turn away when the nightly news offered a solemn recitation of the biography of another dead child. Who loved his family deeply. Who believed strongly in his mission. Who had always dreamed of being a soldier, a Marine, an airman, a SEAL, a corpse. Tears sprang to her eyes each time, but she felt a sense of duty to see the faces. A part of her, the counselor, knew also that what she was doing was putting herself back into her mindset when she and Alex had just been married and he was in Viet Nam. She'd been a child herself. Now veterans would be, were, coming home again, full of the mystery and power and wisdom of their wounds. Not like you and me. Fire-hardened scales closing one by one around their hearts. They'd seen the fucking elephant. At least in this war there were women who'd seen the trunked beast also; men wouldn't have that all for themselves anymore. Though when she saw the women on the news, dusted with Iraqi sand, they and the men all seemed of the same gender. Yes, that was a cliché, but it wasn't a matter of sexual orientation or genitalia or helmets and weapons. They were becoming *buddies*.

She pushed the power button on the computer and held it until the screen went black. Don't turn it off like that, Alex would say. Being bad. Raging against the machine. Big deal. She called Brian and Mary Schulman. Mary answered the phone.

"Listen, my whole family is in goddamn Viet Nam and I'm going crazy," Louise said.

After dinner they sat on the back patio, looking at the river. Brian and Mary had recently enclosed their deck in glass, and the cardinals and sparrows that used to come to Mary's bird feeder there were not yet used to this new arrangement of the world, even though she'd moved the feeder for them. The birds gathered outside, shivering with panic in a small semicircle, periodically taking off, their tiny bodies sweeping back and forth as if searching for the world they'd lost, one or two occasionally thudding into the glass.

"Why didn't you go with Alex?" Mary asked.

Louise shook her head. She picked up the cup and sipped her coffee. Brian and Mary were looking at her expectantly, cocking their heads like the birds outside the window.

"You know, after we adopted Kiet, Alex never spoke about the war anymore; it was as if he had dealt with it. Or made a deal with it; made it into something good."

Brian shrugged. "And now what—he's reneged?"

"And Kiet?" Mary asked.

"I'm worried like hell about both of them, but I resent them also. That need they share to not let it go."

Brian and Mary stared out at the birds now, not moving, as if any motion would jar out their own confessions. It was why Louise had come to them, the mutual language she and Alex shared with the Schulmans.

"Need?" Brian scowled.

"Well, yes. For self-definition. 'This is who I am, this explains everything wonderful and screwed up about me.'"

"It's more like a prison," Brian said.

"Maybe. But prisoners get to feel at home, get afraid of the choices freedom offers."

"What are you saying, Louise?" Mary said.

"I'm not sure. I just need to talk it out. Brian, you've gone back. What was that to you?"

Brian had returned to Viet Nam ten years before, as part of a team looking for MIA remains.

"If the war wasn't part of your experience, it's hard to explain." He held up his hand. "I know how precious that sounds, that it is just what you were saying about Alex. But I don't mean a kind of boys' club exclusiveness. It's more like going back to the house where you grew up; everything will look different, have a different significance to you than to anybody who is just seeing it for the first time. And then to go as I went, to meet and work with the Vietnamese, shifts it again." He hesitated, gathering his thoughts. "See, the weakness in my analogy is to think of the house as my house. But we did. It was really their house, but we ignored that fact—I mean we, there, on the ground, but also the country; it was convenient; it was what got us there in the first place."

"The original sin," Mary said.

"If you'd like. My point is, going back, meeting the Vietnamese, seeing how they see the world, it creates a shift that lets you grow up. Lose your egocentrism. Of course, that's banal; it can be true of any travel. But these are people you once might have killed."

She felt herself losing patience. "For God's sake, Brian, I don't think that's Alex's problem. Or Kiet's. But he's, there's a kind of fragility in him I haven't seen before, not for years. And Kiet—you know her history, drugs, sexual abuse, abandonment, the whole circus." Her mind skated around the central crime of her daughter's rocky adolescence. "She's a mature woman now, one of the most self-assured people I know, but she's like him. They're both strong from what wounded them, but it's all still there and I want to know they'll be all right," she said. "That they won't come back changed or damaged. That's been my experience with that house, Brian."

Mary nodded. "There it is," she said. She put her hand on the back of Brian's neck. "I felt the same way when he went back."

"I'll tell you something," Brian said, "something that happened when I was there. One of the places I worked, we were excavating a site where there'd been a fairly big battle. There was an account of some American corpses, buried with the NVA. We never found them, but I found a plastic bag with a diary in it; it belonged to a North Vietnamese soldier. There was no body nearby, and I don't know how it got there, but the diary was very well-preserved—not just over the years, but you could see how its owner had kept it in the jungle—carefully rebound with tape, carefully buried. The handwriting in it was meticulous also, tiny letters to take up as little space as possible, but all of it precise and neat. It was as if this guy's personality leapt out at you: neat, careful, responsible. Well, his full name was inscribed in it, and the village he came from, in Nghe An, in the north, and we were able to locate the surviving family. There were only brothers and sisters left; the parents and his wife were dead. Luong— his name was Phan Thanh Luong—was the second son in the family to die; they'd never found his body, nor his brother's, and there were something like 200 cases like that from their village. Well, about a month later, we brought back the diary. The brothers and sisters drove out to meet us, lead us in from the highway. They were wearing white mourning headbands, and when they saw us, they burst into tears. I mean, they were sobbing with grief, as if Luong had died the week before instead of decades ago. All the way to the village they were throwing these little pieces of green and orange paper out of the car windows, to guide Luong's soul back home, they told us. I expected some small, private affair, but when we got to the village, the street was lined with hundreds of people, all wearing white headbands, all wailing. I got out of the car, and I walked with the diary down the middle of that road, that wail all around me, just raw and naked with grief. That *wail*. It was as if all the griefs of the village had been concentrated. I can't describe the *immediacy* and depth of it...or later, after we had placed the book on the family altar, and the family held a ceremony welcoming home Luong's soul, the depth of the gratitude everyone displayed. As soon as the ceremony was over, it was as if the grief was switched off. People were smiling at me, touching me, thanking me, their faces peaceful. The belief is that unless a body—or even some physical object, something owned and, in this case, loved by the dead, was brought back home, that person would remain a wandering soul, not at rest himself, and a torment to the living. But, of course the reason I was in Viet Nam with an American team in the first place was to look for the remains of our dead. There was really no difference. The soul has to come home, Louise."

"I thought my husband's and my daughter's souls were at home," Louise said. "I thought that was here, where I am."

PART THREE

THO SON

EARTH

Alex in Cu Chi

The last time Alex had left Viet Nam, he'd flown out of Da Nang, and the Marine Corps had kept him two weeks in Okinawa, to decompress. There was no decompression going back. He flew into Tan Son Nhut after a two day flight he'd handled with Ambien and Bloody Marys.

Tan Son Nhut. Marines were kept up north, away from the fleshpots of Sai Gon, but he'd landed at this airport once, on a three-day R&R in the capital. He remembered his Hemingway; something about certain names meaning more than themselves. But he should be at a point now, he told himself, where the country—the reality of its sights and smells and noises, no matter how resonant—would be shifted into the present, and it would take a conscious act for him to be taken by the fact of where he was landing now. If he let himself, he could be paralyzed with significance, the whole trip a rush backwards into a past that still had red claws in his soul. He preferred to avoid that. He was worried about his daughter; he wanted his attention on her. He had been a cop for three decades and he knew, he told himself, how to detach his emotions and imagination from the mutilated corpse of the murdered, the wrenched loss in the eyes of the victim's family, their lives suddenly re-formed around grief and absence, in order to do his job. You bet he did.

At customs, officials in the uniforms of people he'd once shot at regarded his luggage—a single overnight bag—with suspicion. A girl, her face dwarfed under a large garrison hat with a polished brim, ran her hands repeatedly through his clothing, opened and emptied his shaving kit. On the taxi ride into the city, the driver had kept looking through the rear-view mirror at him, and Alex found himself trying to figure out the man's age. The man nodded at him, smiled broadly, revealing a broken thicket of black and brown teeth, his eyes locked to Alex's even as the taxi swerved and wove through the insane snarls of traffic. He said nothing, just continued to nod, his eyes gleaming with what seemed to Alex a malevolent glee. It kept Alex's mind occupied. During his three-day in-country R&R, he'd been standing on a street corner when a South Vietnamese soldier in a jeep had veered over, insisted on taking him home for dinner, all allies together. He'd been drunk enough to accept. The ARVN had driven as recklessly as this driver, but without his skill. Driving around a traffic circle that looked like the one they were in now, he had clipped a cyclo, sending it into a mad spin, and run over a woman's foot, Alex twisting to look behind, see how she was, seeing a small mob of Vietnamese gesticulating angrily as they sped away, the ARVN giggling gleefully. His present driver's grin in the mirror widened even more, and he nodded vigorously at Alex, as if reading his mind. They were passing places he knew now, not from his experience but from so many photos and film images after the war: the church that looked like Notre Dame, the presidential palace, its gates smashed open on the last day of the war by a North Vietnamese tank. Framed by the slightly fogged window of the air-conditioned cab, driven by a crazed ghost with bad teeth, the city was still a photo. There was no here, here.

"Kampuchea," the driver finally said, as if offering an answer to a question Alex didn't realize he had asked.

Alex nodded. "Sure. Kampuchea."

"War," the driver said. "China. Kampuchea, bad." His smile, if possible, broadened.

"America?" Alex asked.

The driver raised his fist into the air, a power to the people salute. "Ken-a-dy," he said, and shot one finger out. "John-son." Another finger "Nix-on." A third.

"Nixon," Alex said. He was only a one-finger veteran.

"Ha!" the driver exclaimed, satisfied. "War. Bad."

They both agreed solemnly that war was bad.

"Kach San, hotel," the driver said, pulling over to the sidewalk. Alex looked up at the Hoa Binh, a narrow, six-story building, the balconies on its front like drawers pulled out from a tall chest.

"I wait for you," the driver said.

"No need."

"OK, you see. Maybe you go someplace else."

"I'm not."

"No sweat. Then you pay. I wait."

"No sweat," Alex said. "You do that, champ." He grinned, he liked the guy. But he took his bag.

"Kampuchea!" the driver said, grinning.

Miss Kiet was not in room, the clerk said. Alex nodded, asked for a room for himself. He could wait for her to come back. But he was filled with a nervous energy, couldn't imagine sitting in a hotel. He took out the address he'd printed from Nguyen Binh Duong's website—*Duong's Battlefield Tours: Cu Chi Tunnels My Specialty. Welcome Back Brothers.* There had been no reply to his emails, and no one answered the telephone when he dialed the number listed on the site. 1-800-Sorry About That, Alex supposed. In Kiet's email, she had described meeting Duong at Cu Chi. He left a message for her at the desk.

The driver grinned at him.

"'Sai Gon,'" Alex said, quoting a line from a movie. "'I'm still in fucking Sai Gon.'"

They drove out of the city, passing, among other sights, a rubber plantation—he had friends who had fought in the Michelin and had described what he saw now—trees whipping by his window, lined as perfectly as platoons in formation, and a Coca Cola plant with a hammer and sickle flag flying in front of it, like a doctored photo on a website, or a practical joke. He wondered on whom. Hey, G.I., this one will kill you.

At Cu Chi, he asked the driver—pantomimed—to come

with him, help him look for Duong. The driver's name was Hieu, Alex at first hearing "You," when the man pronounced it, pointing at his chest and seemingly saying: "I-you," creating either an Abbott and Costello who's-on-first moment or some portent of linked experience, depending, Alex supposed on how you wanted to take it. How Hieu wanted to take it. They walked into the exhibit area. Closer now, Alex could see that Hieu's face was seamed with scar tissue. Alex felt suddenly, savagely, like laughing. It would spiral into an uncontrolled hysteria, leave him husked and drooling. Pleasure to make your acquaintance. Haven't we met before? I you. He was jet-lagged, worried sick about his daughter, and back in a heat he'd thought he'd forgotten but that stuck on his skin now like the scab of memory. On the mural behind the man American soldiers were dying foolishly and badly, the theme of this theme park. Booby traps, he thought. The trapping of boobies. Now they called them IED's. Improvised Explosive Devices. Better dying through euphemism.

Hieu saw where he was looking.

"Xin loi. I sorry," he said.

Alex laughed. The VC chamber of commerce. "No shit?"

Hieu grinned, his teeth splayed, discolored. "Never happen, G.I."

This unlikely apparition, this three-president veteran who had just made a joke in the slang of Alex's era, a face suddenly edged out from the light of a year that had burned so strongly that all his other years were just flickering reflections on a cave wall, illusionary shades in which he'd protected and served, met the woman he loved and married, met the child he'd saved and raised and searched for now.

Hieu grinned, led him over to a thatch-shaded area, some benches and a desk underneath. A middle-aged man in glasses, a pressed white shirt and sharply creased black trousers stood near the desk. There wasn't a drop of sweat on him. Alex was soaked. He wiped his eyes. Hieu spoke to the man for a few moments, pointing at Alex.

"Please, you are all right?" The man asked him, looking at him.

"Never better." Alex fished out Duong's printout. "I'm looking for this man." *Where VC?* "O dau Mr. Duong?" he said, remembering the word.

He could hear rifle fire, a ragged volley, but he didn't flinch, expected it: Kiet had described the rifle range in her email, tourists able to shoot AK's or M-16s at a dollar a pop. He still refused to be the returning vet, seeing the war under everything. Not the best place for that resolve, he supposed. He watched a line of sweating tourists being led into the scrub jungle, past manikins dressed like VC. But the trails were all too wide and too clean. War World.

"Not here today," the man said, handing the printout back to him, and then told him where he could probably find Duong.

Rehearsal

Kiet climbed up the stained concrete steps to Thuy's studio on the top floor of the theater, clutching a rickety iron handrail that felt greasy from the sweat on her palm. The mildew-stained stairwell was narrow, the heat compressed around her. Laughter, shouts, and music leaked from behind the door at the top of the stairs. As soon as she pushed it open, the noise dissolved. A circle of Vietnamese faces stared at her. The room was large, high-ceilinged, with floor-to-ceiling jalousies covering the rear windows, some of their louvers broken, the broken light coming through seeming to pulse with the intruding street noises from outside. The stained plaster walls were decorated with bills of past performances, a large poster of Ho Chi Minh. The wooden floor was crisscrossed with scuff marks. A piano sat in one corner, an old man with the same beard and build as Uncle Ho sitting on its bench, his thin face wreathed with smoke from the hand-rolled cigarette in his mouth, his hands frozen over the keys. Thuy's drama troupe and Kiet looked at each other for a moment, and then to her relief, the actors returned to what they'd been doing. A dan bau and an electric guitar player started to riff off each other. The actors laughed, bowed, skipped, somersaulted. Thuy grinned at her. She signaled to one of the actors, a tall, handsome boy with an infectious smile. He came over, took Kiet by the arm. She let him lead her into the group. They all smiled at her. She was being seduced, distracted, but she let it happen.

The actors were doing the scene she had witnessed before: a baby being snatched from its mother by soldiers. Thuy's play. It struck Kiet, not for the first time, what the scene might mean, Thuy's reasons for including her. OK, she thought. OK. She'd do it Thuy's way. *Let me stay*, she had pleaded on her balcony. Grasshopper would watch patiently, learn, let things take their course, wisdom unfold like the leaves of the lotus, and so on.

She went over to the actor holding the doll, snatched it from her arms. So much for the slowly unfolding leaves of the lotus. She ran with it, towards the jalousies in the back, turning the run into a dance, seeing in her head, of all things, Eliza running over the ice in the play within a movie, *Uncle Tom's Cabin* done in *The King and I.* Out of the corner of her eye, she glanced at Thuy, frozen, the expression on her face a mask of pain. Was Thuy her mother? She was the right age, she was doing whatever the hell it was she was doing. Kiet brought the doll back to her, thrust it at her.

"Are you my mother?"

Thuy said: "You're very American."

"To the bone."

Kiet watched Thuy smooth the expression from her face, as if she was pulling the edge of a board across ruffled sand.

"No, I am not your mother, em," she said simply, Kiet feeling not let down but simply ridiculous. Thuy took her hands. "Duong told me you are an actor. I can see it is true."

"Not as good as you." But Thuy refused to register the sarcasm in her voice, and Kiet was grateful. She was being petulant, childish.

"My students are curious about your performances."

She would not know how to describe what she did next. How could she describe a dance, except to recite the choreography? She could tell someone the words she sang, but no one would hear what came to her, the memory under those words, that dance; the recall of violations that still thickened in her throat and limbs, whether she wanted it to or not. Her dances all come from the wounds of childhood; they were self-referential, and she had been criticized for that, accused of solipsism. It might be true. She did dance for herself, spun her own demons out of her own memories, or vice versa. But she hoped that her audiences recognized some dark familiars being shaken out of their own heads and hearts. She hoped that fervently, now, in this hot studio on top of the Theater of Then and Now.

At first, though, she started as she always did: assumed the position of the apsaras. As she folded her arms, bent her knees, tilted her head, Thuy stared, her forehead creasing. Her puzzlement puzzled Kiet; she would have thought this pose, the stone dancer known all over Asia, would be something Thuy knew.

The students stirred, restlessly, as her audiences always did. She waited for the dance and its story to come to her. Her gaze fell on the blackboard stretched across the rear wall of the room. A small tinny mirror hung down from a string tacked into the wall. She went to it, picked up a piece of chalk, wrote names on the board, Vietnamese and American. Usually she didn't gloss any of her pieces. She relied on whatever was or should already be in her audiences' minds to connect to the narrative she was bringing them. But she was ignorant of whatever context this audience would have, and anxious, more than anxious, to connect. The Viet Nam war memorial in Washington, she explained—and then began to sing imitating the vibrato she'd heard in their performance. A girl—her name, Kiet found later, was Tuyet—came up next to her, graceful and grave, and began accompanying her, translating, echoing in quavering cai luong also, and Kiet sang how the names of the dead are carved into stone that has the quality of a mirror; when you stand in front of it, the names are written on your face, your body. She was fifteen and she would search for her father's name, and she did not know it, but she hoped it would stay written on her forehead when she turned her face from the wall.

My daddy writes his name on my forehead
but whenever I try to see it another
name nudges it away.

120

She danced along the board and was that fifteen-year-old, kissing, caressing the names, their chalk smearing her forehead. She heard music, notes on a piano, and saw that the old man had started accompanying her, and then a young boy started plucking the monochord zither, the sound rising from his fingers as if he were weaving it into the air. Some of the students, swaying in unison, went to the board, lay down, became—she saw it immediately—a row of the dead. They were dancing with her, their arms rising like snakes, their hands caressing her, drawing her down. The room was filled with music, with flowing, crossing shadows.

The names tug and pinch at my insides.
And where was my mother's name?
she sang, looking directly at Thuy.
And where was my name?
She danced to the mirror, brought her face in close.
My Ma's name is my face reflected in the polished stone.

This is what she danced, what moved her body and in her body, as she told the story, the sing-song of the story, and if they didn't understand her words, they understood the cost that this telling took from her, this weave of her story to their stories. She was at the Wall of the dead, but she was at Hiram Johns' farm also, in a bedroom, legs spread, lips muttering daddy, daddy, daddy, one, two, three. She pushed her body flat, face first, against the Wall, and the actors who had lain down around her, playing the dead, now rose, surrounding her, their hands patting her, comforting her.

The names stitch to my forehead
Daddy, daddy, daddy, daddy, 58,736 times
My name slides away from me like a shadow
I disappear into the black Wall
Black into Black
I push as if into the cold skin of water
It seizes me, fills my mouth, my nose
I tear myself away
She tore herself away from their hands.

I am named and born
from the black living wedge
of the dead.

Her body moved, as if of its own accord, into the posture of the stone dancer. She was finished, and she moved into the apsaras so as to move back into herself, to bring back and hold tight to her everything that she had let come out and twist vulnerable in the dust-speckled broken light of that room. The actors in Thuy's troupe stared, immobile themselves, except for Tuyet, who came to stand next to her, assuming the exact posture, expression: a sister apsaras, who knew what dead lived in her life also?

The actors, dazed for a moment, started laughing, applauding, nodding. Kiet felt dizzy with joy as she waited for Thuy to walk over to her, to bless the occasion: this dance here, with these people, a culmination of sorts. And Thuy was wiping her eyes.

"The cai luong," she said, "How do you know…"

Something dropped in Kiet's stomach. The question disappointed her, seemed anticlimatic.

She shrugged. "It was a form I studied."

The actors were crowding around, applauding, calling out: More, more.

As if on cue, the door opened and she saw Alex, standing in its frame, staring at her as if he could pin her where she stood with his eyes.

She ran to him, crying over and over the same word she had just sung in the rhythms of a delta far from the estuarine marshes where they had first found each other.

A Metaphor

You were right, Thuy said to Duong later. Her mother is telling us the way this must be done.

They were in her dressing room. Since Kiet's performance, Thuy had been listless, moving brokenly as an old woman, as if something vital had been sucked out of her body.

Well, it's getting tiresome, he said. I was wrong. Her other father is here. We should just sit down and tell them what they want to know.

No, she said, her voice strained. You were right. It must be done in the play. She glared at him, with a suddenly revealed loathing that made him turn away.

As you wish, he said. It was no use. Her sense of the dramatic had been aroused, and besides, she was probably right. The serendipity that she had been working on the play before knowing that its true audience would come to see it was not something that they could ignore.

It's not ready. I want them only to see the finished work. We need dress rehearsals, today and tomorrow. Distract them.

How?

She shrugged. You're a tour guide.

He found Kiet and the American she called her "father," in the front row of the theater, staring at the drawn curtain, as if their future instead of their past, were behind it. Duong caught Alex looking at him curiously a few times, Alex's gaze going back to the curtain when their eyes met, but the last time meeting his stare, holding it. For a time, neither of them spoke. Finally Duong broke the silence.

"I can arrange some tours for you." He handed Alex a card. Alex studied it.

"Thanks." He handed the card back. "But I don't do tunnels."

"I thought you'd find it interesting. Where were you in the war?

"What we called I Corps. Mostly in Quang Nam and Quang Tri."

"I was in those provinces also."

They both looked at each other. Did the American see the elusive and killing phantom of his youth, finally fleshed and static? It was the way he had first stared at the American veterans he'd met. But he'd met too many by now. He stared back at Alex stonily, giving him what he wanted, as a good tour guide should.

"Is that where you knew Kiet's family," Alex asked.

"I'm merely a guide."

"To the font of truth?"

"I'm sorry?"

"Kiet told me about you. I think you know more than you're saying."

"Ah," Duong said. "And you'd like to, how-do-you-say, interrogate me? Where are the VC, yes?" He laughed.

"I was a cop for thirty years, Mr. Duong. My sense is you can tell us a little more. Pertaining to my daughter."

"Alex...." Kiet started.

"We all have our own memories, isn't it, Mr. Alex? When you were in the war, did you ever have to defuse an unexploded mine? You must do it very delicately. How do you say? Inch by inch. Do you understand?"

"Is that what you call a metaphor? That whole defuse the mine thingie? I'm afraid I'm just a simple man, Mr. Duong."

"Ah, Mr. Alex," Duong said, "I'm afraid you're not." He rose. Let them sit here, watch the rehearsal, let Thuy deal with them. "Excuse me; if you don't need my services, I have work to do."

"That was rude," Kiet said.

Her father looked thoughtfully after Duong, and then, just as thoughtfully, at her. "The haunted warrior. He does that well."

"He's not the only one," she snapped.

Suddenly the curtain rose. Alex smiled at her, but when he turned to look at the stage, his forehead knit and she saw the blood drain from his face, his eyes go flat, hard. The backdrop scenery was formed from the silhouettes of several hill formations, a dark, dragon-spine shape against a blue sky.

"Marble Mountain," he said, and nodded, as if it had been just what he expected of the day.

In front of the silhouettes were several human-sized cardboard photo cut-outs, their backs, propped by a framework of small wooden struts, to the audience, the two of them. Before Kiet could say anything, Thuy and the rest of the troupe entered, stage right. Some were dressed in traditional robes, silk ao dai dresses, and representations of layered, lacquer armor, but mixed among the ancient warriors were several young men dressed in new-looking American fatigues and green helmet liners, carrying plastic M-16's. Three of those dressed as Americans had white pancake make-up caked on their faces, their mouths outlined in red. The other "American" wore black-face.

An actor—it was, she saw, the boy who had played the dan bau—dressed as an old man, in baggy, work black pajamas, entered from stage left, carrying a stool and a small black box. He sat on the stool and placed the box carefully in front of himself, smiled, and than drew out a small statue of an apsaras, held it between his knees, and then took out a plastic hammer and chisel and pretended to work on it, the statue, Kiet supposed, an acknowledgement of her own performance. She put her hand on her father's arm. A low murmur began to spill from Alex's lips. She looked at him in alarm, but he seemed transfixed on the scene. The "soldiers" surrounded the old man; they began shouting at him, interrogating him, spinning him this way and that. Alex suddenly rose.

She reached up, tried to hold his hand, keep him back, but before she could say anything, he rushed to the stage. Jumped on it. The skit came to a halt.

"You want to do it? Do it right!" Alex stood in front of the actor playing the old man, hulking over him.

She stood up. "Dad, what are you doing?"

"Blurring the lines, baby—isn't that what you always say?"

He bent over, bringing his face close to the actor, the boy cringing back, not acting. Alex began shouting. "O dau, mother-fucker! Where are they? You gonna cop an attitude with me? You think you ain't gonna talk, you gook fuck? Where? Where? O dau?"

The other actors stared aghast. That was the word that came into her mind—she had never before seen that term literally describe what she now saw on their faces. They were not ready for the real thing. She started for the stage. Before she could climb up, Thuy, dressed in black, cartridge belt around her waist, ran across the stage and put a hand on Alex's shoulder. He spun, and as he did brushed against one of the cut-outs. As it fell, he reached out instinctively, caught it, and then froze. A life-sized photo of a Buddha statue with a bullet-shattered face.

Thuy and Duong were both in her dressing room when Alex and Kiet came in. Alex brought the cut-out photo with him, holding it under his arm. Kiet stood with her hand on his shoulder; the gesture—she realized later, remembering the scene—mirroring Thuy's calming clasp a few moments earlier. Her father had nearly been hyperventilating, shaking his head violently, as if trying to dislodge something inside it that was cutting, sharp as a knife, inside his own skull.

"What the hell is this," he managed. "What the hell are you all playing at?"

He seized Thuy's shoulder with one hand. Duong's hand shot out and grasped his wrist. He released her abruptly, sank back down into a seat.

"I'm sorry," he muttered, to someone.

She was furious. "Yes. So you're the apology. So you've finally come." She shook her head, visibly calming herself.

"I'm sorry," he said again. "Please tell me about this photo."

"Of course," she said. "I will tell you. But what is it? What upset you so much?"

"Please."

"The statue is famous where I come from; it's seen as a symbol of the war," Thuy said, nodding at the photo.

"You're from Da Nang," Alex said. A statement, not a question. An accusation. He was still in his interrogator's role, focused and intent. He scared Kiet, her father, this sudden stranger.

"From Ngu Hanh Son. What the Americans call Marble Mountain."

Kiet saw the incredulity tighten his face. "Sure. Right. The statue—do you know where exactly it's located? Is it still there?"

She went over and examined the stand-up figure closely, seeing, for the first time, the resemblance to the statue in Alex's workshop. A chill ran through her. She couldn't wrap her mind around what Thuy had told him, her father's connection to the place this woman came from, this woman's connection to herself.

"No. Not any more," Thuy said.

"Who took this photograph?"

She hesitated. "A man named Trinh Van Hai."

"You know him?"

127

Duong was staring at her, shaking his head slightly. Kiet saw Alex catch it.

"I want to talk to him."

"Of course. But he doesn't live here."

"Where?"

"In Hoi An."

Alex nodded again. "Near Da Nang. Tell me how to find him."

O dau the VC? Kiet thought.

"Afterwards, I can take you to him. But we're preparing a special performance for Kiet..."

"Just tell me where to find him."

"Why is it...?"

"Thuy, please," Kiet said. She suddenly just wanted him gone, this Alex she had never seen.

Thuy sighed, shrugged. "There are other photos from that man, from that place and time, here in Sai Gon," she said to Alex. "I can take you there now."

War Remnants

Alex, as he walked into the courtyard of the War Remnants Museum with Thuy, felt calmer now. It was the kind of flat zone he would get into when a case he had worked hard would come together, the connections suddenly apparent, or when he was working a piece of stone and the shape he hadn't known was there began to emerge. It was not that surprising, he told himself, that the woman next to him came from Marble Mountain, that the peculiar work he'd carved with 7.62 mm bullets that day had become known. War remnants. He studied Thuy with his sculptor's eyes. Her figure was what he thought of as comfortable; what weight had been added to a slim form, the swell of the hips, the slight sag of her breasts, suggested an antipathy to fanaticism, an ability to enjoy the world. In her face, he could see who she would have been, when he was last here. If he carved her, that face shining from among the trees, what would be hardest to capture would be her eyes. They contradicted her body. They contained something he couldn't name, a deep sadness and the resigned humor to bear it, history, maybe—if he saw those eyes anywhere else in the world, he would know where they belonged. How would he put that into clay, into stone?

An old American Huey helicopter was parked incongruously in the courtyard, near a small kiosk and tables. The aircraft's interior had been emptied, but it was otherwise intact. There was no sign to indicate what it was doing there. He stared at it, somehow comforted by seeing the machine here, next to tables and grass, contained and domesticated by the present. Thuy followed his gaze to the helicopter.

"This was called the museum of American war crimes," she said. "But they changed the name so as not to offend the tourists."

Alex walked over to the helicopter. Thuy looked at him, waiting to enter the museum, but he was suddenly apprehensive. He'd arrived at a place which might give him answers, lead him through a door and into the mouth of a cave, and he didn't know if he really wanted what he would find. It was too fast; he needed to slow it down.

He sat in the open hatch of the helicopter.

Thuy climbed in the opposite side. She sat on the deck, her feet dangling outside the hatchway, their backs to each other.

"You were a pilot?" she asked Alex.

He pantomimed holding a machine gun. "I sat behind a machine gun."

"Only sat? At Ngu Hanh Son?"

"What did you do during the war?"

"I stayed very still. It was something I learned from my father. Something about helicopters and the people who sat in them, behind machine guns."

"Don't you find it strange that you're from the place where my base was?"

"I found it strange your base was there at all."

"Me too."

"We say that some lives are tied together by a red silk thread."

He nodded. "Are you a religious woman, Miss Thuy?"

"The only thing I believe in, Mr. Alex, is ghosts." She looked up at him again, her face intent. "Please, tell me about Kiet. You wish to know about your daughter. So do I. It's the price, Mr. Alex. Tell me about how she came to you. How you...what is the word?"

"Adopted. Her mother and I...what is it?"

She was staring at him, the blood draining from her face. She lowered her eyes. "I'm sorry. It was just...the heat. Go on. Why did you come now?"

Her mother and I, he thought. The words had called an image to her. A red thread. He nodded.

"She'd been emailing us, or calling, daily. Then nothing, not for a week."

"But she is an adult, yes? She seems quite capable."

"Sure. But it's…" He didn't finish.

"This country? The war? You are worried about her? But the war is over." She waved at the area around them. "The war is a museum for tourists."

"So it seems."

"I wish we could just bury it all and walk away."

"You sound like my wife."

"She must be very wise."

"Not too wise—she married me."

She laughed. "Please continue. Tell me about Kiet's life in America. Kiet." She pronounced the name as if tasting it. "It isn't a girl's name, you know."

"So we've discovered." He twisted back around, looked at her. "Do you know her real name?"

"I will help her find it, Mr. Alex. I promise. But first tell me about her life with you."

He pressed his foot against the skid. "My wife and I adopted her when she was fifteen. She'd had a rough time of it. My wife was a counselor…"

"What is this?"

"A counselor? Like a psychologist…"

"Yes. I understand. Go on."

"She, my wife, worked at what we call a group home, a place for girls with problems—girls with addictions, or some who had been abused. Kiet had no parents, so she had always been under what we call foster care—kind of like parents who are appointed by the government and are paid to take care of kids like her. She'd been with an older couple, but when the wife died, the state screwed up and left her alone, with the husband. It was on a farm, kind of isolated, and he was molesting her."

"Molesting?"

"Abusing. Sexually. When the system caught up with

him, he was arrested, and she came to the group home. But she was troubled, kept running away."

He stopped. Thuy's face had paled. She leaned forward, her feet flat on the ground, as if she was holding her own body against flight, keeping the helicopter from lifting off.

Alex said, "She's come a long way since then, grew up, went to college..."

"You and your wife," she said, her voice strained. "You are good people. Yes. But tell me; this, how do you call it, foster? This foster. How did she come to America? Weren't there Vietnamese parents who brought her?"

"Well, we were hoping Duong would know more about that. I was hoping you might." He paused, gave her an opportunity to respond, wasn't surprised when she didn't. "The people who brought her over—all we know is that they abandoned her when they arrived."

Thuy looked as if she had been struck. "Abandoned?"

"It means...."

"I know what that word means. Abused. The system," she whispered. "Foster. The group home. Molested. I'm learning so many English words today. So many new words. How helpful they will be in my work." Tears were streaming down her cheeks.

She stretched her arms out, slapped the metal deck.

"I hate this thing. This machine. This *fucking* machine, is that the right word? Let's go inside."

He twisted around to look at her. "Why does that upset you so much. Miss Thuy? I tell you everything, but you tell me nothing. It's not fair."

"Fair?" she said, as if amused by the concept.

"I'm being a lousy cop."

"I don't understand."

"I let you ask all the questions."

"I will tell you everything, Mr. Alex. And I will tell Kiet. But it must be at the right time. Can you wait? Do you have the patience to wait?"

He regarded her curiously. This complex woman whom he once would have seen only as landscape or target or threat. This woman threaded to his daughter. He knew nothing about her.

"Are you married?"

She laughed, wiped her eyes. "Ah, now you are being indirect. Vietnamese."

"Are you?" He was suddenly afraid of the answer.

"I'm a widow," she said, confirming what he'd feared. He didn't want to know.

He asked anyway. "Did he die in the war?"

"No, Mr. Alex. My husband died a few years ago, in a traffic accident. We had gone to a resort, a beach place, Do Son, in the North. He was struck by a motorcycle while he was crossing the street, eating an ice cream cone. He was dead before it melted. I remember that. It is the picture that I always have."

"I'm sorry," Alex said.

"We didn't all die in the war, Mr. Alex. Some of us died eating ice cream."

"I'm glad," he said.

She snorted. "Why?"

He shifted around. The words that slipped out of his mouth next surprising him, as ridiculous as the two that preceded them. "I was afraid I might have killed him."

She stared down at her knees, her hands trembling slightly.

He looked away, tapped the scored side of the aircraft.

"You know, on our police cars, back home, there's the motto 'To protect and serve.' That's all I ever wanted, here."

"Chieu oi," Thuy said. "God help us." They both laughed.

"I was mostly around Da Nang, as you know, and later Quang Tri, the DMZ. But sometimes we flew over Quang Ngai. That's where the My Lai massacre took place. It was after I left. I wasn't there, never saw anything like it, not on that scale. But I used to read about it, obsess about it." He slapped the deck of the aircraft. "There was a helicopter crew that tried to stop it, help people. I always wished I could have been in that crew. To protect. To protect and to serve."

"You're a good man," she said simply. "I'm glad your daughter found you."

"In the accounts, they describe Calley picking up a baby that crawled out of the ditch, shooting it, throwing it back in. And that crew; they pulled a child out, saved it. When Kiet came into our lives, the time we adopted her, I kept thinking of her as that child. As someone I could pull out of that ditch." He said what he'd never thought he'd put into words. "Or out of a cave of the dead." He stopped. "There's something else I need to ask you."

"We will help Kiet find what she needs to find. Soon. Please…"

"No. About the statue. You say you're from Marble Mountain….how do you say it? Ngu Hanh Son?"

"Yes."

"Were you there in 1969?"

She didn't answer.

"Two Marines from the helicopter base went missing that year. In February. Did you hear anything about that? Do you remember it?"

"'O dau?'" she said, turning her voice to a low growl, imitating his at the rehearsal. "'O dau the G.I.'s.' Is that it?"

"Yes, ma'am. That's it."

It would seem you have all the Americans you need, little brother, she whispered in Vietnamese, words coming back to her across a chasm of years. She understood now, with no particular surprise, how this man's life had brushed against the lives of her family, a red silk thread drawn across another thread that tied him to the girl who became his daughter.

He shook his head. "Excuse me?"

"I'm sorry. It's just that—you're not the first to ask about those men. But I don't know. There is nothing I can tell you."

She rubbed her knees. Stared at him, and nodded, as if

coming to a decision.

"I think your vision was correct."

"My vision?"

"The way you saw your daughter coming to you. Like that child coming to you from out of the ditch. That vision is correct. Something seen from the side, from the corner of the eye but surely there."

Inside, photos of various atrocities lined the walls. A few Western tourists glanced nervously at the pictures, looked down at their feet. One middle-aged man, shaven head, moustache, gold earrings, glared at both photographs and other tourists. My Lai, Alex noted, had a prominent place. A French guillotine. Thuy led Alex to one wall. On it was a photo of the Buddha shattered by Alex's bullets, its placement bringing it to the same level of atrocity of the photos of My Lai.

"The photographer..."

"Mr. Trinh Van Hai?"

"This photo...the two Marines who went missing..."

"I don't understand."

"I need to speak to him. To go there."

"Yes, tomorrow, after the play. We can all go up to Hoi An together."

"Is there an evening flight to Da Nang?"

"Morning. Surely you can wait. Kiet—the play tomorrow; we're doing it for her."

"She can stay. In fact, I'd rather she stayed."

"Mr. Alex, why?"

Alex touched the photo, muttered, "Because I am the walrus. Cu-cu-ca-choo."

The Photographer

The telephone rang. Trinh Van Hai, a thickset man in his seventies, his wispy white hair haloed out around his face under a black beret, sighed and put his book—a new translation of Molière—down. He walked painfully across the salon to the phone stand. His house was of the old Chinese style, dark teak floors and low-hung rafters. An altar of the ancestors, with a bowl of fruit and flowers on it, sat in one corner, on it a photograph of a woman. Pictures of ancestors, Chinese mandarins, and authors—Vietnamese, Chinese, American, French— lined the walls, along with Chinese rice-paper paintings, shelves full of bric-a-brac, heavy wooden book shelves, piled haphazardly with books, sagging in the middle under their weight. He picked the phone out of its cradle. Yes. Yes. Mr. Hai here.

———

What name? Kiet. Kiet. His hand trembled.

———

And you gave him my address?

———

Who is this American?

———

Her father? We both know that is untrue.

———

Yes. Of course.

His hand was shaking. He spoke into the receiver, even though there was now no one to hear him on the other end of the line:

The child? he said.

He put the phone carefully into its cradle. He rose, walked slowly into the other room. Turned on the lights. A sudden crowd greeted him; their eyes, when they had eyes, following him, as he knew they would. His photographs lined the walls here; his assistants carefully mounting them for display. But he rarely came in here, did not like to look at his completed work.

One wall contained only the photos he had taken during the war. He'd gone into the profession after he'd been removed from his professorship at the university in Hue, for becoming too vocal in his criticism of the American presence; photography, which had been a hobby until then, had become his only way to make a living, though he'd never taken it seriously as an art. The irony—he supposed there were too many ironies, the term was meaningless—was that his subjects, for the most part, were the representatives of that presence, Americans: G.I.'s who wanted to pose with their weapons in front of exotic landscapes, and later the group photographs, when he was able to get contracts to come on the American bases, selling the idea of books of photographs to commemorate a unit's tour.

He looked at one of the photos he had taken then, before the Ngu Hanh Son sequence. Four American Marines, grinning, their arms around each others' necks.

What he remembers first about that day—strangely enough for a photographer and a bibliophile—are sounds. It is the way he always remembers the war. The sound of explosions, the whistle of parachute flares, the staccato of gunfire from the hills all around, in the distance, and not so distant, the war always there, its noise so constant that it fades into background, becomes meaningless the way a word repeated over and over becomes meaningless. One ignores it until it no longer ignores one, or until years later, on the cusp of old age, one begins to hear what one had tried to ignore.

He wears the same beret under which his hair would later thin and silver, chosen deliberately: as a faculty member at

Hue University it had lent gravitas to his unseemly youth, marked him as a man of letters; in his new career it lent an air of artistic pretension that was a good fit, so to speak, for a craft masquerading as art.

He lines up the four Americans, allowing the peak of Kim Son to be a backdrop. Inevitably they brandish their weapons, fall into what they must see as warriors' poses. Only the large man keeps his rifle slung, is looking thoughtfully at the Cham statue off to their right.

"Please, sir," Hai calls to him. "Look here. Smile. Say 'nuoc mam.'"

"Your mama," one of the other Americans says. Hai laughs. He he he he. Like a fool, he tells himself, an instruction, not a description. He's learned to be an actor as well as a photographer.

He hasn't realized that he is also a subject. Observed, even as he takes that photograph, by men carefully noting his position, the Americans, as if they, the men, are arranging their own composition.

That evening, he is at his desk listening to the pigs die. There is an abattoir near his house and the pigs being slaughtered scream like human beings. One can hear the differences among them in the ways they meet their deaths: some squealing with panic and fear, some with pleading disbelief, some with outrage at the unfairness of the fate which has made them pigs and brought them there. A sudden foul stench makes him wrinkle his nostrils. A gust of air touches the back of his neck. He hears a creak behind him; before he can act, he feels something very cold and sharp touch the base of his throat. He speaks without turning around.

May I see your face? It is a rare privilege, to see the face of one's Death.

Always the hyperbole, the visitor says. You haven't changed.

Ah, do I know you, Death?

The pigs scream. The man doesn't reply. Hai goes to the bookshelves, touches the spines of the books, his fingers lingering. He feels the man's eyes on him, turns to look at him. His assassin wears only a brief loincloth, the knife in his belt, his body and head covered with dark grease. To slip through enemy wire, Hai imagines. Is that how his house was seen now? The man glides over, puts the tip of his knife on the spine of the book Trinh had just touched. *East of Eden.*

Will you murder them as well, he asks, nodding at the books.

Perhaps it's time to do so, my old teacher.

Hai squints at the man, and then nods in recognition.

Nguyen Binh Duong. How good to see a former student getting ahead in the real world. Though you used to be a much better dresser.

Yes, I remember your sense of irony. It was what you had instead of ideology.

Is irony my crime?

Of course.

And the punishment?

But he knew that already.

You know that already, Duong says. Hai sees his hand tremble. He quickly looks away. He wonders, as if he is thinking of another person, if he will squeal with outrage or go silently, with resignation, a good little pig. He closes his eyes.

After a minute, he opens them. Duong is looking at the shelf on the left where Hai keeps copies of what the Americans called yearbooks. His rendition of their year in the abattoir.

Show me these, Duong says. A light has come into his eyes. Hai takes a book off the shelf, opens it. The cover has a picture of a blue eagle, the unit designation HMM-263. The bulk of his income came from the fees the helicopter squadrons gave him to put together these books. The first page contains a map of Viet Nam with the caption *Home of the Blue Eagles*. Ah, Duong says, as if in sudden understanding. He touches the words. Hai shows him the photos. A black-bordered "In Memoriam" page with photos of the dead. Rows of faces, names, ranks. Helicopters landing in various places in the Home of the Blue Eagles, disgorging troops, taking in the broken and dead—those particular stock photos provided by the Marines—he is not, thank you, a combat photographer. Shots around the base: the unit en masse on the flight line, the operations tent, the administrative tent. Duong puts the tip of his knife on one page.

These photographs. They were not provided?

I don't understand.

Duong taps the photographs of the flight line. You have been permitted to go onto this base, to take these?

Yes.

The knife moved down the page, the paper parting smoothly as skin.

And you could, for example, on a map, show me the locations of these places in the photographs?

Yes. I understand.

You will, for example, go back to the base, do more of these?

Yes.

You can, for example, provide us with names and photographs of the Combined Action Company Marines in Non Nuoc?

Yes.

You can, for example, live?

I understand what you are offering.

Duong goes back to the In Memoriam page.

Do you? The object of the lesson, my teacher, would be to move more of the faces from the other pages onto this page. He taps the words "In Memoriam," and then turns to the map page. *The Home of the Blue Eagles.*

140

Until they understand, Duong says. You'll become a teacher again, a teacher of geography as well as of literature and philosophy. The object of the lesson, my professor, is to teach these students why the label they have placed on this map is incorrect.

A Red Silk Thread

Kiet pictured herself slipping through the fringe of woods that bordered Johns' farm, a Viet Cong, blending into a landscape no Viet Cong ever saw: the branches of the trees bare and black against the moon, creaking as they rubbed against each other in the icy wind, moonlight sheened off the frost shrouding the corrugated furrows of the fields. She lay in a bed in Viet Nam with that winter scene hanging heavily in her mind, a coherent waking dream and so more disturbing than the nebulous shifts and portents of a real dream would have been. Her legs had drawn up, an acquiescent parting her skin and her bones remember, it lay dormant in them still, it had come here with her. She dressed quickly and went to Alex's room, needing to see the anchor of him, the rescuer, the true father.

His room was empty.

She felt a flash of anger at his desertion, and then at herself, her abstract, self-conscious "quest," the price they were both paying for it. What had he seen; what was he going through? She went back to her room and began stuffing clothing into her backpack, her hands a blur of motion, as if they were gauging her agitation. The apsaras dancer stood on the table near the bed; looking at it somehow made her angrier.

She heard footsteps behind her and turned to see Thuy and Duong, Thuy's face tightened with concern.

"Alex..." she said.

"He took the morning flight to Da Nang," Thuy said. "Don't worry."

"Why didn't he tell me? That Buddha photo—I've seen him trying to carve it, in his work...what is it?"

Thuy's head had suddenly jerked back, as if she'd been struck. Kiet followed her gaze to the small rose-colored statue. Its eyes calm and detached. Thuy reached out slowly to touch the dancer's face. She picked it up, looking at it carefully, her eyes welling. Duong stared at it also, the question-mark scar on his face seeming to darken, as if the blood had thickened under the thinness of tissue there. Thuy's hand moved to Kiet's face, traced her cheeks, her lips. She tensed, moved back.

"Ah," Thuy said softly. "Of course."

"Excuse me?"

"This statue…what do you know about it?"

"The apsaras? He's always had it. What do you know?"

"We call it a tra kieu dancer. Yesterday, when I took him to see the photographs…there is a connection between us, Kiet. What we call a red silk thread."

"Of course there is." Kiet bit off the words. "Would you please, please stop the fortune cookie shit?"

Thuy flushed. "I mean between your father. And us."

Kiet was out of patience. "I don't know what you're talking about. I'm going after him."

"Then I'll go with you," Duong said.

Thuy's hands fluttered to her throat. "But the rehearsal tonight. The play."

"Fuck the play," Kiet said. "I didn't come here to look for one father and lose another."

PART FOUR

KIM SON

METAL

The Theater of Then and Now

The sunlight coming through the bamboo slats of her father's workshop stripes her skin so that Thuy feels herself dissolve, float among the motes of marble dust that sparkle in the air. She has learned to be invisible. Her name means water; she can be water, sit still for hours, fill any shape she flows into, dissolve into walls or trees. Most people, she has learned, see only what is in motion. Her family is the sixth generation of stone carvers here, in Non Nuoc, and the part of their blood that was Cham here long before that: it was that blood that told them where to find the seams of pure white or rose-colored stone, solid, with no cracks or fissures, in the five peaks of the mountain, how to cut that stone from the mountain, shape it into reflections of the divine. Behind her, against the opposite wall, a line of more than human-sized Buddhas and Quan The Am Bo Tats—Goddesses of Mercy— stand as motionless as Thuy, in front of them a frozen village crowd of other statues her father has collected or imitated: strange Cham gods: Brahma the Creator, with his four faces and four arms, and the Nipple of Uroja, the Mother-Goddess, and the apsaras: tra kieu dancing girls, as well as others, their sampot dresses winged out at their knees, their hair spiked into elaborate Kirita-Kumuta cones; her own features and her sister's sometimes glimpsed in their wide eyebrows, curved noses and lips. She feels their stare on her neck as she herself peers through the narrow opening between the slats at the shaded area under the thatched awning that extends out from the workshop roof, watching the grace forming under her father's scarred and calloused hand. Watching the American Marine, gigantic as a statue himself, who squats in front of her father, staring at the face emerging from the stone. There are Marines who stay in the hamlet, but she does not know this man. He and the other Americans with him, out of her view now except for their shadows on her father, are statues come to life themselves, layered with clanking metal scales.

She fastens her gaze on the hands of the two men, her father's and the Marine's. She has learned to do this also, to sometimes see only in small pieces that she can pick up and examine, so that nothing escapes her. The Marine reaches out, caresses the tra kieu dancer's smile, draws his hand back. There is a tenderness in the gesture that surprises her. For an instant, it seems that his hand and her father's belong to the same person. Her father's hand surrounding the metal chisel, the American gripping only air, but clenched as if around an invisible chisel. But his other hand rests on the rifle barrel slung forward over his shoulder.

Ngu Hanh Son, her father says to the American. Then words that come from his mouth like stones. Mar-ble. Moun-tain. One of the other Americans, a dark, thin boy, says something she can't understand; the others laugh.

The Marine stands, slings his rifle. He goes to the dancer, Thuy's favorite. His fingers still trace her eyes, her smile. Thuy shudders. But her father smiles also. He hands the American something. She fears what it is, and then, seeing the flash of rose-colored stone, she is certain of it: the small dancer; it is hers, his gift to her. She feels a flash of rage, directed not at her father, but at this crude giant, at the price he has made her father pay to get him to go away.

The American disappears, takes the shadows of the others with him. Kim, her older sister, rushes across to their father, hugs him, her eyes wide. Father smiles, caresses her hair, and suddenly Thuy feels like crying, but she is seventeen and no longer a child.

Her father comes into the workshop. She goes to him, puts her arms around his waist. He smiles at her also, kisses her. But his face is tight with worry.

I gave the tourists a little souvenir, Father says. But I don't think they will go home.

I'm sorry, father, Thuy says.

There is a slight noise, and another figure emerges from next to one of the statues, a Ganeesh, moving from the shadows as if detaching himself from the figure. The man stands next to the Elephant God, a statue himself in some future memorial to the war, if his side should win it: dressed in black, a cartridge belt around his waist, an AK-47 slung over his shoulder, a black-and-white checkered scarf around his neck.

You put us all at risk, bringing him here, her father says to her.

Father, Thuy says, this is Comrade Duong.

Le Thach Son looks at him carefully, the way he would look at a piece of stone he was planning to carve. Searching for flaws, places the rock might crack.

You have the book stall in the market, he says, a statement, not a question.

Yes, uncle.

Has it made you a wise man, that façade of books around you?

Uncle, your daughter is a patriot. As you are. I know your background.

Le Thach Son sighs. And I can imagine yours. Serve the people, Comrade Duong. 'Do not bathe in the presence of the village women.'

I don't understand.

No? They are the words of Chairman Mao. And I think you understand them clearly enough.

Don't insult me.

I want to tell you something, comrade, Le Thach Son says. I am proud of my daughter, who looks at you as if you were on one of my pedestals rather than hiding behind it. You know my background? Then you know I fought for this country while you were still sucking your mother's tit. I put a wife who fought for it also, and another daughter into its earth, and what I want to say is this. Living children are our victory. Do you understand me, Comrade Duong?

Whatever Duong might answer is interrupted by the sound of shooting, coming from the flank of the mountain, the direction the Americans had gone.

The four actors playing the Marines stop at the photo of the shattered Buddha. One raises his rifle. Instead of shots, the rapid beat of a wooden drum.

Other actors rush in, place bamboo mats under the thatch awning, take down the Buddha photo.

Do it carefully, Thuy says. She lays down on the mat, stares up into the stage lights. She motions Tuyet to lie down next to her; she has decided for the moment to take the role of Kim, her sister. She is too old, of course, but she wants to, how did Kiet say it? Blur the lines. Later they would switch the roles again, and she would take on the even more difficult task of playing herself. She shows Tuyet how they would sleep, she and her sister, on the mat, in the house, in the hamlet near the flank of a mountain called Water.

Like fish in a pot, the two of them. Their small room separated from the rest of the house by a bamboo partition. They breathe in each other's breaths and groans, entwine in their sleep; their sighs mingle with the sighs of ancestors' souls, woven into the thatch of the walls. Gourds and baskets hang from the joists above their heads, sway and creak, their shadows skittering across the walls. Thuy, waking from an uneasy dream, lies still and listens to their comforting creaking and rustling, to the scurry and whisper of the small lives rustling through the thatch of the ceiling, geckos and insects and sometimes snakes. She remembers her father telling how the first Americans to come to Non Nuoc, the ones before Sergeant Swan and his men came, had sprayed their poison on some of the village roofs, to kill their small residents, and how afterwards the termites and mosquitoes, their enemies annihilated, had been able to come plague the human inhabitants. It is something you need to understand, he had said to Swan, and the American had laughed his big laugh to show that he did.

She feels Kim stirring next to her, keeps her eyes tightly shut. But Kim's breathing becomes even again. Thuy half-lids her eyes, looks carefully at her older sister. She waits for a few seconds, listening to her father's even snore from the room behind the bamboo partition, and then slides off the mat, moving carefully to the door, watching where she places each step. Moves into the night.

Their house is on the edge of the hamlet, close by the eastern flank of Thuy Son. The flank of the mountain, massive and dark, looms over her. Winds moan from its cracks and hollows. She passes the sand-bagged compound where the Marines stay. These are Swan's men, different than the Marines from the helicopter base on the other side of the mountain, or from the patrols that sometimes come through the hamlet. The ones here—a handful—have come to live in the village. Their two houses, inside the ring of sandbags and bunkers, are the same thatched-roof houses everyone else in the village has, except the richest families. A few even speak to the villagers in a language almost like Vietnamese. They are still outsiders, though; physically here, but part of the other world, temporary and uninvited guests. She knows some will be inside, asleep, while others are on the perimeter of the village with the local militia, or out on ambushes. Protecting the village from itself, unaware of the tunnels under them, the caves in the mountain where their enemies, most of them also from the village, sleep, guard, go out on patrols and ambushes. Shadows of each other. Inside the mountain is a secret hospital that is no secret to anyone except the Americans; less than a kilometer away, the Marines have their own hospital, a cluster of tents behind sandbags, across from the helicopter base. She has been in both, seen her mine-shattered mother and sister on bloody cots in the American hospital, next to the shredded bodies of Marines, seen her cousin, a liberation soldier, gut-shot, turn into a shadow on the side of a cave wall. She had seen how the torn and the dead of both sides became the same, slid into each others forms.

But this is her place, not theirs, and she knows how to avoid the Marines. She sticks to the shadows, disappears into a small grove that lies sheltered by a stone paw of the mountain. She can hear the waves crashing into the sand from the sea to the east of Thuy Son, can picture it, the edge of black waves writhing with phosphorescent foam. In daylight, she had watched the helicopters shooting at blobs of green dye on the water. Were they trying to kill the ocean itself? The dragon Lord Lac Long Quan sired one hundred children from the fairy Au Co. He'd taken fifty back with him to the sea, leaving her fifty to live on the blood-soaked land. The Mother of the Nation. Perhaps the Americans are after the other, wet, fifty now. After their flights, children waited on the shore to gather shattered fish.

She goes into the small grove, behind a curtain of wild bamboo, the stalks rubbing and groaning in the wind. Thuy squats in a patch of moonlight. Motionless. There is no one else there. Suddenly, almost imperceptibly, two stalks of bamboo part and she sees Duong, still in black, his back seemingly humped and misshapen. He shrugs off the rucksack. Thuy rises to him, as if to an embrace, but what she waits for is a cartridge belt, heavy with magazines; when he gives her that, he has told her, she will be ready to use it. But there is no belt, no bullets for her; he encircles her waist with nothing more than his arms. She puts her hand flat against his chest, pushes him away.

You know how I feel about you, he whispers.

Thuy shakes her head, puts a finger on his lips. And I may someday feel the same for you, older brother. But that's not why I'm here.

He looks down at her. The stories about me are exaggerated.

And those stories are not why I am pushing you away.

Duong says nothing for a long time, and then nods. You are correct, Comrade. It isn't a world for love right now.

Did he truly say that? Those pretentious words? Yes. And with perfect sincerity. But she would leave them out of the play. Who would believe people once spoke like that. Who today would believe the words she would speak next?

Then let's create that world, she says, and her older self, looking back, doesn't know whether to laugh or to weep.

Let me show you some of this world, he says, and now her older self wants to scream with rage at the vindictiveness of his words. He turns and goes through the trees before she has any time to respond. She goes after him, picking carefully around the flank of Thuy Son, the wind raking her hair. Has he decided to bring her to the war, finally? They are near a statue of the Buddha, its face, she sees with a shock, has been shot off. Two men are dismantling it, carrying it away. He goes down on his belly, motions for her to get down. He puts his finger to his lips, nods at the narrow entrance. But keeps his weapon at his side. They lie in silence, hearing only the trapped howl of the wind in the cave. Then he is gone. She looks around in panic. A hand palm up, appears behind the Buddha, the fingers bend over the palm, beckon rudely. Come. They enter the cave. It is a large space, lit only by some lanterns; smoke from the gunfire drifts in the shafts of light. Several other fighters, AK-47's in their hands, stand in at-ready positions, blinking at Duong and Thuy. They barely register the Buddha statues against the walls, the one large statue in the rear wall, the Cham devas. She sees Hai, the photographer, the flashes from his camera bringing her a series of truncated visions. Four rows of low bamboo platform beds are on the floor, amid a jumble of shattered medical equipment lie about twenty corpses; although they are bloody and torn, she sees many had been bandaged before their deaths—wounded patients, shot by the Americans. Anger and nausea rise in her throat, mix, turn the saliva in her mouth bitter. She spits. The bodies of two nurses lie atop two of the patients, as if they had been trying to protect them, and nearby is the shot-up, torn body of one of the Americans. Next to him another, still alive but badly wounded, is crawling towards them. The photographer takes more photos of the scene. Each flash rolls through her in a wave of nausea and rage. Duong hands her his rifle, nods. It seems to grow heavier as she holds it. Duong stares at her, and then smiles and takes the weapon from her grip. He strides over to the man and quickly—there is absolutely no hesitation in the action; it comes as an extension of his walking—shoots the Marine in the head and then continues to the other side of the cave, lit by the flashes from the camera.

He takes her from the cave. But apparently the evening's lesson is not over. She follows him, the two moving quickly and silently through the village, to the rear of the Marine compound. He motions her to lie down behind a row of cactus. They lie still. Clouds scud across the face of the moon. Two figures come out of the house in the rear of the compound, one large, one small; as they do the moon emerges again as well. Sergeant Swan, the black American, Thuy squinting, recognizing him by his bulk, the way he moves: his features are unclear. Recognizing the person with him, her hand resting on his shoulder, without effort. Her sister

Kim. Whom she had left sleeping on her mat. She looks at Duong, at his hands on the stock and barrel of his weapon, and then into his eyes. A slight smile jerks his lips.

He pushes the rifle at her again. She feels a rush of panic, closes her hands into fists, as if her fingers can delay their grasp. They flutter and then she grips the stock, takes the weapon awkwardly. Duong's eyes are fixed on her, challenging. She points the barrel in the direction of her sister and her lover, lining up the sight on the dark form, as Duong has taught her. A single helicopter passes overhead, intersecting with her life in one brief segment of its spiral towards the base on the other side of Thuy Son. She raises the weapon and fires one shot at the machine, the stropping of the rotors against the rocks drowning out the noise; to her surprise the helicopter jerks, and she sees it let loose a stream of tracers, flashing from the side of the aircraft opposite her, and then veer away. Duong, his face distorted with anger, clutches the shoulder of her shirt tightly, and pulls her away. They run, zigzagging into the shadows.

Back in the house later, she scoops some water from the well and washes the dirt from her face and hands before slipping back inside. In the house, Kim is already on her mat, sleeping or pretending to sleep. Thuy stares at her sister's form, the rise and fall of her chest under the thin blanket, debating whether to wake her, kick her, scream in her face. She lies down next to her. Stares at the ceiling for a long time, a heaviness lying in her chest like grief. Some of it is for their father, who since her mother's and sister's obliteration on Highway One, has, with quiet fanaticism, tried to protect them from the war, urges them to live with the deadly entwinements of the forces all around them, as they lived with floods and storms, as they must live with the locust forms of the helicopters rising and falling and whirling madly from their nest north of Thuy Son. She feels she has been betraying him, her father, has been for a long time, she and now her sister also.

She hears the staccato of a machine gun, an answering flurry of fire, the whoop of helicopter blades, and she wonders if Duong is part of that nightly performance which has become so common that she only hears it now because of the need he has put into her head to be constantly aware of her surroundings, or because now she will join that chorus and she can imagine something new in the world, put into her eyes that night: her sister's American lover as the origin or target of those bullets. Above her head, the thatch of the roof stirs; a gourd hanging from a bamboo joist sways again, and Kim remains silent. Thuy watches the light seep in, bring the gourd to solidity, awaken its yellow skin, watches it delineate her sister's form, the slight tag of saliva at the corner of her mouth. She studies her even breathing. Is she asleep? She will wake her, confront her, scream at her—are you mad, sister? Whatever she did would still be gentler than what Duong would do. Would have her do. She feels another flash of anger at Kim, for her liaison with the American, for the way sparing him had put her in Duong's debt.

.She reaches over and pinches Kim's nostrils.

. Kim jerks up, swatting the hand away. Thuy starts to speak, but when her mouth opens, she hears, strangely an English word shouted, and she shuts her lips, realizes the word came from outside the house, and now the sound of metal clanking against metal. As she starts to rise light explodes in her eyes. Men burst into the room, Thuy suddenly seeing soldiers with weapons pointing at her and Kim, the sight somehow not unexpected, the incarnation of a recurring nightmare that has finally spilled out into the world. An American Marine stands above them, holding a flashlight, screaming something at them. They hear shouts from the rest of the house, crashing noises. They rise, hugging each other, and the Marine pushes the barrel of his gun roughly into

Kim's stomach. Di-di, he yells, Di-di, mau len. And then words in English, screamed into Thuy's face. Terror squeezes her heart. How could they know who had fired a single shot at the helicopter amid the firefights of the night? She doesn't understand the words, but she understands the weapon, the threat, allows herself to be herded into the main room.

Two other Marines are in the room, their rifles pointed at their father, one holding a flashlight along the side of his weapon, the beam lighting her father's face. The man who was with her father that morning; his clothing and face filthy, his eyes wild. Thuy does not recognize any of the others; these are not the ones who live in the village. There is another man, Vietnamese, a government soldier dressed like a miniature American, his helmet too large. She does not know him either. Her house full of armed strangers. The Marines speak to the ARVN soldier in English and he translates their words into screams.

Where are the two Americans who came to you? Speak!

Thuy feels a brief surge of relief that they are here for the Americans who went into the caves the day before, not for her. Then flushes with shame. Her father is the one at risk.

Her father smiles, waves the back of his hand at the Marines.

It would seem you have all the Americans you need, younger brother.

The soldier slaps him.

We stare all day into the eyes of the Buddha. Younger brother, her father says mildly, the Americans stopped here. And then they left. That is what they do. As they will to you, some day.

The soldier slaps him again.

Where are they? Where were they taken? he demands.

On the stage, Phan, pretends to slap Binh, who has taken the role of Le Thach Son. Binh flinches. But it didn't seem right to Phan, is too stylized; he feels like a small boy playing soldier. He wants Binh to cringe, feel terror, not hide his smile at the "interrogation," the breeze of his weak slap. He thinks of the American, the man Kiet called her father: the moment of pure terror he'd felt when that over-sized foreigner had taken the stage, the past his own parents kept locked behind their tight lips, the sudden blankness of their eyes when questioned, the past hidden behind the bright banners and white uniforms and colorful posters of parades, suddenly there, intruding for that moment. The past that was more present than the present. He closes his eyes, seeing the foreigner's eyes, the blue like a mean animal, and when he opens them, he brings his face close to Binh's, so close his breath parts the fine hair on Binh's eyebrows. O dau the G.I.'s, motha-fucka? Phan screams into Binh's face, sees him flinch, the flicker of trapped panic in his eyes. Yes.

———————

Kim is crying in earnest now. Thuy is not. She curses suddenly, in English. Motha-fucka. The word seems to startle the Americans; they look at her in surprise and then laugh. She launches herself at them, screaming, grabs one man's leg, hangs on as he kicks her off, like a man shaking dog shit from his shoe. The man who had spoken to her father the day before has sweat rivulets branching through the cake of dirt on his face, striping it, a distorted tiger mask. O dau the G.I.s, mother fucker? the man says, as if he learned the curse from her. This is the guy who led us into it, sir. Where the fuck are my friends? The other Marine puts the barrel of his rifle against her father's head. Thuy gets to her feet, starts to charge him, but the third Marine, as short as a Vietnamese, but wide-shouldered, his thick, hairy arms tattooed with entwined names and flowers, puts his rifle against her sister's head as well.

Daughter! Stop! Her father demands.

I'll blow her ass away, you don't start talking, papa-san, the tattooed Marine says. Thuy still doesn't understand the words, still does understand the threat.

The door flings open and Swan and four other Marines burst in. Thuy stares at him in hatred. They are dressed differently than the first group: soft hats, black farmer's shirts with their green trousers. Swan wears the same rubber tire sandals that Duong wears. He says something to the others and they spread out, face the first group of Marines. Swan calmly puts his hand on the rifle barrel trained on Kim and pushes it away. He stands between the Marine and Kim.

Let's all calm down here, he says.

Thuy spits at him.

A tall, slender Marine from the first group, a black bar pinned onto each collar, steps forward.

Who the fuck are you?

Gunnery Sergeant Swan, Lieutenant. I head the Combined Action Platoon here.

The flower-tattooed Marine spits. Gook-lovers brigade.

Gunny, do you know we have two Marines from the helicopter base missing, the lieutenant asks.

Yes sir. We've been briefed. But I doubt Mr. Thach Son here has anything to do with it. He's a respected man in Non Nuoc.

Well, we're going to have to take him and these other two in. We have Marines missing, sergeant.

The Marine behind Kim suddenly grabs her again, holds her from behind.

What about the bitch, sir? Hook her up, you'll see how fast the old guy'll sing.

Swan steps towards him. I suggest you let that young lady go, Marine.

The Marine sneers, reaches over, squeezes Kim's breast.

Swan's arm shoots forward and the heel of his hand strikes under the man's chin, snapping his head back. The two groups of Americans raise their weapons, point them at each other. Only the large man, the morning man, Thuy thinks, remains motionless, seems suddenly drained of anger, dazed.

That will be enough, the lieutenant yells. Peterson, you will back off and stand down. Roberts, Minh—let's get this prisoner back to the base.

The Marines bind her father. When they slip a cloth bag over his head, she moans. She and Kim try to run to him. But Swan grabs both girls, holds each under his arms.

He will be all right, he promises in Vietnamese. Be calm. Don't make it worse.

***

Later, years later, when her sister, her belly swollen, cradles Thuy on her lap as if she is the child already born, Kim tells her what Swan did, what Swan said; Kim who knew how to capture and hold spoken words as if they were engraved in stone. Their father brought to a tin building with plywood floors, to a room with a gray metal desk, a gray fan and a gray Major with a clipped moustache, who puts his hand proudly on a metal stove in which he was to burn documents in the event that the base was over-run, he explains in all seriousness to Gunnery Sergeant George Swan, who stands in front of the gray desk. Swan tall, wedge-chested, his head shaven. A strong face, impassive, though in his eyes there is a sparkle of sardonic intelligence made brighter by a lifelong effort to hide it, for his own protection, Kim said. He stands in front of the major with his heels together, his hands clasped behind his back, his gaze fixed away from him, perhaps to some fly-blown calendar on the wall. He is trying to maintain. His words. It is a full-time job, to maintain, he had explained, and the better he got at it, the harder it was to do. And the more he despised himself for being better at it. And therefore

tried to stay away from assholes such as the major. Asshole
avoidance was what he called the tactic, he'd told Kim. It had
been one of the reasons, he had volunteered to be in the
Combined Action Company program. CAC Marines were
assigned to work in small units in Vietnamese villages, living
with the people, training the local Ruff-Puffs—regional
militia; the CAC Marines had to live and act independently.
Away from assholes. It had been the main attraction for Swan.
How noble, Kim had said. You were the other reason, he'd
said. How flattering, Kim said. He didn't believe in the
program, he'd said. Not after a year of it. But he came to love
the Vietnamese. All of us? Kim asked. How unflattering. He
could and was asked to offer counsel and opinion, he said.
He could be a humanitarian warrior in a war in which most
of his fellow Americans, he said, seemed to hold the people
they were here to protect in contempt. He felt tied to a
community in a way he hasn't felt since he lived in his own
village in America, and the Vietnamese he was with—tight-
knit, slyly humorous, despised by the white population next
door—make him feel at home. Necessary. Sometimes even
wanted. Sometimes even loved.

Sometimes, Kim had said.

Sir, he had said to the major, Mr. Thach Son told you
what he saw. The two survivors confirmed...

I have two missing Marines.

Who shouldn't have been there anyway, sir. The four men
who had come out were all air crew, he'd discovered. Tourists
in his village.

I don't give a big rat's ass where those Marines shouldn't
have been, Gunny. All I care about is where they are now.

With all respect, sir, Le Thach Son is an important man
in the village...

And you're charged with winning their little hearts and
their tiny minds. So that their scrawny asses will follow. I
know all about it, Gunny. Do you know what I say about
that? I say: grab them by the balls and their asses will follow.

Yes, sir. I've heard that sir. Quite a few times in fact, sir. The major peers at him. Swan realized, he told Kim, that at that point, he'd crossed a line. In the end, he loves the Marine Corps but one of the games one must learn is to pretend that each worn cliché repeated, masked as fresh wisdom from men masked as superior officers, is truth itself, to be accepted with an obsequious chuckle and a smile, a shuck and a jive. Words he taught Kim.

A shuck and a jive.

Don't you wise off with me, Marine, the major says.

No, sir. But with all due respect, sir, Combined Action is General Krulak's project, and if I have to I will go all the way up the chain of command.

You want to run that by me again, Gunny?

Not unless I have to, sir.

When their father comes into the house, the two sisters cluster around him, fruit from this tree; they hug him, kiss his scarred hands, the bruises on his face. Kim touches his cheek, her eyes glistening. The doorway darkens, fills with Swan. Thach Son smiles at him and nods, and Swan smiles and nods in return.

Sergeant Swan, their father says. Thank him, daughters.

Kim smiles at Swan. Thuy's face has gone to stone.

Does one thank the man who stops beating him? Thuy says.

Kim stares at Swan. For a moment their gazes lock. Thuy sees this. She sees her father seeing this, his face suddenly growing hard as a stone. Good.

Welcome to our house, Kim says to Swan. I thank you for what you did.

***

That night, Thuy follows her sister again, down now to the river. Kim meets her lover near an ancient banyan, the two of them leaning against its wide, tangled base. As if it will protect them. Thuy strains to listen to their conversation.

We have to tell him.

We will tell everyone.

I don't know if it's a good idea, em. Not the way you want to do it.

It's the only way I can do it, Swan.

Swan sighs. "I hope you know what you're doing, girl," he says in English.

Duong's ear always to the ground these days, he feels and hears the barely suppressed ripples of excitement in the village. The scheduled cai luong performance would be more than a break from the war; it would remind them, Hai had explained to him, of their own ties to each other, bind them to a sense of the historical, to what abided beyond the tragedies of the moment. Nonsense, Duong had replied; it is distraction, escape. But unconcerned with either of their definitions, most of the people in the hamlet have come to watch, along with a few Marines. They sit in a semicircle on the ground in front of the communal hall, laughing, eating, and drinking. The drama Kim would perform today is of a village girl waiting for her husband, who has gone to take the Mandarin examinations which, if passed, will elevate him to the highest honor—the scholar-ruler.

A drum beats. The dan bau twangs. The keys of a xylophone are struck. The actors, most from a professional troupe in Da Nang that Kim wishes to join, mill purposefully. Kim takes center stage. She has studied cai luong opera since she was seven; it is her passion.

She sings of her triumphant scholar husband, who will ride into the village like an emperor, escorted by soldiers: *Chong toi coi ngua vinh quy/Hi ben co linh hau di dep duong.*

He has passed the examinations given by the emperor himself. Her voice quavers, stops, and there is a gasp from the audience of villagers. They had expected the "husband" to be Bao Thai, a famous actor from Hue. Expected a grand entrance, the actor dressed in the silken robes of the triumphant new Mandarin. The robes are there, but worn by Gunnery Sergeant Swan, borne in from stage left on a palanquin held aloft by three grinning American Marines and three Vietnamese militia, all from Swan's Combined Action Platoon.

For a moment, there is complete silence from the audience, as if the villagers have drawn in a collective breath. It is the silence before an explosion, the day holding its own breath, and for a few seconds everyone freezes, the Marines and local militia, Kim, her voice caught in her throat. She had planned this entrance for weeks, browbeat the acting troupe into going along, convinced Swan it would secure his relationships with the village. But the silence now passes into her like doubt, and she feels her heart vibrate rapidly.

Trinh Van Hai, off to the side with his camera, takes a photograph, and the sudden flare of the flashbulb seems to release the audience from a spell: a murmur arises. Some of the audience begins to nod and smile, even to applaud lightly, laugh out loud; others look puzzled, yet others angry, though these keep their faces blank. Except Thuy. Her lips tight with rage, she rises and walks away. Her father looks after her, and then looks again at his other daughter, up on the stage. Their eyes meet. Kim throws back her head, tosses her hair, sings again.

Near dusk, the next day, Le Thach Son walks through the hamlet. He carries a gift: the same small, exquisite statuette of a tra kieu dancing girl he gave to the other Marine; he'd finished carving it just moments before, working on it all night and all day. Near the compound, he passes Mrs. Phan's house. It looks sad and ragged, one side of the roof collapsing. Mrs. Phan's husband had been killed by South Vietnamese soldiers during the uprisings in 1966, but before she could even commemorate the hundred-day ceremony, she had been killed herself, as his own wife and daughter had perished, when her bicycle hit a mine as she pedaled down the road to Hoi An. Because she had no family, and because the house is so near the Marines, it has been kept empty. For security, the Marines say. Pinned on its side are several of the posters Son has seen appear around the village over the last few weeks: members of the Marine Combined Action Company, the pictures of their faces captioned with their names and ranks, and the amount of piasters the Front will pay for their deaths or for the deaths of those collaborating with them. Don't Be Seduced by Threats or Smiles, the largest captions warn, in Vietnamese and English.

The Marine compound is ringed with sand-bag bunkers, but inside the door of one of the thatch-roofed houses he sees two Marines, barechested, sitting and playing cards at a small table. At the compound entrance a Marine in a floppy, brimmed hat and a black shirt sits on top of one of the bunkers with Hoang Huy Binh, a seventeen-year-old boy Le Thach Son knows; he is dressed the same way as the Marine. They are both smoking and they both nod to him and then turn their eyes back to the countryside beyond the village, their rifles held loosely in their hands.

He hears a familiar noise and squats in the path behind the compound, waiting. After a time, the patrol, half-American, half village militia, leaves in a line like a dragon dance, their equipment clanking and creaking like musical instruments; the men pulling back the bolts on their rifles. Swan is not with them.

Le Thach Son enters the perimeter after them, the sentries again nodding at him. Instead of going straight to Swan's quarters, he goes around the back of the houses. A line of cactus screens that area from the eyes of the village, the rest of the compound. He slides through a narrow gap between the plants and makes his way to the back door. Next to it is a small bamboo table with an upside-down helmet on it. He glides next to it, into the shadow of the house. A metal mirror is attached to the wall next to the door. He glimpses himself, his face intent. He presses his face against the wall. Through the gap in the thatch he sees what he expects to see, hears what he expects to hear.

He returns to the row of cactus and squats and thinks. He can see the back of the house through a narrow gap between the plants. In a while, Swan comes out. He is wearing Marine trousers but no shirt. He is carved from the black marble of the mountain. He shaves, looking at the mirror, dipping his razor into the water in the helmet. Son thinks about how the helmet has been there, ready, as if kept always for this purpose. He thinks about how long always might be. Swan calls out something he can't understand. Kim comes to the door and he says something else and she laughs, and Le Thach Son can't understand her. He stands up. Kim brings her hand to her mouth, in surprise.

You look like an actress in one of your operas with your hand like that, he says.

They stare at each other and then Kim turns and goes back inside. He walks to Swan. When he speaks to him, he doesn't look into his face. Instead, he watches their two images reflected in the mirror. He hands the Marine the statue.

Thank you, Swan says. It's lovely. His Vietnamese, Le Thach Son notices, is very understandable.

It's a gift. A stone dancer. It is the only dancer I have to give you.

I'm sorry. We meant to tell you. To ask you.

Instead, you told the whole village.

I apologize for that. Kim and I thought….

Do you think it was a secret before then? This is a small place. There are no secrets.

Then…

You understand us better than most of the Americans who come here, Sergeant Swan. You speak our language. But you do not understand that what isn't put into words is not yet true. Now that you have become real, there will be trouble. And nothing good will come of this.

Something already has.

Son is still staring at the mirror, can't look at this man. Something moves across the lower rim.

Is it my foreignness that bothers you. Or my skin? Swan touches the image of his own face in the mirror.

No. It's your heart.

I love her.

What Swan would see, if he would glance back at his reflection, is Duong, crawling on his belly like a worm, along the bottom rim of the mirror. That is, in fact, how Son sees him in glimpses, behind the row of cactus. He is almost naked, wearing only a cloth around his privates, his skin covered with grease. Swan is looking at him, Son, not at the mirror; if he did, Son thinks, he would see his enemy.

He sees Duong fasten something to a cactus.

You love war, he says. Like all of them. That is what you have in your heart. I am grateful to you for saving me. But I have tried all my life to keep that suitor away from my door.

For an instant, behind the cacti, he thinks he glimpses his other daughter's furious face: Thuy staring at Swan's back. He stops looking at the mirror.

Behind him, Duong motions Thuy to get down lower, to freeze.

Let me tell you about hearts, Swan says. Back in '66, before I volunteered into this unit, I was on Operation Hastings, up to the DMZ. A kid in my squad stepped on a Bouncing Betty. It blew up at chest level. He was opened up like an anatomy lesson. Thing was, my mouth was open and parts of him were blown into my mouth. Maybe parts of his heart, because when I looked at him, afterwards, his heart was gone, ripped out. Thing was, I started chewing. That kind of automatic reflex, you know. Chewing and swallowing. Cold and bitter. Live meat, the tick of it against my palate. I vomited, tried to heave it out of me, that taste. But it's still there. That's what's in my mouth. I know what it tastes like, Mr. Son. And I don't love it.

Thach Son looks back into the glass. In it, he can see Thuy clearly, crawling after Duong. Crawling away from his life. He has lost two more daughters today. He leans forward, breathes on the mirror, clouding it, his breath hiding at least one daughter from the eyes of this American.

Private First Class Darren Henderson, a twenty-two-year-old from Eugene, Oregon, steps through the hedge line. He is going to meet Nguyen Huy Dang, a young monk who lives at the Linh Ung pagoda. Henderson, in an early reincarnation he barely remembers now, was a philosophy major at the University of Oregon, and he has been engaged in a running discussion about Buddhism with Dang. Perhaps he is thinking about how he will formulate the question he wants to ask Dang in Vietnamese, when he feels the touch of the taut wire against the front of his left leg and in the split second he has left before he turns into mist, and then into one of the souls whose faces can sometimes be glimpsed in the twists of stone near Ling Ung, has just enough time for a flash of regret that now his question will never be answered. Or perhaps he will now become the question.

Wearing the black peasant cotton whose cleaner incarnation he will wear decades later at Cu Chi, draped with bandoleers, Duong stands in a corner of the cave, deep inside the mountain. Thuy clothed in the same manner, stands next to him, both of them in front of a large map. Pinned up on the crude wooden board next to it are Trinh's photographs of key points on the base; from each a creosote line has been drawn to corresponding coordinates on the map. All of it is illuminated by a lantern placed on a stalactite that juts up from the floor like a squatting bird. The rock gives this small space its name: Shitting Bird Cave. Facing the map, and Thuy and Duong, are eight women from the 443 Viet Cong regiment's Women's Artillery battery. Five mortar tubes lean against the damp rock wall, their shadows elongated like ribs along the curved ceiling of the cave. Boxes of mortar shells are stacked near the tubes. Duong points to sites on the map, gives each two-person team coordinates. As each leaves, they take one of the mortars and a case of shells.

Thuy and Duong set up their own mortar behind a crenellation of rocks on the southern slope of Thuy Son. All of the other guns have targeted the helicopter base, but our tube slants towards the other side of the hill, towards the CAC compound in the middle of the village. Duong adjusts the elevation knob, looks at his watch. They will shoot two mortars at that target, and then move, join in the barrage on the base. He counts off the time on his fingers: one, two, three, and then he points at Thuy. She drops a mortar shell into the tube.

On the base, Alex sitting behind rows of sandbags, sees a helicopter transformed into an orange blossom of fire, sees other Marines running for their sandbag bunkers or fighting positions. And Swan lying in the village, not a mile away, is brought awake by the shell exploding among the cacti plants behind his hootch; perhaps he is even close enough to hear the clunking sound the mortar shells make as they are dropped into their tubes.

On the mountain, Duong watches the mortar shells burst among the helicopters. He has read that the American writer whose book has long been a map for his own life, a book that even now he feels pressed against his back, inside his rucksack, had come to the country, flown over it in one of these insect-machines, cheered on its death. He wills the author inside one now, watches it blow to pieces all over the tarmac.

Thuy looks in the other direction, peering down at the compound, the thatched roofs in flames. Hoping to see her sister's American lover transformed into a blossom of fire.

In the house of the Le family, Thach Son knows immediately where the mortars are hitting, even though the mountain stands between his house and the sound they make. From the northern summit of Thuy Son, he has often looked down at the helicopter base, the insect scatter of the machines, the rows of tents that seem to form some breathing, sucking entity lying half-aware on the land. He can picture the iron tarmac of the airfield ripped, pieces of its metal flying through the air, ripping through tents and bodies; he understands what goaded beasts will do. Even as he strains to hear the sound he knows will come next, he has leapt to his feet, yells to his girls—he believes Thuy is home—Get up, move, get to the shelter tunnel!

He hears the whoop-whoop of the helicopters.

Swan, huddled in the Combined Action Company bunker, feels the sandbags quiver like flesh against his back, as if his terror had moved into them. The sound of the rotors beats down on them, and sand streams down onto his face as bullets rip into the roof.

You're right on top of us! he screams into the handset of the field radio. Lance Corporal Rogers, his head pressed against his knees, looks up at him, and their eyes meet. No shit, Rogers mouths, the words inaudible under the noise, and Swan giggles, can't help it; he is near hysteria.

Rogers and out, he thinks, Rogers and out: the words a litany, a nonsensical chant in his head as he runs out of the bunker, into the streets.

He can't see the helicopters, only feel them above him, hear them as they swoop and dive, strafing the mountain, the village held in the cup of rock. He zigzags through the houses, the roof of one splitting in front of him as if two giant hands pushed through it, grabbed both sides of the wound, ripped them apart. The tripod hearth, bamboo mats, altar inside instantly revealed, as if an exhibit in a museum.

He rounds a corner, sees what he has feared to see. He tastes his bitter heart. The roof of the Le's house has partially collapsed, the thatch on fire. He bursts inside.

Kim is cradling her father's body, stroking Thach Son's face. His chest is split, as if what Swan had felt outside had been visited on this body, as if his connection to the skin and bones of this family had already become that. The noise and wind of the helicopters beat down on them. He wraps an arm around Kim, pulls her up from her father's body and carries her, screaming, to the shelter's trapdoor.

In the Theater of Then and Now, Thuy stood at center stage, staring at the two actors playing Swan and her father. The spotlight swung off them, onto her. Her makeup was webbed with tears.

Fuck the play, she whispered, as fervently as a prayer.

Her Father Returns

A backdrop of brown mountains behind the airfield, and beyond them the green cordillera, the facing slopes of the far mountains liquid with shadow. Across the tarmac, on its edge, Alex could see rusting-tin Quonset-style buildings wavering in the haze, a leftover crust of the war. Some empty revetments, thick dividers whose purpose was to isolate the damage if a plane was hit and exploded, lined the end of the field, and as his plane taxied past now, he saw a peace symbol some G.I. had painted on the concrete wall of one emplacement. Returning to the places of childhood, the common wisdom went, one was to find everything smaller than it had been. But it all seemed the same to Alex, frozen in place.

He walked down the ramp into a solid heat that was very familiar, piled with the others into the shuttle bus. Found himself looking for men his own age. The air was moist and heated, acrid with the smell of sweat. Most of the passengers were Vietnamese, the Westerners young backpackers in shorts, the fronts of their shirts baggy with Velcro-fastened pockets. Two middle-aged men were clutching ceiling straps near the rear, hanging on white-knuckled as the bus swerved, both wearing mesh travel vests that he could squint into flak jackets. One had a book in his free hand and was showing it to the other, his words, Alex, could hear, German or Swedish. He was vaguely disappointed, wanted someone who could move with him through both times this crowded shuttle was traversing. In the window he could see Hill 327, unchanged, part of the crescent of mountains west of the airfield had been where the Marines had put their first positions in this country, their job to protect this airfield, and then to protect the perimeter around the airfield, and then to protect the country beyond the perimeter or the next perimeter, or the day, or the night, until some of them began to realize that what this country needed was protection from them. Marble Mountain would be east and south of here. A map had clicked on in his head, all of the points of terrain around him spinning into place. He was oriented. Un-occidented, he thought. He looked again at 327. A boy he knew had been shot at the end of a resupply mission to the Marine position there; his helicopter was on its approach back to the base, just over the Marble Mountains, when a sniper fired at it, the bullet penetrating under his friend's flak jacket. It was on the last day of his tour. Of course any time you were killed would be the last day of your tour, Alex supposed, and he had witnessed, over the previous year, a series of helicopter crewmen's deaths: by machine gun and by recoilless rocket, by 12.7 anti-aircraft and by rifle fire, by dust and by heat, by wind and by mountain, by rotor blade and by Jesus bolt, by American artillery and by NVA quad-fifty, by accident and by design, by hook and by crook. But that last death had seemed particularly unjust. It was a milk run mission, his friend shouldn't have been flying anymore anyway. Not only unfair, but arbitrary and unjust. It filled him with a bone-deep rage that still, now, trembled his hands. Two other boys whom he had led into those hills, for the dubious pleasure of their company, were encased now somewhere in that stone around him, youthful dancers forever frozen in stone. The boy's death, his lost friends, fluttered like black moths on the edge of his awareness, the periphery of his vision where the hills quivered like mirages in the heat.

The taxi he hired drove through the heart of his past, well-paved now, but the basic topography unchanged, Monkey Mountain jutting out into the bay, and then the Marble Mountains themselves, in front of him, closing around him and unclenching and gone again as they continued south to Hoi An.

Two hours after he'd disembarked from the plane, he was walking in a daze through the Hoi An market, Trinh Van Hai's address in his hands. The market was teeming with people bargaining, carrying baskets filled with goods, but he was oblivious to them, in his own tunnel.

Along the river, women were poling small wooden boats filled with fruits, vegetables, dried and fresh fish. An old woman came walking up from the river docks, a shoulder pole with two trays filled with lychee nuts hanging from it balanced on her stooped shoulders. As her path crossed Alex's, she stopped and smiled at him, her face cracking into a hundred fragments. She squatted, blocking his path, and offered him a bunch of the fruit. For a moment, he stared at her, uncomprehending, and then bent down, took a cluster of the lychees, and pressed money into her hands. She reached into her bag to give him change, but he shook his head and squeezed her hands. He showed her the folded paper. She nodded and plucked his sleeve, motioning at him to follow her, back to the river. He tried to take the pole, but she laughed, showing teeth stained red-black with betel nut, slapped his hand away. At river's edge, one of the cone-hatted boat women had just finished off-loading bunches of green bananas from her narrow skiff. She was tall and wiry, her brown ankles sticking out from too-short black trousers, her wrists bare past the sleeves of her blouse, her hands large and calloused. The lychee woman showed her the paper, and the two brought their heads together, whispering like conspirators. Finally, the woman nodded and gestured for Alex to follow.

Hustlers

Kiet and Duong landed in Da Nang in the afternoon. Duong had arranged for a rental car, and they drove out of the airport and into the place that more than anywhere else was his war. This landscape, the sea where the Americans had first landed, the hills looming over the airfield where the Marines had set up their first perimeters, the rivers and jungles and paddies beyond which he'd help seed with booby-traps and which they'd ploughed with artillery; the great green- flanks of the Truong Son range beyond it, where they had all been locked together in deadly embrace under the strangling triple canopy of the mountain jungle—it was all simply landscape to her, he knew, background for her own mission. As it had been for the Americans. For half her ancestry. They drove down a highway that was paved and smooth now, no longer a strip of buckled concrete, pocked with mine craters, rutted with the imprints of tank treads. Ngu Hanh Son was etched in jagged black, the spine of a dragon on the horizon, simply a strange formation to her. But when he pulled off the road, pointed it out to her and told her the English name, she stiffened.

"My father was there," she said. "He told me his base camp was near those hills."

The place where he had pulled over, he realized, would be parallel to the old base's location, off to their left. But he could see none of it from the road; its rusted remains perhaps lay hidden behind and within a new neighborhood that had erased it more thoroughly than any mortars he had ever lobbed into its perimeter: concrete and tile-roofed houses, parts of the area lush and green with shade trees and bougainvillea, where before it had been an empty sand flat, strewn with the clustered refugee shacks made from discarded tin sheets or pressed beer cans, the refuse of her "father's" base. She was staring at him, waiting for more of an explanation, but he didn't look at her. He drove back onto the road and past the flank of Thuy Son and through Non Nuoc, grown to a large town now, its streets lined with souvenir stores and the workshops of the stone carvers, dozens of them, their products—sitting Buddhas, reclining Buddhas, laughing Buddhas, gigantic eagles, demons, and buxom naked women, myth and kitsch—crowding the main road. All of it was a crust over what he knew lay beneath, but she could see only the crust and for now he was glad of that. For now, let it rest.

Duong had booked a hotel on Tran Phu Street in Hoi An. He called Hai—the photographer was supposed to call his cell phone number if Alex had shown up. But he hadn't and there was no one home when Duong telephoned his house. No use going there now, he told Kiet; he would keep calling. Kiet uneasy, guilty at not looking for her father, but what can we do? Duong asked. He forced her to have a late lunch of cao lau, the noodle dish made with bean sprouts, scallions, and pork slices that, he assured her, was famous in the city. The tour guide speaking. As in Sai Gon, he was trying to see everything through her eyes, to taste the food with her mouth, as if she was new-born and he was her true guide to the world. They walked towards the river market through the narrow streets lined with ancient stone and wooden houses, their Chinese roofs dragon-scaled with red am duong—yin and yang—tiles. The low buildings leaning against each other with amiable haphazardness. Inside the shaded courtyards of old temples huge and sinuous dragons stared in blank malevolence with porcelain cup eyes. We'll find him. Enjoy Hoi An, he told her. Famous for cau lau noodles, Chinese temples, and tailors who could make anything. The town altered and fitted, since he'd last been here, to dimensions that would please the needs of its visitors. They could buy silk shirts, t-shirts, tailor-made linen, souvenir statues, electric bao harps, buffalo-horn pen holders, colorful paper lanterns, lacquerware, wooden carvings, rice-paper prints of bucolic country scenes and graceful girls in ao dais. Anything they wanted. Cyclo drivers pedaled next to Duong and Kiet, screaming at them and waving them to their seats, as if a destination was as easy to buy as a bottle of soda. Dozens of birds of prey plucked at their arms, their sleeves, touting tailor shops, sodas, plastic bottles of water, cheap scarves, postcards, tragic pasts: a legless veteran driving a three-wheel hand-pedal cart, selling turtle-shaped whistles made of cheap black ceramic and a chance to earn some good karmic currency by purchasing from him. Duong bought two turtles, and a group of boys in baseball caps immediately surrounded them, pushed greeting cards featuring pictures of cone-hatted boys their same age, perched on water buffalos, into Kiet's face. He never had this happen when he was alone; the people spotted something foreign in Kiet. Leave, Duong told the boys, and they looked at his face and did, quickly. Beggars and panderers. His dead were all over this ground. The center of the country. He was of a generation that dreamed of liberation, of not being tailored to anyone's vision but its own, the nation as a family of brothers and sisters, the revolutionary love and self-sacrifice that sustained it moving from the battlefield onto the world.

"Well, I think they're great," Kiet said, when he told her some of this. "They're hustlers."

"Hustlers?"

"One who hustles. Energetically pushes, maneuvers, sells you something you don't need but they can convince you that you really want. Why does it bother you so much? A week ago you were telling me about how this country nearly starved when people weren't allowed to be tough and clever. To hustle."

His mind went back, for some reason, to Dottie Simpson: her behind smiling at him, glowing from the darkness of a tunnel in which she did not fit. Of course this young woman was right. What right did he, of all people, have to despise Hoi An? He had become Hoi An, an idea of Viet Nam to be sold as Vietnam: he was what he had fought to free his country from being, all the years of his youth and manhood. *For your sweet dreams, sir.*

What self-indulgent nonsense, he thought. Riotous Hoi An had stirred a riot of self-recrimination in his soul, but, in the end, he knew its root was not grief for a long-dead adolescent idealism. It was her presence. This woman. What awaited him next was what he had delayed until now. If he were still a Catholic, or if he were still a communist, he might at least expect the peace that descends on one's soul from confession or self-criticism. But he was neither anymore. He could expect neither comfort. He was only a hustler, maneuvering his customer towards an ending both of them needed and neither of them would want.

Moon River

At the open market near the river, shallow wooden skiffs filled with piles of fruit, vegetables, sodas, fresh and dried fish, and poled by small, strong women wearing cone hats, docked and unloaded. She asked Duong the name of the river.

"Moon River," he said. Then shook his head. "I'm sorry. It's a joke. A song."

"'Wider than a mile.' I know. My dad used to sing it. Never mind, I like it."

They wandered through the shaded maze of narrow streets and alleys, past stalls selling metal pots, ceramic bowls, chopsticks, underwear, t-shirts and dresses, fish and prawns—dried, fried, steamed, boiled. Which pretty much described herself at this point. She was anxious about finding her father, both her fathers, the known and unknown. But a part of her was enjoying this: Duong showing her something of the country, of what he loved and perhaps wanted her to love. Alex knew what he was doing, she told herself, though he needed to protect her from whatever it was he thought he needed to protect her from all the days of her life. Or to protect himself from her knowledge of it. It was the role he had given himself. He was wrong; she was certain of it, but he'd come alone now because he'd wanted to be alone. So she told herself. A row of women holding baskets filled with lychee nuts squatted in front of a wall. Duong bought a bunch from one woman. He gave one to Kiet, and she peeled it as she walked and popped it into her mouth, as did he.

"It's delicious."

Duong laughed. "It's the taste of my childhood." He smiled. "Is there a particular taste you remember from yours?"

"None that I want to."

Her bitterness seemed somehow a reproach. He peeled two more lychees. His cell phone rang. He took it out of his pocket, listened, his face turning grim. He said a few words in Vietnamese and then turned the cell's power off.

"Everything OK?"

"No problem."

The street they were on ran alongside a canal, the clustered houses on its other side between them and the river now. A man with one leg stood behind a portable cart on which were displayed toy swords, knives, plastic guns and planes, and a row of tiny black ceramic turtle-shaped whistles, like the one Duong had bought from the man with no legs. Was it a special industry for veterans? Duong stopped, picked up one of the turtles, pressed some dong in the man's hand.

"Do you know the legend of the turtle in Hoan Kiem Lake, in Ha Noi?"

"The turtle rose from Hoan Kiem Lake to take back the magical sword of Le Loi, after he used it to defeat the Chinese invaders," she recited dutifully.

"Very good." He squinted at the canal. "When I was a boy, I used to imagine I could see the turtle, its giant dark head draped with tendrils of moss, just breaking the surface, or in a patch of sunlight."

"Can you still see it there?"

He picked up a toy sword, jabbed the air with it. "When I came back from the South, from the war, I looked at the lake and understood that all I had been seeing were pieces of garbage, caught in the duckweed. I wasn't a child anymore."

The vendor started to say something to Duong. He gave the man a look, the same look Kiet had seen him direct at the street kids who'd tried to sell them postcards before, and the man shuddered and retreated to the other side of the cart. Duong put the sword back. He didn't need it, she thought. She picked it up, touched the point against his sternum. He smiled, gripped her wrist with both hands, as if to plunge the blade in, his eyes locked with hers. Then they shifted, caught by something else. She followed his gaze. A low stone bridge spanned the canal, its ends shaded by colorful awnings.

"Where does this photographer live?"

"Not far. Did you see the film *The Quiet American*?"

She'd bitten into another lychee, and didn't answer. She put the sword back.

"They filmed it here," he said. "Hoi An as a stand-in for 1950's Sai Gon. That bridge was supposed to be the place where the American, Pyle, was killed."

They both looked closely at the bridge, as if expecting to see Pyle's body. But Duong kept staring, his eyes narrowed and blazing with a terrible intensity, the question-mark scar on his cheek deepening and darkening, his lips drawn down into a grimace. She felt she was watching a terrible possession, or perhaps his true face, coaxed out and revealed by whatever he saw in that structure.

"Did you like the movie?" she asked tentatively.

"I don't see films about the war," he said. "I have read the book." The grimace transformed into a small smile, full of secrets. "I hated it. Viet Nam as the voiceless dream-whore of a well-intentioned fool or a seedy roué. It's a lie." He closed his eyes and shook his head, his face rearranging back into itself, or its mask. "I'm sorry," he said. "I have an old-fashioned, bad, habit of taking books seriously. Did you see the film?"

"I've seen all of them. They remind me of my childhood. Not the films themselves, but watching them."

"I don't understand."

"When I was a kid, I stole my history from American war movies."

Duong laughed. "You thought of Viet Nam as an American war movie?"

"Everybody did. So tell me about the real war. Tell me a story, Duong."

They walked on. Water lapped against the side of the canal. The sunlight coming off it in undulating sheets of brightness pierced her eyes, her skull. She turned from it, let his face form out of the blur. He was frowning.

"Which story do you wish to hear? There are so many stories, em. They live in every centimeter of my skin."

"When I was a girl I wanted to be you."

"What do you mean?"

"A Viet Cong, moving secretly through the sea of the people."

He smiled sourly. "You mean what I once was."

"I would fantasize that my mother had been someone like that. Is that what she was, Duong?"

"Aren't you afraid you may find out she was not what you wanted her to be?"

"I'm not a child any longer either. I can see the garbage and the duckweed. Tell me, Duong. Tell me a story. Tell me my name."

"Soon," he said, firmly. "Do you know about Trung Nguyen? The Day of Wandering Souls. It's when we bring offerings to those who were killed far away or violently, to bring them to rest."

"Are we waiting for that day?"

She put her hand over his. They stared at each other.

"I'm not a child any longer," she said again.

To him, she would always be a child.

He took his hand away.

An Exhibit

She heard Duong's cell phone ring. Beethoven's Fifth. Vang, he said into it. Vang, vang. Yes. Yes. He flipped the cover back, put the phone in his shirt pocket. "He's home," he said.

Trinh Van Hai's house was at the end of a long street bordering a canal that snaked out from the old section of Hoi An, Kiet seeing a Chagall village, everything slightly out of whack, the green fuzz of moss and lichens on the layered roof tiles of the old stone-and-wood houses thinned in places so patches of muted red showed through. The walls were pastel-colored or age-darkened teak, neat, though to Kiet, Hoi An was wearing on her a bit, all a little too self-conscious and arty, as if the place was an exhibit of itself. Then the light shifted slightly and suddenly the roof tiles were delineated and elongated with angular shadows, undulant and serpentine in the bright lights from the shops and cafés, the cobbled street blossoming with red and yellow and green paper lanterns.

Trinh Van Hai's studio was in one of the teak houses. The photographer was a stocky man but very old; his body shelled over a fragility that made him move very carefully. His wispy hair topped by a black beret, as if he were also an exhibit of an earlier time. He smiled without affection at Duong, a slight ironic tug at the corners of his mouth. His expression remained impassive. Until he saw Kiet. He stared, touched her face as if to pose her for a photo.

"Miss Kiet," he whispered. "Kiet. The child. It isn't possible."

"I'm possible, Mr. Hai," she assured him, his wording sending a current of excitement through her.

"No. You are inevitable." He reached out and encircled

her arm with his bony hand. She didn't mind. "Please, I'm being rude. You must have some tea."

They sat at a low table, small cups of tea in front of them, as inevitable as she.

"I was sorry to hear about your wife," Duong said, in English. Hai started to reply in Vietnamese.

"Please. English," Duong said.

Hai spread his hands. "I'm afraid…it has been a long time." He nodded to Kiet. "I told Duong I'm sorry also that my wife could not be here to see my old student again. My student who became my teacher."

"Your English is fine," she said. "Was my father here?"

"Your father?" His eyes widened, almost imperceptibly. "Ah, yes, of course. Mr. Alex was here."

"When?"

"Earlier—about noontime, I think."

"What did he say—what did you tell him? Where is he now?"

Hai laughed, almost a giggle. "You are very like him. Very direct."

"I'm very worried, Mr. Hai."

Duong said something in Vietnamese to the photographer. The calmness of his voice, the seemingly mild question, maddened her.

"Mr. Alex did not say where he was staying. He was very nervous when he left."

"Nervous?"

"Perhaps this is the wrong word. Upset."

She wanted to shake him. "What upset him?"

"Come, I will show you what he thought he wanted to see."

They followed him into the other room.

When he switched on the light, the first thing in front of Kiet's eyes was a woman in a cone hat, her mouth open in a silent scream. She stepped back, startled, and let her eyes adjust as the other photos come into view. The walls covered with them, a montage of the war; some the shots resembling those on her father's studio wall, except that the group pictures of smiling young Americans posing with their weapons were interposed with photos of smiling young Vietnamese posing with their weapons. Some of the pictures of Americans almost seemed like the kind of wanted posters you would see in a post office, or, more accurately, in an old Western. As she walked along the wall, though, the content of the photographs began to change; more of them were combat shots: North Vietnamese soldiers charging over an earthen berm, a ground view of a helicopter coming down to strafe; another helicopter broke-back on the earth, the mounds of bodies near it.

"The Buddha your father was looking for, the faceless Buddha, is no longer there. Why would a village of carvers leave such a thing?"

At first, the photo in the center of that wall didn't register. She had seen it too often, in too different a context—the bulletin board of her father's studio, next to a picture of herself, play-acting in the clothes the killer next to her once wore. She looked at it, and then slowly allowed it to come into focus: Alex, Baxter, and the two friends whose names he would never tell her. The names he remembered.

"Your father was stationed near Ngu Hanh Son, Miss Kiet. What do you know of that place?"

Was that where you were during the war?

That was the war.

"Nothing."

"Then you were like your father. Like all of them. They saw it a wall against the horizon. How do you say? Flat."

He rose, and gestured at her to follow him to the opposite wall. There were only six photographs on it. He pointed at one showing the entire Marble Mountain formation: from that viewpoint the staggered peaks look parallel.

"They didn't know of the five peaks, each a different element of the universe." He pointed to five separate photos: each a different peak. As he called out the name, he touched each mountain. "Tho Son: Earth; Hoa Son: Fire; Moc Son: Wood; Kim Son: Metal; Thuy Son: Water. Each a shell fragment of the dragon's egg. They didn't know of the ancient shrines in the caves. They didn't know what was in the mountain. Until they entered it."

He stopped himself.

"That is what I showed him, Miss Kiet. What was in the mountain."

She stared at Duong. *You are from the five elements.* She had followed Alex and once again ended back at herself. Her own origins in the place where the Alex she knew, the father she knew, had also been formed. For a second, she couldn't breathe. But only for a second. What was strange was her lack of shock. She had heard enough in Sai Gon, in Maryland, perhaps all the pieces were there, waiting for but one other piece to tilt everything into meaning. Or at least into the next question. But what she felt was a kind of déjà vu—not that what she was seeing and hearing now had happened before, but that it had all slid into the place where it should have been, a place dormant and expectant inside her.

Trinh Van Hai took her elbow and led her to the back wall. It was covered with pictures from the interior of a large cave, furnished with what seemed the wreckage of hospital equipment: grotesquely dangling fluid bags, piles of unraveled bandages. Scattered among the wreckage were the corpses of nurses and patients, gut- and head-shot, some entwined around each other.

"It was one of our hospitals, hidden inside the mountain," the photographer said. "We remained there, of course. Finally, though, the Americans sent a bomb through the cave roof.

The photos were all black and white, giving the human corpses the quality also of statuary. In one, a young man in black VC pajamas, a weapon held loosely in one hand, standing above what seems to be the corpse of an American.

"He found this one very aggravating," Trinh Van Hai said.

She peered at the young man's face, seeing it age and scar, form into Duong's features, the face of the man standing beside her. Her eyes and mind playing tricks. Her heart shelling.

"You must understand," Trinh said. "We were, how do you say? Mixed in the village. The Americans and the VC. The hospital in the cave not a kilometer from their hospital at the helicopter base. Like a distorted mirror." He touched Kiet's arm gently.

She stared at the photograph of the cave, another, from another angle; the torn corpses of patients and nurses entwined in the gloom. The connection came to her in a rush of nausea.

"My father did this?" she whispered.

Trinh Van Hai looked at her with concern. "Ah, my dear—it was the war."

That was the war. The country of her past rippled in front of her eyes as if it were under water; she felt the same sickening wrenching away from herself she had felt when she'd been told her name belonged to a drowned boy. The loss again of a father; had she been the price he'd thought to pay for this? She stared at her father's terrible first carvings, feeling the ghosts of cold hands squeezing him out of her heart.

Weight

Sleepless, Duong walked down through the shuttered river market and along the canal bank. He needed time alone, away from the constant emotion of being with her. The waterfront cafés and restaurants were still open, a few late-night tourists drinking beer, chatting happily, the street and their faces lit in pastel colors by clusters of paper lanterns that made the scene stylized, as if this were still and always a movie set. The water lapped against the stone bank, colored light reflected from the lanterns blending into the silver undulations of moonlight on the black water.

He remembered how moonlight had delineated the boat that had taken her away, the ungainly hump of its rickety bamboo and thatch superstructure, creaking and groaning in the slight swell.

He remembered the day before. It was the second time in his life he had gone to Trinh Van Hai's house. This time he had knocked on the door. When the photographer opened it, his high broad forehead creased a little, but he did not look surprised. He merely nodded as if he'd accepted that Duong's return was inevitable as disease or death.

Since he had last been there, the small house had been stripped nearly bare. There were no screams from the abattoir nearby, as he remembered from his first visit; it had been emptied, the corpses of pigs looted by soldiers from both armies. But since that time, Trinh had also added a wife. She gave out a little scream when she saw Duong. Trinh silenced her with a look.

Bring our guest some tea. There were light patches on the concrete walls where pictures had hung, and the bookcase was empty, a looted city haunted by the absence of its former inhabitants. Duong ran his finger along the wood of its middle shelf.

I'm sorry I can't offer you a chair, Hai said. Unlike the house, he had not changed since the last time Duong had seen him. His long silver hair was combed straight back, the webbed flesh around his deep-set eyes giving him a permanent humorous squint, as if he knew a joke that explained everything, rendered it at bottom absurd.

I want to ask you a question, Hai said. Should one be grateful to someone who has not committed a crime?

His wife had left the room. Duong heard her sobbing in the kitchen.

Tell your wife I am not here to harm you, Samuel Hamilton.

Hai smiled slightly. Why do you call me that?

It's the name of a character in an American novel I love.

I recall it now. A novel I taught you. But I am not that man.

Never mind, I gave you your life, Duong said. I can name you. It is my privilege.

The privilege of power, Hai said. Yes, you're right. You can name whatever you wish now. Sai Gon can be Ho Chi Minh City. Brave soldiers can be called puppets. Slavery can be called freedom. Names call reality to themselves.

Duong smiled. Yes. Corruption and submission to foreign rule can be called freedom. Licentiousness and venality can be called freedom.

What would you name freedom?

You may. That's freedom. Those two words. You may. That's the name of freedom. You should know that, Samuel Hamilton.

Hai shrugged. And what may I do?

I will say some other names. Good Vietnamese names. Your nephew Trinh Van Minh. Your niece Trinh Thi Ngoc Tuyet. Their son, Trinh Ngoc Kiet, and their daughter, Trinh Thi Mai. Names. Do you see what power saying those names gives me? Let me give you another. Nguyen Minh San. Do you recognize it? No? Yes, I think you do. Your family bought fish from San for years, you feel he is a kindly, trustworthy man, a kind of philosopher of the waves.

Trinh Van Hai held up his hand. His wife was standing in the kitchen door, holding a tray with tea cups on it, frozen, her face stamped with horror.

What do you want? We have no more money, no more jewels.

I know. You used it all to buy passage for your niece and nephew.

And knowing this, you can simply arrest me.

Let me ask you a question. Why did you not buy places on the boat for yourself and your wife?

It is as you said before. I exercised my freedom. I chose to stay in my country.

Yes, Duong said. And now I may have you and your nephew's family arrested. Or I may make sure that no one interferes with their journey. That is my choice.

What would you have me do? the photographer asked.

The next morning, for the first time since the liberation, he had worn his full uniform, girding himself with whatever authority it might give him when he went to the prison compound. It was not necessary; the guards knew him. He looked into the eyes of the young corporal who opened the iron gates. The soldier's gaze had fled like a panicked bird. The guard had heard the stories, or perhaps saw the restless souls of the murdered in a cloud around Duong's head.

The corridor had been narrow and dank, dimly lit by a single, filthy bulb. Most of the cells were packed and stank, the usual stench that emanates from unwashed people crowded together in a small space, an acrid stench of sweat, rotting wounds, gas, human waste, and above all, fear; the anticipatory fear of the next blow. It was a stench Duong had lived with in Cu Chi. One can't remember an odor when it isn't there. But the membranes of the nostrils remember it and when they do, time shifts, and the sequence of months and years, the time between then and now, becomes meaningless. For a moment, until he could wrench himself back through an act of conscious will, he was in Cu Chi and this moaning mass of flesh, the flesh of his enemies, was the flesh of his comrades, unified by terror.

He had been able to get Thuy assigned to a separate cell. She sat against the back wall, on the cold concrete of the floor, looking like a black-and-white print of herself in the harsh light of the naked bulb that hung from the ceiling and was never turned off. She had opened her shirt and the child was sucking on her nipple, a gesture only to pacify it. There was no milk in those small breasts.

How did you think to fed her, on the boat? She will starve, he said.

Thuy said nothing, only rocked the child back and forth, pressed the back of its head.

And if she survives, what will she have here? A child with her blood?

She will have me, Thuy said.

And what will you have? I can help you, but only so much. I don't know how long you will have to remain in prison. And afterwards, it will be…difficult. There will be a taint.

What do you want?

He squatted down next to her, and he told her what he had arranged. When he was finished, she closed her eyes briefly, and nodded. Once. And then she had handed him the child and turned her face to the wall. He had taken the weight of it in his arms.

It had been a stupid decision on the part of the people trying to flee, to set out to sea on a full moon night like that. But they had understood, when Duong arrived, that it didn't matter. The young woman, Trinh's niece Tuyet, had stared at him as if she were memorizing his face, would take it with her. She handed one of her children to her husband, but continued to cradle the other in her left arm, as she held out her right hand to him. He looked into her eyes; now it was her face that was being memorized. She kept it expressionless, holding his gaze, her mouth a hard line. Good, he had thought. She had strength, the will that came from hatred. The child slept against his chest as it must have slept in the womb, unaware of the transition it was about to undergo, the rush of water that would carry it to another world. The other people, already huddled in the boat, had eyed Duong uneasily, some muttering. They knew who he was, knew if he wished, if he changed his mind, he could stop this journey before it started, that one of the hands holding the child might at any instance dart to a pocket, pull out a whistle that would itself pull soldiers out of the darkness.

The waves were fringed with silver filigree. Their lap against the shore, the collective breathing of the people in the boat, were the only sounds in the night. Further out, the sea heaved restlessly, and the people waited on the edge of you-may, as if frozen in a tableaux they would one day see, paint, describe, remember as the myth-image of their beginning, their new birth, their new names. But it was not a story yet, not safe yet, not yet the boring and tedious lesson and comparison it will become to their children and grand-children. It was the moment when everything might happen. Or not. Trinh Thi Ngoc Tuyet stared at Duong, their eyes locked. She reached out. He handed her the child, the weight of the child, and she took it from him, and in that second, perhaps, he had convinced himself that he would never feel that weight again.

The Stone Carver

Alex walked along what the driver had assured him was China Beach. It wasn't. But he hadn't bothered to contradict the man. Print the legend. What it was, was as close as he could bring himself to go. He could see the dark humps of the Marble Mountains out of the corner of his eye. He tore his eyes away. But he had a daughter to get back to, one he had abandoned to find her own story while he got on with his. He turned and faced the black silhouettes of Ngu Hanh Son, sighed and started to trudge towards them.

Earlier, when he'd driven through from the airport to Hoi An, he'd kept looking straight ahead when the taxi passed through this area, as if he'd be sucked into a whirlpool or turned to stone if he looked directly at the area around the Marble Mountains and the village nestled among them. He saw now it was thick with casuarina trees, their leaves bright green and fleshy, a richness of vegetation that he didn't remember. He recalled sand flats all the way from the tarmac and perimeter to here, a bleak landscape dotted with the shanty shacks of refugees, the broken snake of the crater-pocked road, the helicopter base's scabrous huddle of tin-roofed hootches, rows of canvas tents filling and deflating on the land like the inhalations and exhalations of a huge beast; he lived in its guts; when he wasn't flying, it absorbed him. He would stare at the not-so-distant, broken black jag of the mountains on the horizon, from the door of his hootch, from the tarmac when he worked on the helicopters, from his sand-bagged position when he was on perimeter guard; he would fly over them when he was on flight pay. They were a rampart behind which the real country huddled and seethed, forbidden to the Marines because of its shrines and secret places. He was a sculptor, a carver, when he saw a beautiful piece of stone, he needed to go to it, open it, reveal its hidden shapes and faces. He'd been pulled to the mountain that day. The bear went into the mountain, to see what he could see. But he hadn't had the guts to go to it alone. He'd taken three others with him, left two, and brought back one for whom this place was the last vision seared on his eyesight. He had no idea what to do now, where to look. Excuse me, but o dau the G.I.'s, mother fucker?

He walked into the town, and down to the river on its west side now; it twisted around the gnarled, fissured, forest-patched peak of Kim Son, like a river in a Chinese print, dyed onto silk. A wooden punt, poled from the stern by a shirtless man in a cone hat, floated by, and a breeze lifted off the water cooled the sweat on his forehead. He was a methodical, precise man; a sheriff for thirty years, a sculptor all his life, and he needed to place himself in the landscape now, grid it and name it, so he knew where he was. Song Co Co, the guidebook he'd bought had told him. The Co Co River. In front of him, Hoa Hal hamlet, in Non Nuoc village, in Hoa Vang district. That's what he'd needed. A guide book. A village of stone carvers; there for generations, since the time when Da Nang, the city he had always thought of as Danang, was part of the Hindu Champa kingdom. If the five peaks rising around him could be compared to a hand, then the village and its hamlets were in its palm. But a hand was his metaphor; theirs, Trinh Van Hai had told him, was the broken shell of a dragon's egg. It had hatched a princess into the sea which Alex used for target practice, shooting his machine gun at dye markers floating on the turquoise water. How could he have not known any of the names, any of this when he was here, touching this land as lightly as a ghost?

He had looked for, found their families in the States. Rodriguez's parents in Puerto Rico, the small town of pastel-colored concrete houses, dusty streets, palm trees: the place Rodriguez came from not that different from the place where he had ended. Hector's parents had a shrine for him in the small neat living room, the tri-cornered folded flag that had been presented to them at an empty-coffin ceremony placed in front of it, medals displayed in a frame over black velvet, and Alex had crossed himself, putting on for them a show of the faith he no longer felt, giving them also a narrative to believe in, to go with the shrine: a fire fight, Rodriguez firing to cover him as he got the blinded Baxter out of one darkness and into another. Nothing about the way they had gone, unauthorized, armed tourists in a war zone. Nothing about his insistence on going. He had thought to confess, would have welcomed the condemnation, the scourging he thought confession would bring, but the Marine Corps had already given Hector's parents a sustaining myth of heroism, and it had seemed self-indulgent for him to buy the pain he needed for his own relief at their expense. It had been the same with Dalton's wife—his father and mother were dead—in Arkansas. She was remarried, to a soldier, two kids from the second marriage, the toy-crowded, lint-heavy carpet in the tiny living room of a tract house near Fort Chafee, the facility already packed with Vietnamese refugees. What the hell do you think you can give me, coming here? she'd asked Alex.

He passed a sign that told him he was in the Non Nuoc tourism zone. The largest of the formations, Thuy Son, was in front of him. He bought a ticket, feeling he was standing for a moment in front of the booth with the three of them, his old buddies. Any discounts for the dead and maimed? He walked up the steps cut into the mountain, joining a procession of foreign and Vietnamese tourists. One of them, he acknowledged, but an unarmed tourist this time. The steps were very steep—had they been here then? He and the other three Marines had entered the mountain from the side, but from which side, where? Where were his daughter, his lost years, his lost men, the faceless statue? The heat and the climb were getting to him, his legs heavy, his heart racing in his chest.

He saw a bullet-scored gate. Stopped. What was the point of this?

"I don't do caves," he said. To someone. Turned and walked back down the mountain.

He walked back to the main street, along the row of stone workshops. Through the open doors of one he saw, through a haze of white dust, a row of squatting carvers working frantically, pounding their chisels into the stone in a clanging chorus. The man who had given him the stone dancer multiplied and duplicated. He walked inside. A woman behind the display counter smiled at him, her face also duplicated in the statuettes. His daughter's face repeated. The dancer he had been given, the dancer his daughter had become, was everywhere, squad after squad lined up on all the shelves, life-sized in the courtyard, near Buddhas and tigers, Confucian Mandarins, elephant-head Ganeeshes and squatting Devas. At the other end of the workshop, younger carvers were using point chisels, working the way he would work, holding the chisels at steep angles to the stone, which meant, he knew, the pink or white stones they were chipping away at were very hard. He watched them scoring lines in the stone with their first passes, at first shallow and then deeper, making cross-hatch patterns, gridded squares that could be easily chiseled off, until the shape in the stone emerged. He wished he could go to the mountain with them, see how they selected the stone, extracted it. His hands tingled, clutched.

He walked farther into the workshop. Most of the carvers were older men, the pieces they were working on in various stages of completion. Some were using claw chisels, refining the shape, smoothing away the gouged lines left by the point chisel, others smoothing it further with flat chisels, the tools all familiar to his hands, connecting him seamlessly to this place. He squatted down. The old man working the flat chisel was wearing shorts and a t-shirt, his eyes protected by plastic swim goggles, his face scored and cross-hatched itself. Alex hunched over next to him, flat-footed, assuming the old man's exact posture. The old man—Alex thinking of him in those words, though they could be the same age—turned his head and smiled at Alex, his teeth broken and stained. Alex stared at the emerging shape in the stone, saw Baxter's blinded eyes, smooth as eggshells. He thought how this journey was to have been his healing journey—so Brian, who had come himself, so everyone had insisted, except his wise, wise Louise. But it had swallowed him. Brian was gone, Louise was gone, Kiet had faded into the landscape; he had never come back from this place.

He would stay here, work this rock. Perhaps for weeks, months. He would squat in this row of men like himself, find himself in them, carve his shape from the stone of this mountain that had once drawn him to itself, had given him a child. He would recarve the face of the Buddha that he had shattered with his fire. He was sixty years old and lost, the anchor of his job gone, his wife deeply into her own life, and in that vacuum, in the knowledge now of his own knit to his daughter's beginnings, he felt again what had scored and split him asunder at his own beginnings as a man. His daughter would need him also, to help absorb the blows of that past, the murders and abandonment Thuy had told him about. She could stay here awhile also. Would want to. The carvers would welcome him, welcome what he could bring. They would see his skill, the brotherhood of art and redemption that was a stronger connection than skin or blood.

He thought he heard her voice echoing from among the statues around him.

He picked up a hammer and chisel, touched its point to an unblemished stone.

The old man next to him snorted in surprise, reached out and seized Alex's wrist. He shook his head vigorously.

"I can help," Alex told him. "No money. It's OK. I just want to help."

The old man still gripped his wrist. He twisted it away, held up the chisel.

"I know how," Alex said. He touched the point to his chest. "I am a carver."

"Buy statues there." The old man jabbed his chin towards the gift shop.

"No, you don't understand. I can help you work." He needed this, he wanted to say.

But the old man was still shaking his head, though he smiled now at Alex, his eyes invisible behind the dust-coated goggles. "No need," he said gently, as to a child. "No need."

Pas de Deux

Perception was a matter of distance. As Kiet got closer to the Marble Mountains they shifted from a single jagged line against the sky into separate formations that finally seemed to encircle her. The town sprawled between the five peaks; the largest, Thuy Son, looming dark above the buildings. She could see the stacked tiers of a pagoda perched on an outcropping, against the sky. Concrete houses fronted by stone-walled, tiled courtyards, food stalls and restaurants, shopfronts and stone-carving workshops crowded both sides of the road. Through the large open doors of one, a sugary white bodhisattva stared at her with compassion, his thousand arms fanned around his body, and continued into the flailing arms of the dozens of squatting men and women nearby, pounding or chiseling relentlessly at white statues or stones in various stages of incarnation. They turned right onto the street that ran under Thuy Son. A sign said Khu Du Lich Non Nuoc/Non Nuoc Tourism Zone, Vietnamese and English. The air was thick with dust and exhaust fumes. She had pictured walking down a dirt road, or along the dike top bordering a green-and-gold rice paddy, to a small hamlet cluster of thatch-roofed hootches. The ancestral nest.

To the left was a car park, filled with taxis and buses. Horns blared. Scooters backfired. Dust. A line of tourists, middle-aged, American or European, was getting off one of the buses. Some of the women, heavy, red-faced and sweating, were wearing cone-shaped hats, lined up at a small ticket booth; beyond it stone steps were carved into the steep slope of the mountain.

"Thuy Son," Duong said. "Water Mountain. The hospital was here. This is where he will come."

199

She shrugged. She felt carried along now, pulled in the wake of some direction Duong felt compelled to go that was no longer hers. The urgency she had felt to find Alex was gone, replaced by an indifference she was constructing as she went along, a wall of the corpses he had carved out of silent rock with his hands.

They trudged up the steps, following the small herd of tourists, all of whom fanned themselves frantically as they climbed. From behind it seemed they were trying to fly. Halfway up the slope, a bullet-scarred gate opened into a small courtyard in front of a small Buddhist temple. There was a line of kiosks selling postcards, bottles of water, necklaces, and Buddhas carved from the stone of the mountain.

The cave entrance was off to the left. "Hoa Nghiem," Duong said, in his tour guide mode. "The smaller cave leads into the larger, into Huyen Khong." They walked into a vaulted corridor. A Goddess of Mercy guarded the corridor into the bigger cave, which was off to her left. The entrance to Huyen Khong was a dark mouth; past it steep steps descended into the cave. So did she and Duong. Groups of tourists and a few monks clustered here and there in the gloom, some around rock cairns and shrines. Flashbulbs popped. A huge Buddha stood in front of the far wall, a small forest of joss sticks, smoking or dead, picketing the altar in front of it. Kiet was unmoved. A dark mouth. To descend into it would be to be swallowed by her father's history. She needed what she had come for. More now than ever. A different father. A different name.

She looked around anyway. The huge space wasn't completely dark, cave black: there were several openings in the roof, far overhead, shafts of light streaming down through them. They must have been the holes left by the bombs, when the Americans found there was a Viet Cong hospital here.

But Alex had already made his visit, before the bombs.

"Let's get the hell out of here," she said.

They walked down a street lined with stone carving workshops. Coy nude nymphs delicately touched their ankles next to lions, laughing Buddhas, another Goddess of Mercy, sitting cross-legged, her left hand palm-up on lap, her right raised in karate-chop mode. Kiet stopped. Through the entrance of one shop, above the cashier's counter, she saw shelf after shelf of apsarases, as if she had arrived at the homeland of the girl that had danced across the sea to her.

Duong followed her gaze, saw where she was looking. For an instant she thought she saw him flush. She walked in, ahead of him, tired of his secrets. The dancing girls, the tra kieu were everywhere. She shuddered. From somewhere a kind of hiccoughing crying began; it took her a few seconds to realize it was coming from her. Duong put his arm around her.

She touched her face, brought away fingers covered with white powder. "Bui doi—dust," she said.

They walked a few more steps. Suddenly she was face to face with a life-sized tra kieu dancer, the first in a row lined up on the floor. She touched it, and briefly, assumed its position. Duong looked at it, touched its face also.

She relaxed from the posture, spun away from him, to the opposite side of the statue and began to walk down the row, the statues between them, as the lines of boats had been in Sai Gon. He moved hesitantly, parallel to her, his face showing momentarily between the faces of the apsarases, disappearing, revealed again. She stopped, stood directly behind one statue, crooked her arms and legs in opposition to its arms and legs, the stone cold against her chest and stomach.

He stared at her.

"Tomorrow is Trung Nguyen, the day of wandering souls."

"Is it?"

"How do you say? Close enough. Thuy will be here."

She was at the end of the row. They faced each other.

"We'll find him," Duong said.

"I don't know if I'm still looking. When I saw those photographs I wanted to rip off my skin." She shuddered. "How could you sit with him?"

Duong was silent for a long time. When he spoke, his voice was strained.

"I thought you said to me that you were no longer a child."

Kiet's Dream

She hides in the reeds, crouches beneath the paddy dike, clutching her weapon, an old musket dripping with mud. It is a straw broom, prickly in her hands. It is a pistol, cold and hard as fact. Minnows and crabs nibble her toes, which wiggle under the sheen of the water. A turtle breaks the surface, stares goggle-eyed at her, bearded with moss. Her stomach knots and she has to pee. Tom Berenger hunts her, stalks the other side of the berm, amid swaying palm and pine trees, an olive-green do-rag around his head, an M-16 in his hands, his face scarred. The rifle in his hands is a straw broom also. He points it at her, grins, reaches up and peels off his scars, leaving his face smooth as a baby's bottom. The baby suckles at the clay statue's breast. She shatters the glass, reaches in for it, tears the baby away, her wrists and hands bloody. She crosses the bridge, shoots Brandon Frasier, who falls into a huddled heap in the black water beneath it. She runs through a jungle bleached by moonlight. That was the war, her white father says. Don't go to that place, her black father says. He follows her like a weighted shadow through brittle frozen stalks. A swing set gleams silver in the moonlight, near a thatch-roofed hootch. Her black father and her white father swing in tandem, shaking their forefingers at her. She is next to a tobacco barn, every other board winged up. She peeks inside. A skeletal man is probing the moist interior of a tobacco plant, with a filthy, broken-nailed finger. She runs to the thatched-roof hootch, slithers through her window, into her bed. Rows of Buddha and demon statues stare at her from the shelves. She can't bear their painted eye-sockets. She clutches her stuffed Raggedy Ann. She clutches her father's pistol. She pulls the blanket up over her head. When she peeks out, she sees that the face of one of the demons has grown and fills the window. She fires and the trigger moves through the metal smoothly and liquidly. The metal is like butter. The face shatters into crystalline shards. Her hands are gloved in blood. Her black father, his face sad, takes the pistol from her nerveless fingers. Her white father, his face sad, takes the pistol from her fingers and puts it into his empty holster. Her hands are gloved in blood. Johns, his face cracked like a mirror, sits up and licks her fingers clean. I always knew you were my daughter, he says.

Her Skin

Duong felt a touch on his back and was instantly awake. Confused. The hotel, he thought. I'm in the hotel in Hoi An. The room dark except for the stripes of light coming through the window trellis. He sat up. She was sitting on the edge of the bed.

"I can't be here alone," she said. "Em yeu anh. I love you. I want to be you. Let me stay."

Have you come to me in the night? he might have said. Have you come back to me, beloved?

She put a finger to his lips, stopping the words she couldn't understand and then leaned forward and stopped them with her lips. Duong drew back, held her by the shoulders. She began unbuttoning her blouse, counting aloud, like a strange prayer.

One.

Two.

Three.

He was awake now. He tried to take her hand, stop her. She moved back from him, and when she slipped under the sheets, her body was striped with shadow and then covered, and her skin was cool, she was the apsaras, she whispered, whose job was to guide the heroes who have died in battle to paradise. Stop the nonsense, he started to say, but she pressed her lips to his again, drew his hand to her sex. A groan escaped him and he began to return her kiss, fit his body to hers. He held her to himself, stroked her hips, her back. His hand touched a ridge of scar tissue, and as it did, she moaned, touched the scar on his cheek. They were caressing each other's wounds. This thought formed in his mind in exactly those words. The banality of them, even more than the knowledge of the origin of those scars, stopped him like a splash of ice water. He pushed her away and closed his eyes, let something in himself close tight as a fist. She reached over, but when she touched him, she could feel that he had not responded. He pushed her hand away

She covered herself with the sheet. Shuddered. They sat in silence.

"I'm sorry," she said. "I'm very fucked up."

She brushed his face with her fingers, got out of bed and quickly dressed. Then she sat again on the edge of the bed, reached over to his nightstand and picked up his pack of cigarettes. She offered one to him. He shook his head. She drew one out, lit it, inhaled deeply and then exhaled, staring at the glowing tip. The she pushed down on the top of her head, and ran her hand back hard over her hair, following it all the way down her neck. It was a gesture that put a cold blade into his throat.

The Names of Things

Alex worked his way around the Marble Mountain formations: Moc Son, Hoa Son and Huyen Vi cave, Kim Son and the Quan Am cave, the Long Hoa pagoda at Tho Son. Finally, he let himself go back to Thuy Son, but to its eastern flank, facing the sea. He entered the courtyard of a large, seven-tiered pagoda made of a pale blue stone. Chua Linh Ung, the two old women squatting at its entrance told him when he asked. It was his mission now, to learn the names. One of the women stroked his face, muttering, and then took him by both hands to a small cave, inside another cave. Dong Tang Chon. He pronounced it, and when she laughed, tried it again, until she nodded. Chua means pagoda. Dong means cave. Names. Secret chambers inside secret chambers. To the right of the entrance, on top of a natural ledge halfway to the cave's ceiling, he saw an ancient Buddha, sitting in a position of meditation, hand raised. The old woman, her back so bent she scurried over the ground like a reverse capital letter L, scrambled nimbly to the top, waved at him to follow. He did, with difficulty. Needed to be more crabbish, he supposed. On the other side, he could see nothing—the ledge dropped into cave blackness. But there was another statue, hidden behind the first—a reclining Buddha, lying on its side, larger than life-sized, there for no one's eyes except those who knew where to look, who brought their own lights. He touched down the length of the statue, a work of perfect art that didn't need to be seen to be completed, that could and did lie in solitude and darkness. He played with the notion that this was the Buddha he shot, crawled here to heal in the darkness, to recarve its own face.

The woman was staring up at him, as much as her crook

allowed. He sat on the ledge, said, *cam on,* thank you, and handed her a wad of dong. She smiled, put it in her pocket, left him alone. He lay down, just enough room on the edge behind the reclining Buddha, placed his face against the back of the statue's head, the cold press of it into his forehead. The Buddha would enter the secret soul of Alexander Hallam and it would tsk: so much tumult to be soothed, surrendered. Or some such. His mind reeled with fatigue; he was drained. He fell asleep behind the guarding statue, dreamt Rodriguez and Dalton melted into the rock, the brush of bat wings fanning him all night, sweeping the dreams from his mind before they had time to root.

He only knew it was morning when a dim glow illuminated the face of the statue. Alex rose, covered with dust, his body stiff, climbed down, and then brought his folded hands to his forehead, thanking the Buddha.

He walked around the flank of Thuy Son. It was just past dawn, but to his surprise there were already a few tourists in line at the ticket booth before the carved steps that went up the mountain.

A ticket? Say what? Rodriguez said.

He shook his head. The two men in front of him, one white, one black, were middle-aged, his age, looking at him with something like concern, their faces puzzled. Had he spoken out loud? He got his ticket, labored once again up the stone steps set into the steep slope. The two men stayed near him; his new companions on this hill. They stopped at a stone bench, peered worriedly at Alex.

That was then; this is fucked, Dalton said.

No need for this, old man, Rodriguez said. You are not needed here.

Alex pressed on. It was what you did. One foot in front of the other until you got where you needed to be. Or shouldn't be at all. In front of him was the bullet-scored gateway before a courtyard and the small Tam Thi monastery building. Old women were selling souvenirs, bottles of water, and incense from some stands in the courtyard. He looked around, confused. One of the vendors plucked at his sleeve, and pointed to a walkway to the left of the pagoda. "Hoa Nghiem," she whispered. But he already knew the names.

Booby traps, man, Rodriguez said.

Sarge, come on, Dalton said. We tell the grunts. Let's go.

"Some of this shit's thousands of years old," Alex said.

One of the pair of American tourists glanced at his friend. "Excuse me, bro?"

So was that mama-san I balled at the dump, Dalton said.

The old woman plucked at Alex's shirt sleeve.

So is this old lady. Who gives a shit?

Dong Hoa Nghiem, the old woman said again, insistently.

So that's what they call it, said Rodriguez. Everything we never knew, right, hombre?

"You OK, bro?" one of the tourists asked.

"Copasetic," Alex said.

"Sure, old hoss. No problem," the other said.

He walked down the path and then stood still, sweating, staring at the entrance to the first cave—Hoa Nghiem. He passed through a bullet-scored gate—he remembered none of this. Old women selling souvenirs, postcards, incense, and bottles of water guarded the black mouth of a cave. He was confused, drifting. One old woman plucked at his sleeve, as if to draw him back to earth, pointed at the opening. "Hoa Nghiem," she said.

He bought a bundle of incense from her, walked into the cave. The Goddess of Mercy stood in front of him. He considered lighting the incense here. But didn't. The old woman had come in with him; she pointed him to the left. Four statues, two of them in armor, warriors, guarded the cave entrance. The other two looked like scholars, mandarins.

"Dong Huyen Khong," the woman said, giving it a name after all these years. He nodded, staring at the blackness of the cave mouth.

He advanced enough to see the Goddess of Mercy statue, inside the entrance. Then he descended into the final cave, held like a secret behind the entrance to the smaller cave.

Kiet in Heaven

They were back at Thuy Son by late morning. Duong led her up the steps, to the area in front of the small Tam Thi pagoda. Kiet puzzled. Why there? she'd asked earlier, but Duong had said he'd rather not tell her yet. To trust him. She let herself be led. Had he located Alex? What would she say to her father, his face carved from the inside by the fingers of his victims? Duong was looking around anxiously now, searching for what? Running his hand over his face repeatedly. His agitation was catching; she found herself wanting to move away from him.

She wandered over to one of the stands, little thatched-roof kiosks alongside the small square. Wooden and shell necklaces and bracelets, hung with amulets or tiny Buddhas, were looped around a corner peg, under the thatch. The woman looked at her face and smiled a betel-stained smile at her, and said something in Vietnamese that started with words she knew, chao em, hello younger sister. The first time anyone in this country had not pegged her as a foreigner. It was probably just sales technique, another Viet Kieu recognized. But she felt an exaggerated rush of gratitude. The old woman picked up a bundle of incense sticks and pressed them into her hands anyway. She pointed to a steep path, and said, "Heaven," and as if to prove she knew what the English word meant, pointed her finger up at the sky.

Duong had come over. He looked up at the slope, and then at his watch.

"Do you have an appointment?"

He was still looking up. "Let's go," he said.

"Kill some time?"

He froze, his eyes widening; she felt she could see her words enter them; how they would sound to him.

"Yes," he said. "We will kill some time."

They worked their way up the path, from rock to rock, using the slippery roots as steps or as pull-ups. At the top, they passed into a small tunnel, slanting upwards, a hole in its ceiling through which the sunlight poured, and then a natural chimney. They climbed rock to rock, at the top emerged into heaven.

It was a shallow cup on top of one of the sub-peaks of Thuy Son, the small indent of it jaggedly rimmed, the ground horizontal but floored with a jumble of stones, and the ones that didn't stick up sharp and vertical were smooth and very slippery. Kiet walked carefully, holding the incense in one hand, but as she stepped out, her right heel suddenly couldn't find purchase and slipped out from under her. She fell forward, her forehead cracking. When she sat up, she touched her skin, felt a trickle of blood, tasted it in her mouth. She touched her finger to the stone; if the mountain wanted more blood, her blood, so be it. The incense was still clenched in her other hand.

Duong was staring at her intensely, his eyes preternaturally bright in the clarifying, wind-raked light, his face pale, so that the question-mark scar on it seemed redder, newer. He touched her forehead, looked, almost puzzled, at the blood on his fingers. He put them into his mouth, cleaning off the blood, and then pointed at a jumble of rocks on the edge. A cluster of burnt-out joss sticks had been stuck in a crevice, the slight lip of rock over it sheltering it from the wind. He went over, knelt by them.

She shook her head, clearing it, joined him. She wanted to ask him what this place meant to him, to her, but she held in the words, other words she had once said to Mai Becker forming in her mind: if I could say it, why would I go though the great trouble of dancing it? Whatever was here had pulled her to itself, taken her blood into itself. She pushed the ends of the incense sticks into the crevice, next to the burnt-down bases of the other cluster, and Duong handed her a lighter and she brought the flame to them, watched it release the smoke from their cores, watched it curl out into the air. Standing, turning slowly, she could see the country and the ocean, the jagged mountains and the green and gold patchwork of rice fields, the patches of green forest, a white thread of sand, the turquoise sea. The word in Vietnamese for country, she understood, meant Land and Water, and she understood also now how one of the other names for this elemental mountain was another way of saying that same marriage, the edge and thread of water plaited into the edge and thread of land. The wind that touched both blew in her face, sang in her ears.

Hat Chau Van

Duong felt her eyes on him, her presence here an accusation. Enough. It was a mistake to bring her here; what had he thought to accomplish? He had let her light incense; he would be forgiven, was that it? By whom—the rocks?

He looked at his watch. "It's time to go."

"Where?"

"Thuy will meet us at the pagoda."

He turned and started to climb down, then stopped and tried Thuy's number on his cell phone, connected.

We're here.

Yes.

She was waiting in the courtyard in front of the small pagoda. Kiet smiled. Thuy rushed over, embraced her.

"Come, em. We have prepared everything for you."

Kiet said nothing. Duong glanced at her, her odd passivity. Not like her, he thought, and then he thought of the strangeness of it, that he knew what was like her, what was not. Thuy led her up the path to the two caves, Hoa Nghiem and Huyen Khong. He watched Kiet take in the row of blue plastic stools, the roped-off stage area in front of the cave. The first cave was an antechamber to the larger: Thuy, he realized, must have gotten permission from the local authorities to use it as a dressing and staging area. He supposed her family was still that well known here. But who could say no to her, to him, in this place? It was their mountain, its caves and crevices the configurations of their history. A sudden babble of voices echoed from the entrance and Kiet stiffened, turned towards the noise, and Duong saw the members of Thuy's acting troupe, boiling out of the cave's mouth, some already in costume. She had always been the organized one, Thuy, helping him decide where to hide the mortar tubes, where to set the ambushes, knowing the labyrinth of chambers and secret hollows of the mountain; it was more truly her place, for hundreds of years her family had taken its stones, given them back carved into the shape of their stories as if they were the formed dreams of the mountain. The actors greeted Kiet effusively, hugging her, patting her. She stared, but Duong could see she was not surprised. She knew why they were here. One of the students propped the life-sized photo of the shattered Buddha near the entrance.

He led her to one of the stools and sat her down and then sat next to her. She sat stiff and straight, her feet flat against the earth, as if she might spring up and run at the slightest opportunity. Some of the vendors from the mountain, several orange-robed monks, and a few tourists, Vietnamese and foreign looked at them; some sat down also. Thuy and the actors were setting up a few simple props: a table, four bamboo poles holding up a thatched awning.

To the side of the cave, he saw the musicians, in classical dress, and stopped. A moon-shaped dan nguyet, lute, with its accompanying phách, the bamboo struck to mark the rhythm; xeng clappers; the trong chau drum; a chieng gong, a 16-stringed dan tranh zither, and a sao, flute. They were the instruments, he knew, not of cai luong but of Hat Chau Van—the music of incantation, the chants sung as an invitation to the spirits to seize the singer, the players. He shuddered; Thuy had hidden the form from him—what he had seen in rehearsals was cai luong, like most of her plays. But he knew her, knew what she would do—it would still be cai luong; she would combine the two forms, spirit and story; it was what she did. She would call ghosts. He was not a religious person, but to invite in the spirits here, of all places, seemed suddenly so desperate as to be insane.

The rest of the troupe went into the cave. After a moment, from the monastery building nearby came a low murmuring chant, and then the sound of someone beating the trong chau, the phach echoing it. With each beat another actor emerged from the mouth of the cave and took up a position in front of the audience. An old man squatted near the table, pantomimed chiseling stone. Two peasant girls squatted on their heels under the thatched awning. A VC guerilla lay on his stomach nearby. The beat stopped. The chanting stopped. Four actors dressed as American soldiers, one with blackface paste makeup, the others with whiteface paste, emerged from the cave mouth, stood before the stone carver. He lifted his cupped hands to one, opened them to reveal a statuette of a Tra Kieu dancer. As if what she had given to the mountain had been returned or refused. He sang, in Vietnamese and, as he did, Duong spoke the English translation:

Today is Trung Nguyen, the day of wandering souls.

Thuy, dressed as the tra kieu dancer, danced onto the stage. She was holding another statuette, another dancer, also cupped in her hands.

Thuy's strange cai luong began.

Once there were three sisters, born here, and named for the elements of the mountains by their father. Thuy, now the cung van, the mistress of ceremonies, who would open herself up to possession, circled her hand at the mountain behind her, and to her side, and in front of her. And then she pointed at Kiet.

Named by your grandfather, Le Thach Son, which means Stone and Mountain; by your grandmother, whose name was Tung, pine. The element of wood. Wood that bends but never breaks—but who did break and was gone before you were born.

She pointed south.

Moc Son, Wood Mountain, Duong said.

And thought of Thuy's mother and sister, dead on Highway One, on their way to market. Act One of the usual tragedy that poisons the blood of everyone born in or of this country.

Once there were three sisters. The eldest was Nhat. Sun. From the element of Hoa—fire.

She pointed west.

Hoa Son, Fire Mountain, Duong said.

A female actor dressed in peasants' black cotton danced onto stage.

And in fire she died, along with her mother, in the Year of the Horse.

Act Two, curtained by an exploding mine. The phach was beaten, the cymbals clanged.

The actor exited. Kiet gripped his arm, hard. "Was she my...?"

"No. Patience, em."

The youngest was Thuy. Le Thi Thanh Thuy. The spoiled darling. Thuy, the element of water, that flows into whatever shape it finds....

Thuy pointed at the mountain behind her, and as Duong watched, she transformed. Duong gasped, overwhelmed by the illusion; he had seen her act before, knew her exquisite talent but what he saw now was the young Thuy herself, in her steps the skip of the young girl with whom Duong had once fallen in love. Act Three. The particular and peculiar cai luong that was his life and the life of this woman next to him, to be unfolded before his eyes,

And the middle daughter was Kim. Gold.

She pointed south. Gold Mountain.

Gold Mountain, Duong said.

Tuyet, dressed now in a traditional ao dai dress came onto stage. She pressed both hands against her breasts. Duong held his breath. He knew the part the young woman would play.

Nhat's sister. My sister. Le Thi Ngoc Kim.

The sao flute wailed.

She pointed at Kiet.

Your mother.

Kiet was crying now, silently.

217

Thuy drew herself up to her full height, stood on her tiptoes. The phach beat out a rhythm, the sao carried it spiraling up, smashed it against the mountain. When she sang, it was in English:

Today is Trung Nguyen—the day of the wandering souls.

Today is 1969, in Chua Hamlet and our lives are tied together by a thread of red silk...the father you never knew woven by war and place to the father your soul found....

Duong watched Kiet as she watched Alex's story fit to her own, the beginning brush of their lives. Under the awning, the cai luong actors danced into her grandfather and the Marines, her adoptive father again given the gift of the stone dancer, again shooting into the face of the Buddha, as he and his men disappeared into the cave, the actors going off-stage, disappearing into the cave, the sound of the bamboo phach beating faster and faster from inside the entrance, its hollow echoes that represented the murder they did and the murder Duong brought to them. Binh, the actor playing, Duong assumed, himself as a young man, appeared, Duong watching, wanting to scream at the figure, warn him, change the play. "You?" Kiet whispered, her voice strained. Several flashbulbs went off, and he heard a Western woman behind him, her accent reminding him of Dottie's, ask plaintively, "What's going on?"

The play was going on.

O dau the G.I.'s.mother-fucker? an actor screamed.

Hien, his face covered with black paste entered.

Kiet started to rise. Duong put his hand on her shoulder.

Let's all calm down here.

Who the fuck are you?

Sergeant Swan, sir. I head the Combined Action Company in this area.

Kiet, meeting her father. Swan. Swan. She said it aloud. Duong saw her lips form the word, hold it as if it might fly off or float away as lightly and gracefully as its namesake.

Thuy, her eyes fastened to Kiet, came out from the stage.

The music played faster and faster, echoing off the mountain, into the cave and then back out, as Thuy wailed, calling the spirits into herself, into them. Hat Chau Van. Tuyet disappeared into the mountain, and Duong felt himself sigh, as if the actress had taken the soul of the woman she was playing back to the tomb. Thuy took Kiet by both hands, and led her back, the actors touching her gently, passing her back into the cave and the dressing area and when they emerged, it was Kiet in the formal ao dai blouse and dress, and she was her mother. Thuy signaled Duong to join them, in the sacred square, he thinking of it with that name, the way he imagined Thuy did. The family altar was at the edge of stage left, draped with a red cloth. He pulled the cover off. More flashbulbs went off. On the altar were framed photos, flowers, bowls of fresh fruit, a statue of Buddha, a small bowl containing sand.

Kiet came over to it.

What was happening, there didn't seem any story to it, why didn't something happen, it didn't make sense, the tourist complained loudly.

Kiet looked at the sepia-tinted photo of a man in mandarin clothing. The woman in an ao dai almost identical to the one she wore now. Two young women, their arms around each other, on top of the mountain. A Black G.I. The same man dressed as a mandarin. Her fingers, trembling, she touched each picture. As her fingers brushed the last one, it fell forward; behind it was a bundle of letters, tied with a red thread. Next to them, a diary. She picked up both.

Duong went into the dressing tent and changed his clothing. The black shirt and trousers, the gray ammunition belt, the checkered scarf. Changed, he thought, into himself.

He came out, carrying a bundle of incense. He stood to the side. George Swan, the actor playing Swan, came to Kiet. He removed the objects she had taken from her hands, put them back, and then sat with her in front of the altar. She would not look at him.

Duong stuck the incense sticks into the sand, lit them, and stood still for a long time, feeling the light from the candle flickering on his face, feeling it melting years from him. He brought his hands together and dipped them three times towards the light, bowing his head. Some religious thing, the foreign woman said, her voice breaking the hush, and the flashbulbs started again. He raised his head and turned, facing three quarters towards the audience, but his attention on Kiet.

The flashbulbs exploded in his eyes and the audience disappeared. He was aware of the actors behind him and around him, his words, his cai luong, his Hat Chau Van twisting and forming their bodies into the stream of story, and then he was no longer even aware of them, only of the story, only of its true audience, this woman, tears streaming down her face, in front of him in the sacred square of the stage.

PART FIVE

THUY SON

WATER

East of Eden

Gunnery Sergeant George Swan and Co Le Thi Ngoc Kim, two lovers, stand in front of the altar of the ancestors in the Le house. They had, as is the tradition, first burned incense and asked permission to enter of the Spirit of the Soil whose altar was outside the entrance, and then—there being no male relatives left alive, and no elders, male or female, to whom the groom could kow tow—had placed tea, rice wine, and fruit on the altar, lit two candles, and held them high in front of the ancestors, to tell them of this marriage. Now each gives the other a round box filled with areca leaves and betel nuts, to symbolize the union of these two different people. Afterwards, they climb to one of the summits of Thuy Son, to a place which was a favorite of Kim's father's. It is Kim's desire to create their own tradition in this place, and the couple stands with the wind and the sea breeze blowing against their faces and bodies, and burn incense they have stuck into the rocks. From below them, they can hear the height- and wind-dulled noises of the war, bursts of machine-gun fire, the thud of exploding shells, like distant but rude reminders. Some helicopters lift from the base. Kim had wanted her sister to be with her, but Thuy did not come. The organization to which she belonged, the fighting arm of the National Liberation Front, did not approve of the marriage, nor was it sanctioned by the United States Marine Corps, which had its own peculiar traditions. Swan's superior officers knew nothing about the ceremony.

***

Duong, dressed in a white shirt and black-market American jeans, walks to the highway market in Hoa Hal: a string of dilapidated stalls made of discarded tin sheets fastened helter-skelter to bamboo frames, along Highway One. Except for old, stone-carving families, many of the people here are refugees from the countryside, trying to survive by selling whatever they could make, steal, or grow, including, sometimes, their own daughters. The Americans have a dump not far from the northern side of Thuy Son; a few times a day one of their trucks, three or four armed Marines guarding their precious loads, stops there and the Marines toss down the trash: scrap metal and wood, paper, tin cans, broken wire. It is a treasure trove for Duong and for the locals, and for that reason he makes sure the trucks are never ambushed, even though some of the Marines throw boards or cans at people walking or bicycling down Highway One—another windfall for the resistance. The day a ten year old boy named Ninh was blinded by the jagged edge of a ration can, Duong had ten recruits from the village, one for each year of Ninh's age.

His book stall, a sagging affair of bamboo poles, thatch and galvanized tin, is located in the middle section of the highway market, the business a front for him, an excuse to be in the village, a way to get and send messages, living, as his unit does, clutching the belts of the Americans. He sells scrap paper, treated with lime, re-used notebooks, pencils when he can get them, and other junk—some of it from that dump, though he still did have some stacks of old books, bourgeoisie writers from the Thirties: Khai Hung. The Lu, and Nguyen Tuong Tam, and occasionally some tattered foreign books, in translation.

He looks now at the new book that has shown up, second from the left on the sagging shelf, and he feels a deep chill. A ragged, dog-eared copy of *East of Eden*, not a translation, but in the original English. He has seen it before. But not lately.

Somewhere in his file, he imagines, someone—a classmate from Hue who was now in the Party?—had once noted that this novel was the Steinbeck he loved the most, though *The Grapes of Wrath* was the more officially approved work. After victory, Ho Chi Minh had promised, the victors would turn this land into an earthly paradise, but, looking deeply into himself, one of the designated builders of heaven, Duong recognized the same human flaws of Steinbeck's characters—everything which had kept them from paradise, from Eden. That is, he had his doubts about any paradise that contained and depended upon Nguyen Binh Duong.

It was this novel that led to his failure to eliminate Trinh Van Hai. The decision has turned out well; he'd turned Hai around instead, moved him from the abstractions of art to revolutionary practicality. But he had disobeyed orders and after suffering the obligatory boring and lengthy sessions of self-criticism as a result, he had been transferred here, to Ngu Hanh Son. He didn't mind. His assignment, his *work*, after Cu Chi was close and needed silence, knife more than rifle or booby trap, and too many times also, he'd wrapped his hands around the throats of the condemned and traitorous, felt their final breaths explode into his nostrils and mouth. After a time, he couldn't stop tasting those sour kisses.

The book code had been his idea. An asterisk next to the name of a character in the Steinbeck kept in whatever book stall he operated; the character keyed to a secret list of potential targets he'd memorized. He would think of them by their names in the novel. It was easier that way. Easy to see the corrupt Sai Gon colonel—a vicious torturer of Front fighters who fell into his hands, a man who kept a fourteen-year-old Chinese mistress while he beat his daughter (who brought his daily schedule to Duong) and had her lover sent to the front—as Cyrus Trask, the father who twisted and shamed the souls of his two sons, and built a fortune stealing money from the veterans he represented. Easy to see Madame Ninh, the former whore and madam he eliminated in An Tan, as Cathy, the whore and madam, the heartless corruptor of the innocent.

And easy to see Trinh Van Hai as Samuel Hamilton. He had linked his old professor's name to Hamilton's in the code he gave his superiors, but had hoped never to see that name starred on the dog-eared page. That poor Irish peasant was his favorite character by far in the novel; as much as it is possible to love a fictional character, he loved Hamilton. Of course he reminded Duong of his own father, a poet, editor of an intellectual journal, always in trouble, possessor of a sly humor that protected him by enabling fools to see him as a clown, his keen, passionate and non-utilitarian interest in everything: the workings of a machine, the earth, the human heart. Duong delighted in the passages in the novel when Hamilton and Adam Trask and the Chinese cook, Lee, would sit and drink and strive to understand human beings and the light and the dark they would do in the world, speaking not out of expectations of power or gain, other than the knowledge itself. Whenever he reread the novel, he would take a subversive delight in their impractical excitement.

The sad irony was that his designated target not only fit that character's name, but was also the man who had introduced him to the novel in the first place. Hai was an eclectic man, a free thinker; he had criticized both the corruption and toadying to foreigners of the Southern regime, and what he saw as the cruelty and rigid ideology of the NLF and Hanoi. His outspokenness had gotten him dismissed from the faculty at Hue. His insistence on the ambiguity of truth, the grays in a life-and-death conflict, had made the asterisk next to the name of his literary shadow inevitable, Duong supposed, perhaps had known all along. When he'd seen Duong, covered in the grease that had allowed him to slip quietly into the window of the house near the abattoir in Hoi An, his first move was to touch the books within his reach, gently, as if saying farewell.

What Duong had loved truly, mostly, about *East of Eden,*

was the human complexity of the characters. But what had never impressed him until that moment—the very moment he'd watched Hai caress the spines of his books—was the central conceit, the central discourse that gave the novel its title: Samuel Hamilton, Adam Trask, and Lee, the Chinese cook, naming Trask's twin boys, and drawn to names from the Christian bible, their excitement about the story of the brothers Abel and Cain. The first murder. The first assassin. Was God unjust? Did He not cause the jealousy in Cain that led to the killing? Lee, the Chinese cook, suggests looking at the passage in its original language, Hebrew, to see what is there in this story that has made it what he calls a map of the soul. He brings it to some of the old wise men in his family, and for years they study Hebrew (how Duong loves that Lee and those old men decide that this is the best way for them to spend their years). And what they discover is that a sentence translated into the English, God telling Abel that if he is a good man, he will rule over his passions and anger. What the Chinese discover, though, is that the Hebrew word *Timshel* actually means *may*—you may. Not that you *will*, but that you *may* rule over sin.

Duong never understood, nor shared, Lee's excitement for that seemingly mundane wisdom, until that moment, when he saw Samuel Hamilton in his incarnation as a professor of literature further reincarnated into a Hoi An street photographer. Hai's fingers on the spines of his books. The words burst in Duong's mind like an exploding grenade. They shattered him. *You will*, Lee says, is a promise. It requires only a passive loyalty to obedience, and whatever is gained is the reward for obedience. But *You may* is choice. You may, Lee says, is the mark of humanity. Those two words in Duong's mind, as clear as if that character in a book had spoken them into his ear. Those words as powerful, as needful of action, as the names that had been starred for him in the book. They had looked at each other, Mr. Trinh Van Hai and his would-be assassin; Mr. Samuel Hamilton and Nguyen

Binh Duong, former student of literature, and Duong did not bring his knife to Hai's throat. Only the threat of it. Perhaps to see what Hai would do. Perhaps hoping Hai would disappoint him. Perhaps to murder the possibility of Samuel Hamilton.

East of Eden once again pressed into Duong's hands, he passes into the mountain. Passes the four statues of mandarins that guard the entrance to Huyen Khong cave, and the concrete Buddha, ghostly and white in the dark, and enters the field hospital chamber beyond two stalactites, one dripping water that comes from Heaven, the other dry, supposedly touched by the Emperor Tu Duc who, as emperors do, took all the water for himself. The wounded lay on their mats in the darkness, groaning softly, rustling in the gloom like dried leaves. They had been evacuated before the G.I.s searched the caves, now they are back. Thuy, the element of water, retreating and then flowing back into its space.

Behind a mushroom-shaped outcrop, Duong moves aside a mat covered with a crust of latex and stone and lowers himself into the tunnel beneath. He lights the candle he's brought with him. The fierce faces of ancient Cham gods grow suddenly from the rock, exemplars of the entombment of their race, that people his own people had erased from this land and who, some believe, he believes, cursed Viet Nam to eternal cycles of war. The tunnel ends in a wall split by what seems a shallow crack. But when one slips inside, one can move sideways, to the right, deeper into the mountain. He slips inside. The stone is so close to his face it scrapes his nose, and in several places he has to let his breath out in order to squeeze past the tightening rock walls. A claustrophobic panic starts scrambling in his chest. Never mind the many times he's done this. He stops and presses his face, his lips, against the cold dank rock, the dampness of it thick as moss in his nostrils. It is something he learned in the

tunnels at Cu Chi when he'd been trapped for hours, after a
bomb had collapsed the earth around him. Become part of it.
He extinguishes the candle. Standing still now, in the perfect
darkness, he seals himself to the inside of the mountain, a
small, live thing of flesh and beating heart subsumed by the
mass of it, petrifying, the stone dusting into his veins until
they fill and harden, as he imagines the bodies of the two
Americans they'd encased in another small hollow in the
mountain have done, metamorphosing into stone. For months
afterwards, the doctors and nurses heard their souls
screaming, confused, until some of the fighters burned
incense in front of the Americans' burial place, held a
ceremony to bring peace to their wandering spirits. Dead,
they were no longer enemies; their bones were part of the
mountain, the land.

The panic is gone. Duong knows that if he stands there
any longer, the mountain will trickle its substance into his
eyes and lips, fill him with its weight, and he will never leave.
It happened that way in Cu Chi, and when his comrades
managed to dig him out, they found him smiling as peacefully
as an earthen statue. But he isn't ready yet to be a reclining
Buddha. He thinks of Thuy, imagines her in this space with
him, and presses his loins against the rock, feels himself
swelling. He groans, inches sideways, away from his own
thoughts, until the walls widen, and he can go around a corner
into the small vaulted space he keeps as his "office" within
the mountain.

He lights a match, touches the wick of the candle in his
hand. The light defines the small cave around him, reveals
the table made from American ammunition boxes, another
candle on top of it, a lip of melted wax along one edge. He
lights that candle, softens the base of the candle in his hand
in its flame, and presses it to the wood. Puts the book down.
He could have opened it in the market, but he'd felt the need
to be alone when he did, to drag it into his cave. He didn't,
for that matter, need to open it at all. He finds the dog-eared

page, runs his finger down it. There are asterisks, faint, in pencil, after two names. *Aron** and *Abra**. The letters elongated and contracted in the flicker. He has known since the wedding. East of Eden. The fanatic, delusional boy manipulated into going to war, the woman he thinks he loves, when what he loves is merely an idea of what he wants her to be. Perhaps his analogies are strained. Neither character, he thinks, truly fit the real people. It doesn't matter. They are not literary figures. They are his mission. The book a kind of mockery. a reminder of past sins of omission, its code not really needed. He knew what gift he'd been given.

You may, he thinks, and then he says it aloud, in the darkness of the mountain.

He had been taught how to move without sound by Hien, a sapper who specialized in slipping, stripped naked but for a loin cloth, his body greased and blackened, through the concertina wire hung with cans and other noise-makers and strung around the perimeters of American and puppet-soldier base camps. Hien would reverse the claymore mines under the wire, plant explosives, and sometimes even cut the throats of sleeping soldiers, before escaping back through the wire. There were other sappers who would infiltrate in the same manner, and, strapped with explosives, would explode themselves in key positions. Hien disapproved. Duong agreed. They were not, if they could help it, a people attracted by suicide. Duong would be amused, many years after the war, hearing about an American film that showed Vietnamese betting their lives on the spin of a pistol barrel, gambling on whether or not there was a bullet in the chamber when they pulled the trigger. It was, he would think, a brilliant metaphor for the emotions one feels in combat. But his countrymen and women had always had more than enough ways to die, and more than enough people willing to help them do so, without doing it to themselves for sport. Hien would say that the best weapon for a poor army was one that could be used over and over again. You will be that weapon he'd told Duong, and showed him how to blend into the ground, move over it as slowly and silently as a lengthening shadow.

Although he had not used the skills Hien taught him against enemy bases, he still prepares for kills as his mentor did, stripping down and greasing himself, not only for silence and to avoid having his clothing catch on snags, but also to terrify anyone who might see him. Naked now, he opens the can of grease—scavenged from the American garbage dump—he keeps stored in the cave. He will use it mixed with dirt to both darken himself and disguise his smell. He closes his eyes. Thuy came to him again, her body momentarily against his in the grove, her refusal, and he eases himself with his hand, before applying the grease, watching, with amusement and disgust, his own shadow's futile human dance against the wall of the cave.

Dark. The middle of the night. He opens a hinged thatch window and spills himself into the house he knows so well. He is in the cooking area, set off from the rest of the house by a bamboo partition. He peers through the narrow slot between the stalks. The two of them are sleeping on a mat, covered by a thin blanket. It rises up and down with their breathing, a form that has been stolen from his own life. Duong stands perfectly still, letting whatever sounds there are come into his ears, separating them. Her soft breathing. Swan's, harsher, interrupted by the occasional snort, moan. The breeze rustling the roof, the creak of the joists. An insect scurries in the walls. He looks again, letting his eyes adjust, seeing it all come clear. The Marine's rifle and cartridge belt are on the packed earth of the ground next to him.

There is a soft exhalation near Duong's shoulder. A touch on his back. He spins, his knife at the throat of the person behind him, holds back his stab just in time when he sees

Thuy's face. A thin line of blood trickles down her neck. She takes his wrist in both her hands and moves the point of the knife down and forward a little until it is touching her left breast. They stand in that position, breathing in tandem, almost panting. As much a twisted image of the configuration of love as his shadow on the cave wall. An image of the blanket in the next room, rising and falling, comes into his mind. He pries her fingers from his wrist. With their eyes still locked, he backs up to the window and then, silently as he came, leaves the house.

In the morning, he stands at his book stall, trying to think what he will say to Command after this, his second failure. He scans the people in the market. To his surprise, he sees Thuy moving through them. She stops at a stall selling kitchen utensils, glances uneasily in his direction. Their eyes catch for a moment, and she looks away. She picks up a clay pot, speaks to the merchant. Duong stares, as if he can draw her to him. She is pretending to be casual. He feels a flash of anger and resentment; he is her superior officer, she has thwarted a mission. It's time, he thinks, she learns about Party discipline. It's time he ends his own foolish fixation.

Mr. Tran, the charcoal seller, sidles over to his stall. Though in the Front, he is not a party member, not fully trusted. Like Trinh Van Hai, he had also been a professor of literature at Hue University, fired and then imprisoned by the Diem regime after the Buddhist protests. He wears the vestiges of his imprisonment in the gray pallor of his skin, a cautious sideways shifting of the eyes, a permanent cringe frozen in his shoulders.

Mr. Tran's arms and fingers had been broken on Con Son island, and he often had trouble gripping the books he wished to bring down from the rickety shelves lining Duong's thatch-roofed stall. Now he points at one volume and Duong draws it down: a Vietnamese translation of *The Quiet American*—

the title striking him as ironic after his failure the night before. The American had been quiet. He should have been quieter yet this morning. He hands the book to Tran. He has read the novel before; he can see that Tran wants to talk about it. Normally, he enjoys their chats, even though Tran's observations come in broken questions and querulous whispers, a ghost trying to remember words he might have used when he was alive in order to hang on to his former incarnation.

The dangerous, bumbling altruism of the Americans, Tran says. The novel was prescient. The Americans are killing us with their kindness.

He wonders how long Tran has been waiting to try out that phrase on him. He looks over to the stand where Thuy had been, but she is gone. He tries to untangle the knots of the crowd, find her. Kindness! Duong spits out the word, a part of him aware they stem from his self-disgust at his foolish, unrequited entanglement with the stone carver's daughter. He pretends to love so he can fuck Phoung. That's all. Tran winces at the vulgarity. He deserves to die, Duong says, his voice rising. For using the pretense that he loves in order to delude others into loving him.

He stops himself. These quiet, early-morning chats with Tran are simply ways they both remind themselves of who they had once been. Tran, he can see, is taken aback by his raised voice, staring in shock at the finger Duong is impolitely shaking at him.

He lowers his hand and looks away. Spots Thuy walking towards him again, smiling, as if she has come to a decision. A ghost suddenly looms behind her. A tall man with an empty rice bag over his head, two crude holes cut so he can see, pointing exactly as Duong had pointed a second before. ARVN soldiers appear behind the hooded man. Mr. Tran drops the book, pushes on Duong's shoulders with both his broken hands, shoving him down behind the counter, with its stacks of rotting books and papers. The hooded man is pointing at Thuy. The soldiers run over to her, people scattering out of their way, surround her. Duong starts to rise, but Tran holds him down with an astonishing strength, his crippled arms locked at the elbows. One of the soldiers pulls an identical bag, without the eye holes, down over Thuy's head. Makes her a ghost also. Before her face disappears Thuy looks quickly in Duong's direction, her eyes pleading with him, not, he understands, to come to her, but to stay down. She is right. Of course. He has no weapon, except the knife in his pocket. All he can accomplish is his own arrest or death. If he remains free, he may be able to help her. His mind flees to Swan, to the way he had been able to free Thuy's father. But even as this thought comes to him, as he comes to the American as a figure of salvation and aid, he feels a backwash of revulsion, a swell of helplessness and loathing so strong it makes him nauseated, a lemony bile rising in his throat and mouth. Who could have betrayed Thuy, identified her? Her sister would not have. He knows with the certainty of hate that it must have been the American. And then he can't think about anything except the mixture of utter terror, utter resignation, and utter self-sacrifice he sees in Thuy's eyes before the hood is pulled over her face, canceling her.

He knows enough people who had have been tortured by the South Vietnamese puppets and the Americans. He knows Mr. Tran's hands. Two of his friends, both women, who move through their existence on withered limbs, broken by torture. He knows others blinded by the lime enemy soldiers would throw into cages that had been dug like graves into the earth. He knows the shovel handle, the water, the telephone which must be answered, attached to the most vulnerable portals of the body, the entries and exits of love and sustenance which are always the enemy to be shattered and erased.

He does not know what they used with Thuy. He didn't need to ask. He knew all the methods. They were all extant

234

within him. He knew the ways to fill and empty and shock and carve to visions of perfection that shimmered in an inner vision. He knew that they would take from her what she had never given to him.

After a week, Duong is able to bribe the commander in charge of the prison. A door is opened, and a bundle thrown out, into the dust. Duong unwraps her, this broken present the war has given to him. He bends to pick her up. She throws off his hands.

Don't touch me, she hisses, through clenched teeth.

They are the last words she says to him for a year. It is the last year that the Americans will stay in the war. George Swan leaves during it. Before Duong can kill him. Swan had come back for three tours, to stay with Kim, but his request to stay on after the troop withdrawal as an advisor to the South Vietnamese army is refused. His marriage is never recognized by the American authorities.

Thuy spends most of her time lying on a bamboo mat in the house she shared with Kim, two women alone in their father's house. She rises occasionally—more so as time goes on—and helps Kim in the family garden plot, or at the little roadside shop Kim ran, selling cheap statues and religious objects. Kim is pregnant, but it is Thuy who lies in a fetal position, as if she wants to float in a safe womb. Kim takes up the burden.

Whenever Duong enters the house, bringing food or money if he can, he sees Thuy curled up on that mat. At times, she does not even get up to go outside to urinate, and Kim, very pregnant, patiently cleans her sister, feeds her, gives her something to drink, and then goes back to writing her endless letters to her husband, letters she knows cannot be sent.

He squats by Thuy, and she turns her face from him. When he tries to touch her, she curls back into her fetal ball.

He looks at the wall, where Kim has hung a framed photograph of Swan.

Why does she blame me?

You're what she has.

He gets up, walks over and taps the photograph.

I spared him. And he betrayed us.

Don't be absurd.

He betrayed you as well. Left you with his get and fled. Like all of them.

He snatches the letter from her hand, and begins to read, in a mocking voice:

Thanh yeu, Beloved…

Her Mother's Letters

On the stage, Thuy took the bundle of letters away from Duong and sat cross-legged in front of the family altar, Swan's photo on it. And she sang, in Vietnamese and English, the words of Kiet's mother. Not all of them—they were too much for her little drama. But enough, and the rest Kiet read later, and many times, and she still does.

Beloved, thanh yeu,
You will never receive these letters, for there is no way by which I can get them to you. But they are for me, in some ways, what you are to me. There are people in the village who regard my love for you as abnormal, and for village people, as you well know, my darling—we spoke so often of your own village—that is the one sin that can never be forgiven. It is not only that, but perhaps it is that strangeness is what first drew me to you. The red thread that binds us. The others here call me the Cham girl, and it is true that our family of stone carvers carries that Cham blood, and of them all, I look most like those old carvings, and my skin carries the Cham darkness, among people to whom a sickly pallor is considered beautiful. But there are many here with Cham blood, and what they mean by that name is not how I look, but to say there is something a little to the side in my nature, something not quite right. Too much tinh and not enough hieu. You will understand if I tell you it is the way your fellow Marines look at you, not only because of your own beautiful color, but because of whatever strangeness in you that makes you love Viet Nam, love what they hate.

Beloved,

My father once told me a Chinese proverb, or perhaps one he made up—you remember his sense of humor—and gave dignity to by calling it a Chinese proverb. I think it is more the proverb of someone who worked with stone and earth. He said that when two people truly love, it is as if two clay pots have has been shattered and then their shards mixed and fused in the kiln. I love you like that. I miss you as if I have been shattered again.

With you, my dear husband, my dear paper, I can speak of things that would not be acceptable, normal, to those around me; I can speak to you with the small, secret voice I speak to my own soul. This is what this paper has become for me. I need to express my secret thoughts, though I did not know I did until I loved you.

A poet whose work I love wrote:

> I need a secret place to kneel
> To keep my minuscule soul
> Which fears the vicious dog
> The colorless hungry dog

Beloved,

It is Tet now, and today my sister and I went to fix the family tombs. We carried the items necessary to bring peace to our ancestors' souls to their tombs—the votive papers, the paper money, and so on—and we asked the Spirit of the Soil for permission to disturb the earth around the tombs, so that we might weed and clean. I wept at the tombs of my mother and my sister, who seem one entity now; more of us now dwelling in those little houses than in the house Thuy and I now share. I wept at my father's tomb, not only for his loss but also for how little of him we had to place in that grave, and how he would have carved it if he had been able to carve his own tomb, and how many souls in this country wander now without tombs, without family to burn joss and clean

*their tombs at Tet. And I remembered how much the earth
had been moved on the day of his death (we may not say his
name anymore, my love, nor of the others), and how no one
had asked the Spirit of the Soil for permission to disturb the
earth on that day, and how cursed we all must be.*

*There are, as you remember, three stones in the kitchen
on which our cooking is done. Those three stones are for Ong
Tao, the spirit of the hearth, who leaves the house—this sad
house of two women now—on the 23rd day of the 12th month,
and who goes to the heaven and tells the Jade Emperor
everything he has observed of our family over the year. On
Tet, at the altar of the ancestors, Chi Thuy and I burned a
picture of Ong Tao leaving, riding a phoenix. On the 30th
day, Ong Tao and the spirits of our ancestors will return.*

*Do you know, my love, that you left on the 23rd day of the
12th lunar month? What can you tell the Jade Emperor? Will
he let you return?*

Beloved,

*The war closes in on us. Before, it was always there, the
way bad weather is always there for our peasants: a slow
killing drought, a sudden storm or flood. But now it is as if it
has all gathered on the horizon, drawing all the evil energy
of the past years to itself, swelling up for one last and terrible
blow. It is inevitable the way it will end, and in spite of my
love for you, I am glad that your country will be erased from
mine. Of course all of your soldiers are gone now anyway.
They have slipped away like a hand that tightly gripped a
thorn, pressed it into its palm, and then slowly, slowly
loosened its grip and let it fall. I remember when you left the
first time, and then how the marines in your unit were gone,
and the American soldiers who came, none of whom lived in
the village as you did. I remember how, before they left as
well, the new G.I.s seemed even more full of hate at being
here, at why they had to be here, and how when they came by*

they threw cans and boards at people walking on the road.
Nguyen Van Viet, a boy you don't know, was run over by a
jeep, left broken as if for a game; people saw him running to
get away. I remember how the helicopter base was shelled
again, and they said 19 helicopters were destroyed. I thought
of you and tried not to feel good, victorious, but my love, I
don't know why, but more even than the faces of my mother,
of my father, of my sister, I saw the face of that child form in
each one of those explosions, as if they had all become
encased in that one form. How can I love you? How can I
not? How can we forgive each other and live? How can we
not forgive each other and live?

Beloved,
   I feel your child moving in me, and I want to laugh and
weep. A child, we are always told, is a sign of hope in the
future, but we have learned in this country that there is no
future; it is a tale for children. The only hope I feel is in the
miracle of our finding each other. But that miracle has to be
enough.

Beloved,
   It was this way. Some of the men in the village who still
revere my father enough to have not ostracized me, came to
the house and built a special bamboo bed, behind the altar
of the ancestors. And when the time came, Old Mrs. Hao
helped me bring our child into the world. You would have
been proud of me, and my father would have also, because,
like a dutiful daughter, I did not cry out and embarrass myself
by drawing the attention of the neighbors. So much of our
pride lies in being silent, doesn't it? In not letting out the
scream we all lock in our chests, where it grows, day after
day, like a monster in a cave.
   Our daughter was born, and she did not hold that scream

inside her, and for that I love her even more, if that is possible. And afterwards, our daughter was washed, swaddled, and brought to me, and a brazier with burning wood in it was placed under the bed, to restore the heat of my body. And we buried her umbilical cord in the earth outside, so that she will always be tied to this earth. Our daughter, I wrote before, because I was afraid to tempt the jealousy of any malevolent spirit. But now, because of all else I must tell you, I must also tell you her secret name.

My Khanh. Precious Jewel.

I have needed you so much, my love. Now I hold a living, screaming part of you in my arms. My Khanh.

But now you must listen to me carefully. Through Mr. Han, the village chief, I have received your letter telling me of your plans to return, as soon as you are discharged. It is madness. The end of this terrible war is near; we all feel it, and there will be many who cannot forgive all the death, all the murders. Would you put the burden of your death on my soul as well? I will try, through Mr. Han, who has contact with the last American consul in Da Nang, to send this letter, and send the others I have written. I had never thought to do so, had feared letting them go from me, as if I'd be releasing my spirit. But it is necessary that you receive this.

My love, there are those leaving now, at night, in the boats. If I can I will come to you. If anything should happen to me, sister Thuy will come to you with our child. Wait for me. Do not come.

Kiet reached over and touched the letters, the paper soft and worn as skin. My Khanh. "My Khanh," She said out loud, saying her name for the first time in her life. Feeling born on that stage whose borders had finally dissolved into her life.

Duong squatted next to her and Thuy, their heads almost touching.

"But she never sent it," Duong whispered, as if it were part of the play.

She turned to Thuy. "And she didn't come. Is that how you were arrested—trying to take me out?"

"Yes. After liberation."

"I could have helped her," Duong said, "but she…"

"My father, did he…?"

"Oh, he came back."

"He came for her," Thuy said. "He came for you. He came to finish the story."

The audience shifting uncomfortably on the low plastic stools, applauded.

"I don't get it," a voice said in English, from the second row.

Her Father Returns

As soon as Swan's plane lands at Da Nang, it is swarmed by people trying to get on, screaming, holding small children and suitcases above their heads like sacrifices to whatever gods mattered at that moment. He had been able to hitch a ride on an Air American transport from Sai Gon. The crew chief, an ex-Marine, thought he was crazy, but it was a quality the man admired. He had insisted on giving Swan a 9-mm pistol he kept under one of the web seats. You'll see, he said. Now Swan has to push aside South Vietnamese soldiers—weapons and in some cases boots and uniforms gone, the men in their underwear and some of them panting with fear—in order to descend. The families of some of the soldiers mill on the runway, watching their men push into the aircraft and disappear, abandoning them. Some shove forward, weeping; others simply squat and stare into nothing. Swan glances behind himself, sees the crew chief punching down into the crowd at random, trying to clear the ramp, men hanging onto his knees, dragging his pants down and exposing his buttocks, like some last farewell gesture of contempt. Several of the ARVN soldiers who had stayed with their families notice the American—in spite of his civilian clothes, what else could he be? Their faces harden and they begin to close in on Swan. He stares back at them, puts his hand in his pocket and pulls out the handle of the pistol, hoping the threat of it will be enough. One soldier stands, staring at him with naked hatred, and raises his M-16. Swan takes out the pistol and points it at the man's chest. If he kills him, he knows he'll be torn to pieces by the mob. He might be anyway. The two face each other, pointing their weapons, and then the

ARVN spits on the barrel of his American rifle, and throws it clattering down onto the tarmac.

A young man on a motor scooter yells to Swan, and he walks over to the grinning man. End of the world, boss, the young man says, in English.

Swan pulls a wad of dollars from his shirt pocket, yells his destination, and the young man nods, pats the back of the scooter. Swan climbs on. They weave into Da Nang through the surge of refugees clogging the road, at first heading with that surge towards the sea, and then turning south, towards Ngu Hanh Son.

Duong climbs to the same jagged, rock-ringed place where Swan and Kim had gone to perform their second wedding ceremony. To create for themselves a new tradition, Thuy had told him. To be a new tradition. To twist into a private and convenient vision that should remain sacrosanct. To betray the past in the name of an impossible future. To become, in a word, American. It is a place he comes often now, though usually at dawn—not like today, at sunset. He is not sure why he comes. Perhaps, he thinks, to make it his instead of theirs. To reclaim it, as the country has been reclaimed. It is surely the reason he has come today. Reclamation. A small Cham statue has been left in the crack of a rock, some burnt-down joss sticks before them: two dancers, male and female on a small pedestal, their left legs raised behind them, their out-raised arms hooked so that the couple is linked, arms draped over shoulders, the female's other arm crossed over her breast, her long fingers pointed at the earth. Had Kim brought these dancers, or had they already been here, the place itself calling the couple to it? He holds the statue in his hand and then flings it over the rim, hearing it bounce metallically off the stones below. Then he rises and climbs back down the shaft and into the mountain, to his hidden room. The last of his string of hollowed and secret chambers, nexuses of the veins netted under the skin of the country.

He uses the candle he has brought to light the candle near the blackboard. The teacher is alone, his students gone. An AK-47 lies against the table. He checks its magazine, and then undresses, once again smears his body with grease. He could put on his People's Army uniform now, march to the house with a platoon of soldiers, arrest Swan. But he will go instead as he has gone into the houses of the enemy countless times before. The American thinks the war is over.

He glimpses something, a fleeting form, in the corner of his eyes; it vanishes when he tries to look directly at it, sliding away from his sight like a drop of mercury. A coldness brushes the back of his neck, and his hair at that place bristles and stands. The air seems smudged, the stone softened and blurry at its edges. A single word forms in his mind, as if something had pushed it in through the skin over his eyes.

No.

It takes him a second to realize that the word is not just in his head. It is the first word she's said to him in a year. No. Thuy stands in the entrance, the flicker of candlelight melting her features and expressions into a fluid succession of masks. Without a word, she goes over to the stacked ammunition crates and picks up the book, opens it at the dog-eared page. She stares at it intently, as though if she looks hard enough she will be able to read it, or perhaps erase it. The English words must dance before her eyes, elusive as that shadow on the wall.

He puts his arm across her shoulders, squeezes her to him. She rests her cheek against his chest and closes her eyes.

He has returned, he says.

She doesn't open her eyes, doesn't look at him.

I know, she says. We all know.

He looks down at the gun, bends and tastes it with his tongue. A melodramatic gesture; he feels suddenly ridiculous. Once again making a fool of himself for this woman.

You must not do it, she says. You will send yourself to hell.

Duong laughs.

He did not give me to the soldiers. All he did was to love.

Her words fill him with hatred.

That is enough to condemn him.

She looks at him, draws in her breath slightly, as if suddenly becoming aware of his nudity. Her hand lingers on his lips and then traces down to his chest and side and hips and stomach, the glide of her fingers making him aware of his skin and nerves as if her touch is creating him. She finds him, encloses him firmly. He hears a low mutter, almost a growl in her throat. But then, in that sound, he senses a pleading. It fills him with a sudden, heart-shaking rage. Did she think she was the heroine of an epic, Thuy Kieu protecting her family with her body? She slides her thumbs under the waist of her pants, works them down and kicks them away, and he shoves her roughly against the wall, presses himself against her cool belly as if love is a knife. Filled with hatred and with anger, he finally enters her, as he never has before and never will again.

On the stage, the reenactment of violation becomes a dance of shadows. Becomes what his memory has become.

The violation became a dance of shadows. He leaves the mountain, a shadow. He enters the house through the same window he had on the night Thuy had first stopped him from killing the American and Kim. Now she has asked the same of him. He pictures himself, greased and naked, and suddenly he feels foolish, a bare boy playing war. He sheathes the knife, but still holds the automatic rifle; he does not know how he will be greeted in this house. Kim is on her bamboo bed, nursing the baby at her breast, cooing to it. He stands still until Kim sees him. She stands, startled and frightened, holding the child off to her side, as far away from him as possible, her arm over her breast like the tra kieu dancer.

On the stage, Thuy places Kiet as if she is conjuring her form out of air. Kiet is My Khanh is Kim is her mother is holding out the doll is holding out the baby is holding out My Khanh is holding out herself, an offering, in supplication, to him.

He looks for the first time at the child. She smiles at him. His enemy's face and the face of the woman he loves are seeded in her features. Perhaps this is only what he wants to see. It doesn't matter. It doesn't matter. At that instant, everything changes.

Don't be frightened, younger sister, he says. Don't you recognize me?

That is why I am frightened, brother, Kim says. She presses the child back to her breast, and then raises one hand to the back of her head, presses down and smooths her hair, a nervous gesture that she shared with Thuy, that he saw Thuy in also. She stares into his eyes.

Have you come to kill us?

I came to kill him.

It is the same.

He holds up his hand, in a gesture of peace, or surrender.

I will kill no one.

It will be his third failure. It occurs to him that perhaps he is not made for this type of work. He begins to laugh.

She stares at him. Then why are you here?

You must leave. Take your child, take your American, and get out. There are already people fleeing from Da Nang by boat. I can get the three of you on one, and make sure it is not stopped.

She looks at him. Why would you do that? she asks.

Timshel, he says. Because I may.

***

Or doesn't. Or thinks. Or should have said. It was his grand gesture. But this wasn't a play. Swan steps into the room, dressed in the black cotton shirt and trousers of a peasant. He is with Thuy; she went to meet him, to warn him and now she stands behind him, her face frozen in horror. He has not heard the conversation, or his Vietnamese is not good enough to understand what had been said. Duong raises the rifle, offering it with two hands.

—

On the stage, Duong offers the rifle with both hands to Kiet, to My Khanh, a gesture of exquisite grace, but she does not take it from him, does not understand.

—

Duong raises the rifle, offering it with both hands, a gesture of exquisite grace the American does not understand, and Swan pulls the pistol out from under his waistband. Kim cries out, steps between them as he fires, as Duong fires. Only a short burst. They carry, the two of them, the war in their nerves and muscles. The flashes light the room, burn what they illuminate into Duong's brain. Something slaps his face he is on the floor Thuy is screaming Kiet is screaming. His face burns and Thuy's scream does not stop; she is kneeling over the heap on the floor, drawing the wounded child—the bullet that killed its mother first burning along the skin of its back—away from the hands of the dead, her face stamped with horror and premature resignation, as if she is a midwife pulling some unwanted monstrosity into the world.

Timshel, he may have said. But he doesn't say that word on the stage. Thuy was right; it is too complicated to put into the play.

Thuy Son

Alex doesn't know how long he has been in the cave. He sits against the rear wall, a line of cold ridges pressing like counter-vertebrae into his spine. He is near a white concrete Buddha, faint in the dim light from the dusty beams of sunlight that stream through holes in the cave ceiling. The walls are pocked with niches containing more Buddhas, figures of mandarins, Cham devas, carved inscriptions. Next to a squat stone shrine, a narrow, deeply shadowed corridor stirs his memory like a finger. He goes to it. Another Buddha, its stone sooty, streaked with age. One more Buddha for the road, dear Jesus. The flashes from the tourists' cameras make the shadows switch and jump, illuminating the statue's face from different angles, so it seems to be flowing around the head, the shadows of the people in the cave black and fluid against the rock walls. Their voices mutter and buzz around him, echoing in the chamber. He and his friends must have entered from somewhere else then, a side tunnel, rock was always opening its secrets to him. There had been no hole in the ceiling of the chamber, only complete darkness, the beam of his flashlight finding the statues in the niches, face after face, Rodriguez shuddering and crossing himself. From the mouth of the cave and then echoing from the rock all around him, he hears strange music, the jumble, clanging, twanging cacophony of Vietnamese instruments, a woman's wailing song, the voice vaguely familiar.

The actors looked confused. On the ground in front of the cave were the remnants of the reenactment: a toy pistol, a plastic AK47, the doll that represented her. Kiet. My Khanh.

She pressed the flat of her palms against her ears, blocking the story. The name. She stared in hatred at Duong. "I want to burn away any part of me you touched."

Thuy tried to embrace her, but she moved back, away from her aunt.

"It was how I felt towards him as well, em. But you can't know what those times were like."

Kiet shook her head vigorously, refusing her words. Refusing My Khanh.

"I am not blameless," Thuy said, her lips trembling.

She didn't want to hear it. Her mother's words, written in her language and translated by her mother's murderer, came into her mind. *There will be many who cannot forgive all the death, all the murders.* You bet.

"He regretted it for many years," Thuy said.

"Who didn't?"

Thuy tried to embrace her again, and this time Kiet stood still and shook in her arms, her ancestors looking from the altar at both of them. Her aunt Le Thi Thanh Thuy.

Thuy looked over at Duong. "Don't be too harsh."

Kiet laughed. Harshly.

"He meant to save them. When I was arrested trying to escape with you, he used his influence to get me out of jail. He arranged for the Trinhs to take you, for their boat not to be stopped."

Kiet looked at her, an unspoken question between them. She shook her head, her eyes on the ground.

"You would have kept me," Kiet said. "Your sister's daughter. You would have raised me. He wouldn't let you, would he? He wanted to get rid of me. To get rid of the evidence," she said, and remembered a gun taken from her hands, brought back to Alex's empty holster, the image pressed into her mind like an opportunity for forgiveness. She chased it away.

"You can't know what those times were like," Thuy said

firmly. The actors were milling around, confused, the people in the audience muttering to themselves.

"Come back. All of you," Kiet screamed.

They did. Her new family. Starting with a lie, just like her old family. "Do it again," she demanded. "The last scene. Do it again."

"Please," Thuy said. "My Khanh."

But even hearing that name, her true name out now in the world, did not bring her any peace. She was filled with maniacal energy. She pushed the others into position, arranged them like furniture, went back into the cave and pulled them out until they were all there, crowded onto the stage—Alex and Baxter and their friends, her grandfather, and her other father, his blackface scarred by rivulets of sweat. She pushed Duong, hating to touch him, but needing to do what she did, to rearrange curses into blessings as he had tried to do, pushed him next to the actor who'd played him, next to Thuy, and, her hands trembling, handed the doll to the actor who had first played her mother, Kim. She stood alone. Duong and her mother and Swan and Thuy faced each other, all of them standing with their own ghosts. Only the real Alex MIA. They stared, unwilling to move, to change the tableau she'd created, unable to play it out once again to its inevitable conclusion. Duong, his eyes dull, began to raise his weapon, and Kiet leapt between him and Swan, snatched the toy rifle from his hands. She pointed it at the actor playing Duong and then at Duong himself. And stood, sweeping the barrel back and forth frantically, as if unable to decide what to do, caught up in something that would never end. She would stand here forever, swinging the barrel of the gun back and forth. Her left hand, cupped under the plastic barrel, pulled up, as if of its own accord. Duong took a step toward her, his eyes pleading, and she screamed words at him, *Don't touch me,* the only weapon she had. She saw it hit home. The other actors started to back off the stage, get away from her, and out of the corner of her eye she saw the actors who had played her father and his three companions looking at each other, laughing nervously, walking away. They disappeared into the darkness of the larger cave. Kiet threw the rifle down. My Khanh threw the rifle down. She didn't know where to go. She needed Alex, cursed him for being the murderer to whom she could no longer go.

Alex sees that the floor of the cave is littered with bodies. At first they seem to be more statues. In neat rows, uncovered, some naked, some in draped tatters of uniform. Their blood on their faces and bodies black as tar, gouged and cratered. Utter silence. Then the sound of Vietnamese, as if coming from all the walls, the ceiling, and the shadows in the far corner of the cave shift, elongate, separate, and clarify into rows of litters, the wounded moaning, the echoes of their groans filling the cave. Flashbulbs pop, their sudden light washing the color from the people on the litters, as the tourists take pictures. The light chips and dissolves a dark wall that has been in front of his eyes, as if he were Baxter, suddenly given back his sight. Alex sees four women and two men come into the cave. They are carrying more corpses; one a pregnant woman, her belly pocked with bullet wounds. The two groups stare at each other. The Vietnamese freeze in the beam of the flashlight. Alex drops it and fires.

She was fleeing to the moon. She came back to the row of thatched-roof kiosks in front of the small pagoda. The old woman selling souvenirs and plastic water bottles smiled at her. Her eyes and nose and lips were scrunched very close together in the center of her face, sitting on top of a nest of wrinkles like the topping on a salad.

She sat on one of the stone benches, near the bullet-scored gate. She heard a sharp cry. A little tribe of teenage girls, hawkers, swarmed towards her. Some had flat trays, filled with the same junk the street kids in Ho Chi Minh City had been selling, hung from their necks, their arms bent at the elbows, holding them in front of their chests; some lugged plastic-net bags of sodas and bottled water. Their clothing was ragged, and most of them wore conical hats, tied under their chins with colored ribbons. Their faces were shadowed. They gathered around her, thrusting their trays forward. She smiled weakly at them, shook her head. To her surprise, they didn't insist—you buy, you buy—instead stood staring at her, their faces shadowed under the brims of their hats, eyes gleaming. One, a tall girl, some of the buttons on her blouse missing, sighed, and as if it were a signal, they all sat down around Kiet, put down their trays and bottles. She had the same feeling of connection to them she'd had in Ho Chi Minh; if she hadn't left she could have been them, dust, hustling here instead of hustling there, sleeping in Sai Gon alleys and the edges of rice paddies instead of sleeping on grates on D.C streets, in doorways, in the beds of strangers. The tall girl reached over and touched Kiet's face, her finger finding the trail of the tear that had leaked out of her eye; Kiet hadn't known it was there until she touched it.

"Doan be sad," the child said, sadly.

Kiet grinned at her, shook her head. "No problem, little sister."

She and the others instantly reflected the grin, the same wise-ass, I-can-take-whatever-you-got grin of the kid Kiet once was, repeated on all those tough, beautiful little faces.

They began to pat her, their hands on her shoulders and back. "No problem, no problem," they muttered. The first girl touched Kiet's cheek again, stroked it, touched her own, traced the shape of Kiet's eyes. "You same-same? Viet Kieu?"

"Sure," Kiet said. "*My*. America. Half-half."

Half a dink, half a spade, her group-home homies would say. Kiet-Keisha. *Bui do.* No My Khanh about it.

The girl stroked her hair, nodded, said something in Vietnamese to one of the others, a chubby girl wearing stained black trousers and a tattered Pittsburg Steelers jersey. She got up, ran over to the line of thatch-roof kiosks. A few moments later, she came back, holding the hand of a short woman. The woman walked bent forward, as if permanently bowed at the waist, looking at her own feet.

When they were closer, the woman raised her face and smiled at Kiet, a thousand wrinkles spreading out around her grin. It transformed her face, as if an internal light had gone on under the thin crepe of her skin. She had three discolored teeth, one top, two bottom. Her lips were somewhat thicker than you would see on most Vietnamese, Kiet thought, and her skin was chocolate brown. She squatted in front of Kiet, the girls making room, two of them draping their arms around her, and one of them resting her head on the old woman's shoulder. "Me," the girl said, and pointed at her mother. "My me. Same-same, you."

The old woman took off her hat. Her gray hair was thick, tight-curled. She touched Kiet's cheek, it seemed the thing to do, drew her fingers back to her own. She might not be an old woman, Kiet thought, repeating her gesture. She might be her own age. She leaned over and kissed the woman's cheek. A sigh passed through the girls, like a breeze, and they tightened their circle around Kiet.

The woman waved at knobby hand towards the mountain. "Heaven," she said. A command.

Kiet climbed again to Heaven. She saw they had set up a small altar, just under a jagged crenellation; the real deal, she thought, what she saw on the stage below its shadow on the wall of a cave. She looked over that natural rampart and down at the turquoise of the South China Sea, its surface patterned with shifting crinkles of silver. The breeze from that sea dried the sweat on her forehead and carried to her nostrils a faint sting of salt and dust, a whiff of seaweed and silt: an odor in which, she supposed, if one had the right history, one could detect the scent of blood. Thuy Son. Water Mountain. The element of water. The beach below would be crowded with sunbathers; the frothy surf dotted with bobbing bodies, lovers clinging to each other and shrieking as the waves hit them, kids on rubber inflated rafts and tubes. Some would strike out further, head in a straight line at full speed, as if going for the green peaks of the distant island she could see. Or further, drawn east and east, towards the Beautiful Country. There was nothing she could look at in this place that wasn't resonant. She was tired to death of it. The swimmer she couldn't see drew her, pulled a coil out of her heart, something greasy and filthy that lay wet and steaming in the sun. She sat down and drew her knees up to her chest, hugging them, shivering, held her thighs tight against her breasts, against the shivering that was moving through her core. She wanted to descend the mountain and swim as far as she could go, into the sea that had taken her from this place.

She heard, from somewhere below, the sound of shouts or screams. But there was no war here, except for her.

Suddenly the vendor girls were all around her; they had come up after her. She smiled. It is impossible to be alone here, she thought. They formed a knot around her. Occasionally, absently, one or more of them stroked her skin as they spoke quietly to each other, staring at the altar.

Now she saw Duong, climbing over the rocks towards her. Her head edged a little taller than the others in the cluster. The girls looked up, in unison, their faces hard. But then Duong was in front of them and said something Kiet couldn't make out and their circle opened, exposing her.

He squatted down in front of her, put his hands on her shoulders. She closed her eyes and then let her face rest against his chest.

"Your father," he said. "You must come."

She nodded. But when she rose, she first went over to the altar: a bamboo tray on which there had been placed two framed photographs: a photo of two women in traditional slit-sided ao dais, another of a couple, a bride and groom. To her, to My Khanh—though she still, she understood, would think of herself as Kiet, the name of a drowned boy, a twin by need and by deed—the people in the photographs were still legend, Swan and Kim, though now she ached with love and loss for both of them. Swan, she thought. She preferred the single name, the mythic, flawless, fleeting grace it called. Swan and the element of Gold. Of Metal. This was the place where they had wed. It was the place where, one way or another, they conceived her, and one way or another their tragedy birthed her to the flawed and beautiful and generous flesh and spirit of those she would always think of as her real parents. Yes. She thought of Alex, who forgave her a murder as she hadn't been able to forgive him his own murders, the father that she had found her, and she thought, somehow the girls' gift, their own accepted legacy bringing her to it. I knew from the first moment I saw you that you were my father.

She turned again to the altar. They—it must have been Thuy and Duong—had placed a small bowl of rice, a small plate on which oranges, bananas, and rice cakes, arranged in front of the photos. Next to the plate was a vase of lotus flowers, curving over the food so that the miniature canopy of blossoms cast shadows on the flesh of the fruit.

She took the stone dancer from her pocket and nested her among the stones from which it had been carved, and then she lit the incense. The heads of the joss sticks glowed deep red in the breeze, and she was afraid they would be extinguished. But the smoke curled upwards and twisted, and as it did she felt something that had been clenched inside of herself for years, for years, unclench, the way those seeking blessing will open their hands and release a captive bird into the open and possible sky. She wished they were here with her, all of them, the parents she found and who found her, and the aunt who let her go to save her. The wind touched her face and she strained to hear the rest of her mother's words, speaking in a voice she never heard:

How can I love you? How can I not? How can we forgive each other and live? How can we not forgive each other and live?

The tourists' flashbulbs strobe the darkness, the faces around Alex there-gone-there. Flashbulbs for flashbacks, he thinks. But he is aware of where he is, when he is. The beginning of one century, not just past the middle of the last. The Theater of Then and Now. The images are simply written in the air here, ready to be called, like dust motes, invisible until they are caught in a shaft of light, seen by the right eyes. Everything erratically illuminated by the waving beam of the flashlight, rolling on the floor, the flashes of rifle fire. His rounds tearing into the group, the corpses, the pregnant corpse, sweeping over, hitting the wounded. Had the others fired? The Viets are all down. Echoes of the gunfire rolling through the chamber. Yes, the four of them continue to fire, raking the patients on their litters; they dance animatedly. The gasps and ahh's of the tourists. One of the women rising from behind the pregnant corpse, as if to a strange birth. Baxter yelling, Alex, over there, as she struggles up, a grenade in her hand. Throws it as he fires, splitting her, splitting the corpse. Someone screaming. Someone laughing. The tour group leader waves a green flag, gathering his troops. Flashbulbs. An after-image: Baxter, clutching his face, hands over his streaming eyes, Dalton and Rodriguez statues on the cave floor, Dalton's arms stretched over his head, his hands turned in at ninety-degree angles from his wrists, palms down, like a Cham dancer. Then they are alive again, running past him, laughing crazily. Baxter, his eyes restored, Rodriguez and Dalton, their lives restored, but their uniforms wrong, like representations of uniforms, their features crude masks molded onto Vietnamese faces; they have been reborn here, been translated. It is the only way to live. He has found them at last. He sees himself, his own younger self in his jungle utilities, hung with bullets and weapons, his face also made Vietnamese and he reaches his arms out to embrace, to stop himself, but he flits past himself like a shadow. Alex kneels by the Buddha, sees it has reclaimed its face also, as if it had carved itself. He touches his own face. He feels the Buddha's calm smile form on his own lips; he closes his eyes. Someone presses his shoulder, and he feels a twitch of fear, but when he turns another flashbulb explodes, blinding him. He hears, in the strange echoes of the cave, the voice of his daughter, the pure goodness that had come out of all this, out of beds of murder, calling him to the light.

Author's Note

There was a somewhat unusual genesis for this novel. It began as a sequel to my 1998 novel, *Prisoners*, which tells the story of the 15-year-old Kiet and how she came to be adopted by Alex and Louise Hallam. I'd wanted to continue the story, and had become interested also in the stories a number of my Vietnamese friends, who had fought on the other side, told me about reading American literature during the war—usually London, Hemingway, Whitman, Steinbeck. How did my well-read Vietnamese friends feel toward the American enemy? *It made us hate you more because we felt we had no choice*, one of them told me, and Duong was born.

Another friend, the film director Judd Ne'eman, asked me to develop a script based on *Prisoners*. But when I started writing it and speaking about it with Judd, the new story kept clamoring to be told. There was a new war, and it seemed very little learning, and Kiet would have been in her thirties—what had happened to her and her parents, Judd asked. I began writing the novel and the script simultaneously and the differences and tensions between film and page became part of the creative energy that went into the work. In the past, I had become used to working with good editors, and occasionally sharing my work with fellow writers I trusted, though normally I would not do so until at least a first draft of the book was finished. The process of working with Judd was similar, but became much more symbiotic; we would meet and speak for many hours about the plot and direction of the script narrative, our conferences often confrontational, but always creative, and Judd's insights about the way story needed to be presented in film gave me many different ways of looking at both script and novel, many challenges in finding the words that would bring those concepts and characters to life. Script and novel, of course, both became different, as each grew into its own life, but

Judd's contributions were invaluable and I'm grateful to him.

Last, my son Adam went to Marble Mountain a year before I gathered the courage to go back to that place. Adam went to see Viet Nam for himself, and also to climb to "heaven" on Thuy Son, and light some incense, in gratitude to a friend who had taken my place on a mission and had been killed, flying out of the Marble Mountain helicopter base. Thus, as it should be, and as it is with Kiet/My Khanh and Alex, the child led the father to the place he had to go.

photo by Phan Trieu Hai

WAYNE KARLIN has previously published six novels: *The Wished-for Country, Prisoners, Lost Armies, The Extras, Us,* and *Crossover,* and two works of creative non-fiction: *Rumors and Stones: A Journey,* and *War Movies: Journeys to Vietnam.* As American editor for Curbstone's Voices from Vietnam series, he has edited and adapted translations of writers from Vietnam, including (with Le Minh Khue and Truong Vu), *The Other Side of Heaven: Postwar Fiction by Vietnamese and American Writers,* which received a Critics' Choice Award for 1995-1996, and (with Ho Anh Thai) *Love After War: Contemporary Fiction from Vietnam,* an anthology chosen by the *San Francisco Chronicle* as one of the 100 best books of 2003. He was a consulting producer and writer for a six-part National Public Radio series on the aftermath of the Vietnam war. Karlin has received five State of Maryland Individual Artist Awards in Fiction, two Fellowships from the National Endowment for the Arts, the 1999 Paterson Prize in Fiction, and the 2005 Vietnam Veterans of America Excellence in Arts Award. He is a professor of languages and literature at the College of Southern Maryland.

Curbstone Press, Inc.
is a nonprofit publishing house dedicated to multicultural literature
that reflects a commitment to social awareness and change, with an
emphasis on contemporary writing from Latino, Latin American,
and Vietnamese cultures.

Curbstone's mission focuses on publishing creative writers whose work
promotes human rights and intercultural understanding, and on
bringing these writers and the issues they illuminate into the
community. Curbstone builds bridges between its writers and the
public—from inner-city to rural areas, colleges to cultural centers,
children to adults, with a particular interest in underfunded public
schools. This involves enriching school curricula, reaching out to
underserved audiences by donating books and conducting readings
and educational programs, and promoting discussion in the media.
It is only through these combined efforts that literature can truly
make a difference.

Curbstone Press, like all non-profit presses, relies heavily on the
support of individuals, foundations, and government agencies to bring
you, the reader, works of literary merit and social significance that
would likely not find a place in profit-driven publishing channels, and
to bring these authors and their books into communities across
the country.

If you wish to become a supporter of a specific book—one that is
already published or one that is about to be published—your
contribution will support not only the book's publication but also its
continuation through reprints.

We invite you to support Curbstone's efforts to present the diverse
voices and views that make our culture richer, and to bring these
writers into schools and public places across the country.
Tax-deductible donations can be made to:
Curbstone Press, 321 Jackson Street, Willimantic, CT 06226
phone: (860) 423-5110 fax: (860) 423-9242
www.curbstone.org